SOMEONE IN BLACK

I turned my head back toward whatever had hit me. All I could see was the open door on the Dumpster and someone in burglar-black running away from me.

I tried to get up, but my head hurt too much. I heard footsteps coming from the opposite direction, and I rolled over toward the sound. Someone was yelling at me in a flood of words I didn't understand. *"¿Qué pasó? ¿Qué pasó?"* It was Manuel.

"What happened?" I asked groggily.

"Sí, qué pasó," he said.

I staggered to my feet. My leg almost buckled under me. I could see a pickup backing up in the parking lot across the street. The taillights came on when the driver put on his brakes to shift gears. It was the person from the Dumpster. I was sure of that. It was probably the killer as well.

I headed for my car, but Manuel tried to stop me. I shook him off. "Let go, Manuel. Call the police and tell them I'm going after the guy."

Dell Books by Dolores Johnson

TAKEN TO THE CLEANERS
HUNG UP TO DIE

HUNG UP TO DIE

A Mandy Dyer Mystery

DOLORES JOHNSON

A Dell Book

Published by
Dell Publishing
a division of
Bantam Doubleday Dell Publishing Group, Inc.
1540 Broadway
New York, New York 10036

The trademark Dell® is registered in the U.S. Patent and Trademark Office.

ISBN: 0-440-22353-9

Printed in the United States of America

Published simultaneously in Canada

December 1997

10 9 8 7 6 5 4 3 2 1

WCD

To my husband, Dale, who has always given me the support and space to write. Thanks for hanging in there with me until I was finally published.

I wish to thank the following people for their help: Joe and Kaye Cannata of Belaire Cleaners, Denver, Colorado, who convinced me that a body could hang from a conveyor; Jim and Sarah Parham of Acme Cleaners, Orlando, Florida, for sharing information about personnel records; and Detective Donald Vecchi of the Denver Police Department and Lt. Thomas Bay, Arapahoe County Sheriff's Office, for answering my questions about law enforcement. Any errors are mine and not the fault of the people who provided me with information.

In addition, I wish to thank the members of my Boulder critique group, and the writers who meet at Lee Karr's house, for their advice and support. A special thanks to my agents, Meg Ruley and Ruth Kagle, and to my editor, Jacqueline Miller.

CHAPTER 1

Strange things had been happening at Dyer's Cleaners for the last few months, so I wasn't really surprised when Uncle Chet's old baseball bat turned up on Lucille's worktable.

Lucille, the middle-aged matriarch of the mark-in department, collared me the moment I came to work Monday morning and began to complain about the bat. Unfortunately Lucille complains about a lot of things on her job, which is to put tags on the clothes so they can eventually be matched up with their rightful owners when she or someone else bags them.

"Mandy," she said, brandishing the bat. "Someone must have been playing around with this and knocked half my stuff on the floor. Now my tags are all mixed up."

I grabbed the bat before she hit me with it. Uncle Chet had kept it at the front counter in case he was ever robbed, but I'd moved it back under her table when he died two years ago and left me the cleaners. I preferred a more high-tech and less confrontational form of protection, so I'd had an alarm installed for my counter people to push in case they were ever held up. It's called a panic button and is hooked into our security system.

"I bet it'll take me an hour to get everything straightened up," Lucille said as she lifted a dirty clothes bag from a laundry cart and poured its contents and the owner's ticket onto the table. "I think you should tell people to leave my stuff alone."

I reminded myself to ask Sarah McIntyre, the quiet but conscientious woman who'd closed for me Saturday night, if she'd noticed anything out of order at the mark-in table when she left work. Meanwhile I said, "I'll just put the bat back under the table for the time being." I slipped it behind the laundry cart of clothes and heard it drop to the floor. "How's that?"

Frankly this problem was a lot easier to solve than some of the other weird things that had been happening at the plant: garments filed away on the conveyor in the wrong places; a single item missing from a customer's order; slashes of lipstick or Magic Marker on freshly cleaned clothes as if some demented cosmetologist or out-of-control kindergartner put them there.

"And people are always leaving their junk on here." Lucille patted the table. "I have to clear it off before I can even start my work."

"Just put anything that doesn't belong here in the lost-and-found drawer like you always do."

She sighed heavily and motioned to another cartful of clothes to be marked in. "I still don't know how I'm going to get everything done."

Personally it made me happy to see so many clothes in the plant. We'd been losing customers lately, due mostly to a discount cleaner named Farley Mills who'd moved into the neighborhood and siphoned away a lot of our business. But maybe now that Easter was coming up, people had decided not to entrust their Sunday best to a competitor who promised to clean any garment for eighty-nine cents.

"I'll send Ann Marie back to help you, and I'll open

up," I said, heading through the door to our call office, where customers drop off and pick up their clothes.

Ann Marie was a bouncy teenager who'd just graduated from high school at the end of fall semester and was now working for me full-time. Unfortunately she and Lucille went together about as well as a miniskirt and a plaid flannel shirt.

"Do I have to?" Ann Marie asked in her high-pitched voice.

"Yes, you have to," I said.

She stomped off to help Lucille, and I unlocked the front door for the first customer of the day, a white-haired woman named Emily Grant whom I hadn't seen for far too long. I escorted her to the counter, but before I could wait on her, the phone rang and I picked it up.

"Amanda," a woman on the other end of the line said, and I knew immediately that the caller was my mother. Everyone else calls me Mandy. "I wanted to let you know I've decided to come up and visit you for a few days."

"When?" I hoped I didn't sound as panicky as I felt.

"I've booked a flight from Phoenix this morning. I'll be in Denver at two. I hope you can meet me at the airport."

"Two—today?" I stopped before I started stuttering for real, grabbed a pencil, and wrote down the flight information for her arrival at DIA.

The only thing I could think about was "why now?" Mom hadn't been here since Uncle Chet's funeral, so why was she coming now when customers were casting me off like last year's fashions? Unfortunately Mom's my worst critic, and I never seem to have the right answers to her complaints about the way I look, where I live, and the lack of a "significant other" in my life.

Of course, she hadn't seen me since I'd put away my easel, cut my long, dark hair, and abandoned the jeans and paint-splattered sweatshirts of my starving-artist days. Now that I was a thirty-three-year-old business-woman, I wore dry-cleanable clothes—wool suits in the winter and crisp linens in the summer—as a subliminal form of advertising.

But Mom was a hard sell. She favored frilly blouses and flouncy skirts and thought a woman was nothing without a man. She was still upset that I'd divorced Larry the Lustful Law Student, as I called him. In fact the only thing I could think of worse than Mom paying me a visit right now would be Larry showing up at my apartment unannounced.

Mom was saying something, but I stopped her. "Look, I'm with a customer. I'll be at the gate at two. We can talk then."

When I hung up and turned back to the counter, I tried to put a smile on my face for Mrs. Grant, who always reminded me of a small, twittery bird. She'd been one of my best customers until she and dozens of other people had taken flight to Farley's One-Price Cleaners.

"Oh, Miss Dyer," she said. "I'm glad you're here this morning. I owe you an apology." She flapped her thin hands in front of her as if they were wings. "I never should have taken my clothes to one of those *other* cleaners. They didn't get the stains out of Marvin's suit, so I had to bring it here. One of your people said she thought you could fix it."

I gave her what I hoped was a reassuring nod. "I'll go get your order now, and we'll take a look at it."

Mrs. Grant put her hand over her heart as if she were pledging allegiance to the flag. "I swear I'll never go anyplace else again."

Her promise warmed me, and despite Mom's imminent arrival, I decided to look on the bright side. Business was picking up as customers like Mrs. Grant began to return to Dyer's Cleaners, and I was hopeful that we'd been able to remove the stains from her husband's suit.

My optimism lasted about thirty seconds. That's how long it took to turn on our up-and-down conveyor, which starts in the back room, goes through an opening in the wall, and rises like a stairway to circle the high ceiling above the call office.

The conveyor started to move, like a carousel for clothes, but suddenly it came to a dead stop. I tried to reverse it, but it was jammed. Any noise it made was drowned out by Mrs. Grant. She began to scream at a decibel level to shatter glass.

I shut it off and ran out front.

"Oh, my God," she yelled, her hands now waving in double time. "There's a body up there."

I froze as I saw what she was pointing at. It was a pair of red cowboy boots hanging down below the plastic bags of clothes on the conveyor, almost at the ceiling.

"I'm sure it's just a dummy, Mrs. Grant," I said, hoping to calm her down. "Someone must have put it there as a prank."

Ann Marie was the first employee to reach the counter. "Oh, yuck and double-yuck," she said. "That's totally gross."

Lucille was right behind her, and she put her hands on her hips. "It's probably just some dumb April Fool's joke," she said, looking disgusted at yet another interruption to her work.

Call it denial, but I wanted to agree with Lucille even though it was only March. Maybe it really was a dummy that had been placed on the conveyor as the ultimate practical joke. A dirty trickster's version of industrial sabotage.

Mrs. Grant kept screaming while wild possibilities flitted through my head.

"I'll get it down," I said, and started to the back room to get a pole with a hook on it that we use to untangle hangers that get stuck in the conveyor.

Before I reached the door, McKenzie "Mack" Rivers, my production manager, came running from the dry-cleaning department at the back of the plant. He's a big black man with a deep baritone voice. "What the devil's going on?" he boomed, an instant before he saw the cowboy boots.

"Someone was just trying to be funny," I said for the benefit of the rest of the crew, who were right behind him. Sure, Mandy, and if you believe that, a clotheshorse is a pinto pony in a party dress.

I grabbed the pole and came back out front just in time to see Ingrid Larsen, my ponytailed silk finisher, elbowing everyone else aside to get a better look at the dangling boots.

"Holy shit!" she said, and popped her bubble gum in exclamation.

"Everybody, stay back," I ordered as I handed the pole to Mack, who's over six feet tall compared to my five-five. Together we moved under the up-and-down part of the conveyor.

Mack reached up with the pole and tried to push the plastic bags of clothes aside to get a better look at whatever was attached to the boots. It looked like a pair of jeans.

"Maybe it's a scarecrow like in *The Wizard of Oz*." That was Kim Il Chong, Mack's new Korean assistant. Ever since Mack had suggested that he could learn English by watching movies, Kim compared every life experience to a film he'd seen.

"It's pretty heavy," Mack whispered.

"This has gone too far," I whispered back. "I'm going to get to the bottom of these dirty tricks if it kills me." It was perhaps a bad choice of words, standing as we were under an object that could fall and squash us at any moment.

I'd bet anything Farley "The Sleazeball" Mills was

behind this. Nothing strange had ever happened until he appeared on the scene. He was a skinny little guy with a thatch of red hair and a permanent leer on his clean-shaven, freckled face. An evil Howdy Doody with a habit of playing hardball. Before he opened his discount cleaners, I'd caught him sneaking around the parking lot, trying to get a head count of my customers. For his grand opening, he'd handed out discount coupons just outside my front door, and he'd gotten in a fight with the shy Sarah when he tried to pass himself off as a customer to get information about our delivery service. Furthermore, since I'd never heard of a poltergeist in a dry cleaners, I suspected that one of my employees was working undercover for the Howdy Doody of Mean to try to destroy my business.

"Maybe it's a mannequin from one of the stores over at Cherry Creek," someone suggested, referring to the nearby shopping mall.

At that instant Mack managed to push one of the garment bags aside, and I saw what looked like flesh-colored hands. The dangling figure seemed to be attached to the conveyor by an orange cord that was wound around the conveyor. The cord had apparently stuck in the sprocket beneath the drive chain. That must have been what made the conveyor stop.

"Okay, everybody out," I said, turning to my crew, who were still staring up at the boots as if they were a couple of UFOs in the sky. My eyes were drawn to the gum-chewing Ingrid in one of the bright red KANSAS CITY CHIEFS T-shirts she liked to wear. "Ingrid, will you see that everyone gets back to work?"

Reluctantly she started to herd the rest of the crew out of the room through the far door. That's when I noticed Mrs. Grant again. She was leaning on the counter, as far away from the boots as possible, and she looked as if she were about to faint.

I grabbed Lucille. "Would you and Ann Marie take Mrs. Grant back to the break room and try to calm her down?"

"Do I have to?" Ann Marie whined.

"Yes, you have to." This would also get them away from the nearby mark-in table while Mack and I tried to sort things out.

I detoured to the front door, locked it, and put a CLOSED sign in the window. Then I returned to Mack and said the dreaded words: "It looks like a real body, doesn't it?"

"I'm afraid so," he said.

"I'll call the police."

Mack nodded, and I dialed 911.

But I couldn't help hoping we were wrong. Maybe after the police arrived, we could all have a good laugh when the body turned out to be one of those inflatable love dolls. In your dreams, Mandy.

Unfortunately this wasn't a dream. This was my worst nightmare, and if it were a real body up there, I had a hunch that Uncle Chet's baseball bat had something to do with the person's death.

CHAPTER 2

The body had to be someone I knew. How else could a person get inside my locked plant overnight? And how could the person's death be anything but murder? A stranger wouldn't wander into my place of business from the street and hang himself on my conveyor. It just wasn't the method of choice for someone contemplating suicide.

The 911 operator had asked me to stay on the phone, but I covered the mouthpiece with my hand. "Is everyone here this morning, Mack?"

"Everyone who's supposed to be here."

That relieved me, but only a little. Several of my employees didn't come in until later, including Sarah, who'd closed up on Saturday night. Oh, please, don't let it be her.

Mack shook his head at a customer outside the door, watched her walk away, then turned to me. "How the hell could a body get up there?" he asked in a voice that's trained to project to the back row of a theater.

In addition to being my cleaner/spotter and production manager, he's a part-time actor who'd once played a lawyer in a local production of *The Caine Mutiny Court*

Martial. I found myself wishing he could run interference for me with the police right now, but I knew it was up to me. Mack had always seemed a little skittish about the cops.

I hadn't minded a few months earlier when I'd gotten involved in a murder case after a bloody suit wound up in one of our dirty clothes bags. But this was different—a body strung up to the conveyor inside my plant. This could be big trouble, the kind that made my money problems and Mom's visit pale by comparison.

I went to the door, waving a few more early-morning customers away, and waited until I saw a patrol car pull up to the curb outside. A policeman got out, and I opened the door for him and escorted him to the conveyor.

"There's something up there," I said. "In case it's a body, I thought I'd better have you check it out."

He took one look at the cowboy boots and called for backup. Then he turned to me. "When did you discover this?"

"Just now when I went to get an order off the conveyor. It stopped, and I came out here to see what was wrong." The officer looked at me skeptically, and I continued, "We've been having a lot of weird things happen around the plant, and at first I thought this was just another trick of some kind—" I stopped to take a breath. "I mean, that was when we first saw the cowboy boots—before we decided it might actually be a body."

Mack frowned at me, which I took to be a bit of legal advice, garnered from his onstage experience with the law. Never volunteer, it seemed to say.

"Mack, why don't you get a ladder from the back?" I suggested. Fortunately we had a tall one that we used for changing light bulbs and getting lint off the overhead pipes.

Mack hurried away, probably relieved at not having to talk to the cops any more than was absolutely necessary.

When I was a kid, working at the cleaners, I'd been sure there was a dark secret in his past that made him leery of the law. No one was born with a name like McKenzie Rivers. It had to be an alias.

By the time he returned with the ladder, the place was beginning to look like the site of a law enforcement convention. Two of the officers set up the ladder, and one of them climbed up to get a closer look at the thing on the conveyor. I still didn't want to think of it as a person.

"It's a body, all right," the man said, climbing back down to the floor.

My stomach, which was already queasy, went into a fast-spin cycle. "What did the person look like?"

"The person looked dead, Miss," the officer said. "That's all I can say right now."

Okay, so the police weren't going to tell me if the person was a man or a woman, but I didn't think it could be Al Pulaski, the salesman and driver for the pickup-and-delivery route I had started operating to office buildings in the area. He wasn't here yet, but he was such a big guy that surely no one could have lifted him up onto the conveyor. And Theresa Emory, my front-counter manager, had wanted off early Saturday so she could go out of town for the weekend, so it probably wasn't her. That left Sarah . . .

"I'll call in Homicide," the man said to one of the other officers, then turned back to me. "Is there someplace we can put your employees where we can make sure they don't talk to one another?"

It was probably a little late for that. I glanced into the plant and could see that very little work was going on. Most of the crew was clustered around Ingrid's silk press. Even from here I could see flashes of her tight red T-shirt and hear her popping her bubble gum.

"I guess they could all go in our break room." I pointed to Mack. "Mr. Rivers can help you see that they go in there."

Mack left with one of the officers while I answered a lot of questions, wrote and signed a statement, and went with another policeman to see if anything seemed to have been disturbed in the rest of the plant. I was numb, and wondered if this is what it felt like to be in shock.

I couldn't really spot anything out of place, but it was a little hard to tell with so many clothes in the building waiting to be done. I tried not to think what this was going to do to my business. All I could see was the idle equipment. Some of the forms we used to steam the clothes looked eerily like dismembered body parts to me now.

We'd reached the door to my office when someone came up behind me and tapped me on the shoulder. "You doing okay?"

I recognized the voice and swung around, almost jamming my nose into the breast pocket of a sports jacket, worn by a very tall man. It was Stan Foster, the handsome, blond homicide detective who'd collected the bloodstained suit from me in that other murder case.

He reminded me of a young Clint Eastwood, and at one time I'd even thought there'd been some chemistry between us. But I hadn't seen him in three months—and I still had his clothes. He'd left them here to be cleaned about the time he'd gotten the mistaken impression that I had a live-in boyfriend. I'd planned to clear up the misunderstanding when he came to get his clothes, but he never returned.

So why did he have to show up now—when I had a whole lot more important things on my mind? Was he the only homicide detective who worked this end of town, or was it just the luck of the draw that he'd been on duty when the call came in?

"Are you sure you're all right?" he asked again.

I came out of my trance. "I—I've been better."

"So how do you think a body got on a conveyor inside your store?"

"I'm sorry, I haven't a clue." I suppose he was expecting more from the woman who'd analyzed every inch of the bloody suit and came up with a profile of the killer.

"Have you spotted anything unusual in the rest of the plant?"

My police escort spoke for me. "Miss Dyer says everything seems okay as far as she can see."

"Why don't you take her to the break room when you finish up and have her wait with the rest of the witnesses." I hated it when people spoke about me in the third person, and I was about to object when Foster turned back to me. "We'll need to use your office to interview your employees. Okay?"

I nodded and started to leave, then turned back to him. "Could you talk to Emily Grant right away? She was my first customer of the day, and I'd appreciate it if you would let her go home soon."

Foster nodded.

When I got to the break room, my crew was jammed into the small space like cattle corralled in a pen to await the slaughterhouse. It was not a pretty picture, and the thing that was even scarier was that there was a strong possibility one of these people or someone on my afternoon shift could be a murderer. There was no sign of forced entry. The doors had been locked and the burglar alarm set when I came to work this morning. But no matter how hard I tried, I couldn't shake the feeling that this had something to do with the dirty tricks going on for the last few months and that one of my employees might be a turncoat who was working undercover for Farley Mills.

I took a seat by Mack. The only thing I could see from the front of the plant were occasional flashes of light from cameras as the crime-lab people went about their work. One particularly bright eruption made our uniformed guard glance out the door.

Mack took that opportunity to nudge my arm. "Did you find out who it was?"

I shook my head and looked around at the stunned faces of my crew. At least Mrs. Grant seemed to have calmed down finally. Perhaps the arrival of the police was a soothing influence on her, even if it was disconcerting to the rest of us. The only sound, besides people shuffling nervously in their seats and scratching with pens on the statements the police had asked them to fill out, was Ingrid and her bubble gum.

Pop. Pop. Pop. She sounded like a kid at a carnival taking potshots at a string of ducks. I tried to get her attention so I could make her stop, but she was staring off into space as if she could see some invisible target.

Not for the first time I wished that Uncle Chet had put in a nonchewing ban when he'd put up the nonsmoking signs inside the cleaners. That's why Ingrid had taken up chewing gum, and I used to have nightmares about her gum landing on a five-thousand-dollar bridal gown as she worked on it, but she was a whiz at pressing even the most elaborate silks and satins, so I held my tongue.

I'd noticed that the more nervous she became, the more bubbles she blew. She was tall, big-boned, and blond and reminded me of a Nordic goddess. The image was only slightly marred by her addiction to bubble gum, the Kansas City Chiefs, and the slot machines at Colorado's three nearby gambling towns.

Pop. Pop. Pop. My head was beginning to feel like a dryer with a couple of tennis shoes banging around inside. I finally caught her eye and slapped my hand over my mouth. Apparently she got the point of my creative body language. The incessant popping stopped long enough for me to take a head count of the crew.

I saw that Al Pulaski, the ruddy-faced, sandy-haired driver for my business route, had arrived. Al had never met a man—or woman—he didn't like, and in true salesmanlike fashion he was trying to start a conversation with the policeman at the door. He was politely rebuffed for his efforts.

I couldn't spot Juan Martinez, who worked in the laundry. "Where's Juan?" I whispered to Mack, taking advantage of Al's attempt at conversation with the cop.

Mack glanced around the room. "I don't know. He was here a little while ago."

A policeman at the back of the room came forward and told Mack and me to be quiet. Al finally went over and sat by Kim in the only empty chair in the room. He looked totally bewildered as he mouthed a silent "What's going on?" to Mack's assistant. Kim shrugged and ducked his head.

Now only Theresa Emory, my front-counter manager, and Sarah were missing. But what the devil had happened to Juan? I looked around the room for him again, and as my eyes moved to the door, I saw Detective Foster motioning at me.

I jumped out of my chair and went over to him.

"We need you to take a look at the body and see if you can give us an ID," he said.

I didn't want to see it, but yet I did. I had to find out who it was. Surely it couldn't be Sarah in jeans and red cowboy boots.

I hurried to the call office, trying to keep up with Foster's long strides.

The corpse was in a body bag, already on a gurney.

"Do you know who it is?" Foster asked.

Unfortunately I did, and I lurched to a stop. My stomach kept right on spinning.

"Who is it?" he repeated.

"It's—" I gulped, trying to stop the bile that was rising in my throat like soapsuds. "His name is Farley Mills. He owns another dry cleaners in the neighborhood."

It couldn't be Farley Mills, but it was. My competitor was staring up at me with that same awful leer that he'd always had.

But what was his body doing inside my cleaners? I couldn't even hazard a guess, but I knew someone was bound to tell the cops about the time I threatened to put a permanent end to his cleaning career if I ever caught him hanging around my plant again. I pushed the thought from my mind.

"Why don't we go back to your office so we can talk?" Foster suggested.

I lagged behind him as I followed him to the back of the plant. My thoughts returned to Sarah, who looked as if a strong wind could blow her away. She was a single mother with two small children and a background she never talked about. I'd hired her six months before when she'd arrived in town and seemed desperate for a job. Everything had been fine until about a month ago when she'd had that fight with Mills and had tried to eject him from the call office. She'd wound up with a bruise on her arm and a burn where he'd grabbed the chain of a locket she always wore around her neck.

I should never have let Theresa talk me into letting

Sarah close Saturday night by herself. What if she'd had another run-in with Mills? But for the life of me, I couldn't see her having the strength to kill Farley, much less string him up on the conveyor.

"Was there a bruise on the back of *his* head?" I asked as I trailed after Foster.

He slammed to a stop. "What do you mean?"

"There was a baseball bat up front, and the woman who marks in clothes found it on her table this morning."

Foster turned around and had me show him where it was. He called someone from the crime-lab team to take possession of it.

"It'll have our fingerprints on it," I said, realizing this could be incriminating, particularly for me since I was the last one to touch it. I watched as a member of the crime lab bagged the bat with as much care as I hoped we bagged the clothes.

When we finally got to my office, Foster seated himself at the swivel chair behind my desk. I was forced to take the seat across from him. It put me at a distinct disadvantage, which was probably what he wanted.

He opened a small notebook and reached into a shirt pocket for a pen, making a show of depressing the top so the point would come out. "See," he said, giving me his lopsided grin, "I remembered your advice about retracting the point so I won't get ink in my pocket."

If he was trying to make me feel at ease, it didn't work. I couldn't even force a smile.

He seemed embarrassed. "I'm sorry." He stared at his open notebook for a minute. "Okay, how well did you know Mr. Mills?"

"Not well at all. Mills opened a store in the neighborhood right after Christmas. It's called a drop shop because people take their clothes there but the work is done someplace else. I think he had a plant up north of town."

"But I gather you had talked to him."

"A few times."

"What did you talk about?"

I decided I'd better come clean, as we in the dry-cleaning business say. "He was always handing out coupons for his cleaners right outside my front door. He would block our entrance so customers couldn't get inside. We exchanged words a few times about that."

"I take it these weren't friendly conversations?"

"No." I was beginning to sweat, and I brushed a stray lock of hair back from my forehead. It didn't help.

"So were you angry enough to kill him?"

I half rose out of my chair. "No, of course not." I eased back down, not wanting him to think I had a problem with control.

To his credit, Foster looked embarrassed again. "Hey, I had to ask."

He wanted to know who had keys to the building, and I told him: Mack; my route salesman, Al Pulaski; my front-counter manager, Theresa Emory; and me. He asked who knew the code for the burglar alarm, and I said the same people did.

"So who locked up on Saturday?"

"Actually that night a woman named Sarah McIntyre did. Theresa gave her a key for the back door, then all she had to do was lock the front door and turn on the burglar alarm as she went out the back."

"Was the alarm set when you came to work today?"

I nodded. "Yes, I shut it off myself when I got here."

"So someone must have turned it off and reset it over the weekend in order to get in and out without being detected?"

I gave a tight little nod.

"Did you notice anything suspicious when you came in this morning?"

"Not until I started the conveyor and found the body. . . ."
I told him about the "dirty tricks" and how I'd even thought

for a minute that the body might be another trick. Unfortunately this time Mack wasn't around to stop me.

"Are you saying that you think Mills was behind the—uh, dirty tricks?"

"I don't know."

Foster continued his rapid-fire barrage of questions. "Did any of your people have a connection to Mills?"

I thought of Mack's Korean assistant. "Kim Il Chong actually worked for Mills before I hired him, but he came here after the dirty tricks started." I paused. "Everybody calls him Kim, but that's actually his last name."

Foster wrote down Kim's name. "Anyone else?"

I couldn't quite bring myself to tell him about Sarah's problems with Mills the night he'd tried to pass himself off as a customer, especially when she'd probably be grilled enough about closing up Saturday night.

I could see Foster was waiting for my response.

"Well, Ingrid Larsen, my silk finisher, had a fight with him in the parking lot one day. She said she told him to shove off when he'd started coming on to her." Actually what she'd said was that she'd threatened to "bust his bubble," metaphorically speaking, if he ever crossed her path again.

She'd also told me that her husband, Warren, would have killed Farley with his bare hands if he'd heard the remark. It hadn't been a serious threat, but I had no doubt that Warren could have done it. He was a big burly truck driver whom she'd met last fall at a Broncos-Chiefs football game. He was a rabid Broncos fan and had orange and blue paint smeared all over his face and torso at the time. She'd been decked out in her red-and-white Kansas City Chiefs regalia, and against all odds they fell in love and were married at a tailgate party before the final game of the year.

"Anyone else?"

"Not really." I began to itch, a slight tickle on the nose, which is what I do when I lie. Still, I didn't mention Sarah.

Of course maybe all of my eighteen employees had decided to get together to kill Farley to help out their beloved boss, whose business was going down the drain because of him. I didn't tell Foster that or the fact that the only person I could think of with the means, motive, and opportunity to kill Mills was the beloved boss herself.

"Are all your employees here today?"

I glanced at my watch. "They should be soon." I explained that a couple of them didn't come in until eleven, and gave him Sarah and Theresa's names. "And—uh—Juan Martinez in our laundry isn't here right now."

Foster never missed a thing. "Was he here earlier?"

"Well, yes, but he's had a stomach flu." That part was true. "He probably got sick again and had to leave."

Foster looked down at his notebook. "Why don't you tell me where you were this weekend?"

I hesitated, thinking that it was not only incriminating but embarrassing to have no social life. "I was home most of the time—except yesterday afternoon when I went to the supermarket."

"Was anyone with you Saturday night or Sunday?"

I shook my head, wondering if this might be the time to tell him that Nat Wilcox might be my best friend but he was *not* my lover. Nat is a reporter, and I'd only let him claim to live with me to help him get a scoop for his newspaper. I decided this wasn't the time to bring that up.

Foster turned over a page in his notebook. "Do you have any long extension cords in the plant?"

I was puzzled for a minute and then I realized that's what must have been used to secure the body to the conveyor. "Yes," I said carefully, "we have them to use with power tools when we need to work on the equipment." I wasn't about to tell him that there'd been a twenty-five-foot cord back by Mack's spotting table the last I'd known.

Foster closed his notebook abruptly. "Why don't you go back into the break room now, and I'll start talking to your employees."

I couldn't leave yet. "Could you tell me when you think he was killed?"

"We can't determine that until there's an autopsy."

I got up. "Right, and you wouldn't tell me if you could."

He nodded.

"One last thing. Could we at least get the work out of the machines and shut down the place?"

He agreed and told me he wanted me to remain in the plant in case he had any other questions for me. As far as I was concerned, that was a given. I wasn't about to leave until my employees were allowed to go home.

Then, in the company of another cop, Mack and I were permitted to remove clothes from the washers and dryers and the dry-cleaning machines. During our rounds I managed to tell Mack that the murder victim was Farley Mills. He looked as bewildered as I felt.

I noticed that Mrs. Grant was gone when I got back to the break room. Apparently Foster had heeded my request and allowed her to leave. After that, all I could do was watch helplessly as, one by one, my employees were interviewed and then sent home. Theresa was among them, but Sarah never did show up for her afternoon shift, and Juan didn't return to work. I wondered if they'd called me, but I had no way of knowing because the police were letting my voice mail pick up.

Finally only Mack and I were left. Instead of calling him, the cop at the door asked if I'd return to my office. My stomach was in a permanent knot by now.

"You're supposed to call this number," Foster said, handing me a piece of paper and vacating my chair. "You can do it here."

I was puzzled, but I grabbed the receiver and punched in the numbers.

"Amanda, is that you?" Oh, geez, it was Mom. "I'm at a pay phone at the airport, and I've been trying to call you for half an hour. I finally had to call that Mexican restaurant behind your place and ask them to give you a message."

I couldn't believe that I'd forgotten she was coming, and to think that only a few hours before, her visit had been the biggest problem in my life.

"You'll have to take a taxi, Mom. Go to my apartment and ask the manager in One-fourteen to let you into my place."

There was a silence on the other end of the line. "I'd think," she said finally, "that when your mother comes to town, you could at least break away from what you're doing long enough to come get her."

"I'll be home as soon as I can, but I can't leave now."

Mom began to sniffle. "I didn't want to tell you this on the phone this morning, Amanda, but I've left Herbie."

Suddenly the knot in my stomach became a noose around my neck. Mom ran through husbands like most women go through panty hose. I'd had four stepfathers after my dad died when I was a year old, and I'd kind of hoped Number Five would last, mainly because I liked Herb better than the others.

"I'm sorry, Mom."

"I really need to talk to my daughter."

There was nothing to do but tell her the truth. "Mom, listen, there's been a death here at the plant, and I can't leave until the police are through."

She let out a gasp. "Oh, my god. Are you all right? I'll come down to the cleaners right away."

"No, please, just go to my apartment." My words were firm, but unfortunately my hands were shaking so hard I could hardly hold the phone. I turned around so Foster wouldn't see me falling apart. "Look, I have to go. I'll see you soon." As I hung up, I could hear Mom protesting at the other end of the line.

"That was my mother," I said to Foster, compounding the obvious. "If you're not through with me, do you suppose I could ask Mack to go stay with her until I get home? She's very upset."

I also thought, knowing his aversion to police, that it would be a way to get Mack out of the plant as soon as possible. It was arranged, but actually I'm not sure Mack dreaded the police any more than he did the thought of entertaining Mom. He'd known her since he started working for my uncle years ago.

"I've obtained a search warrant," Foster said, causing all other thoughts to flee from my mind. "We'll probably be in the plant all day tomorrow."

I didn't ask if the cleaners could be open while the search was going on. I wasn't about to expose my employees, much less my customers, to any more of the investigation than was absolutely necessary. And I didn't even ask if I could be here during the search. I didn't want to give even the slightest impression that I had anything to hide.

"We'll have a guard posted outside the plant tonight, but I'll need a key so we can lock up when we're through."

Mack gave him a key off of his key ring.

"We'll try to get out of here as fast as possible, and I'll call you when we're through."

"Fine." I didn't know what else to say.

He had me leave the office so he could talk to Mack alone, but the interview lasted only a few minutes. Then it was my turn again.

"I wanted to remind you that nothing can be removed from the building while we're here."

For some reason I took a small, perverse pleasure in that. "Which reminds me," I said, "we still have some of your clothes. I guess you won't be able to remove them now, either."

Foster looked blank.

"You brought us some clothes to be cleaned in December."

He whacked himself on the forehead. "Oh, damn. I forgot all about that."

"I'd have called you, but you said you couldn't believe anyone would forget their clothes at the cleaners."

"I've been looking all over for my brown sports jacket. . . ." He gave me a sheepish grin, and I couldn't help wondering if his smile was crooked or if the cleft in the middle of his chin was just a little off center. "I bet it's here."

My moment of satisfaction was short-lived.

Foster got back to business. "Who has keys to your company van, by the way?"

"Al and I do, and I guess Mack has a set too. Why?"

"You still take the van home at night?"

I nodded.

"Did you take it out someplace after you got home from the grocery store yesterday afternoon?"

"No."

"Well, one of our officers talked to someone in the neighborhood who said he saw the van here at the plant last night. Who could have been driving it at eleven-thirty?"

"I—I don't know."

I'd already figured out that I was a prime suspect in Farley Mills's murder, but now I realized someone had been working overtime to set me up.

CHAPTER 4

Who would want to frame me for murder? For that matter, who would want to play dirty tricks on me? And if Farley had been the one behind the mysterious goings-on at the cleaners, why?

I had never even set eyes on him until he started bombarding my customers with discount coupons for his store. He could have targeted a dozen other cleaners. Why me? And I didn't really think it was coincidence that Farley's efforts to lure customers away from Dyer's Cleaners began about the same time that the Magic Marker and lipstick slashes began appearing on our freshly pressed clothes. No way was it just some new fad of garment graffiti.

Now the company van had mysteriously appeared behind the plant in the middle of the night. Another dirty trick? No, this was much more scary. I'd always viewed the van with its Dyer's Cleaners logo on the sides as advertising on wheels. But last night it had falsely advertised my presence at the cleaners. The police had hauled it away and were now searching its interior for evidence against me in the murder of my competitor.

I'd given Foster the key to the van, which left me without any transportation at all. He said he'd get one of the patrolmen to give me a ride home when he finally finished talking to me. He also let me take a roster of my employees so I could call them and tell them they shouldn't come to work the next day.

I went out the back door and waited for my police escort. I didn't even know what the weather was like until I got outside. It was as cold and dreary as I felt, and I pulled up the collar on my new tan coat and looked across the expanse of parking lot to the strip center behind the cleaners.

Al and Ingrid were coming from the direction of Tico Taco's, a Mexican restaurant where they'd obviously gone to have a drink and talk about the murder. They waved at me as they stopped beside Al's new Blazer. It was parked beside the little red convertible—what else?—that Ingrid had bought for herself last fall after she won a big jackpot at the slots. I couldn't help wondering why all my employees could afford fancy cars when all I had was the company van, which I used when Al wasn't driving it. I must be doing something wrong.

I went over to them, and Ingrid tapped out a cigarette from her pack of Marlboros for me. "You look like you need one," she said. It was probably a major mistake since I'd quit smoking two years before, but I took it anyway.

"So who do the cops think killed Mills?" Al asked.

"Your guess is as good as mine."

"He always reminded me of Hitler," Ingrid said as she handed me a book of matches. "Everyone who knew him probably wanted him dead."

I wasn't sure that was an apt comparison, but I let it go. I was too busy trying to light the cigarette in a mini-whirlwind that blew across the lot. Four attempts, and I gave up.

"Where's your lighter?" As I recalled, Ingrid always used a red lighter to go with her all-red wardrobe and her jazzy car.

"Huh?" She seemed surprised.

"Your lighter—where's your lighter?"

"God, you have been quit a long time, haven't you? Nobody can use the childproof lighters they have anymore—except maybe a six-year-old kid."

Al took the matches, cupped his hands around one, and struck it as I dragged on the cigarette. "Ingrid was saying maybe Sarah got in another fight with Mills," he said. "We never saw her come in today. Where was she?"

"I don't know." I puffed on the cigarette and almost choked. "She probably called in sick but couldn't get through on the phone."

"Miss Dyer." It was the uniformed officer Foster had found to take me home. "I'm supposed to give you a ride."

If I'd known Ingrid and Al were still around, I would have asked one of them for a lift. As it was, I told them not to come back to work until I called them, and then left with the cop.

I felt like a prisoner all the way home. And why not? After all, someone had gone to a great deal of trouble to set me up. They'd apparently taken the van from the street near my apartment for the rendezvous with Farley. I tried to remember if it had been parked in the same spot this morning where I'd left it yesterday afternoon. If it hadn't been in the same space, I was sure it had been parked close by. I didn't have to wander around the neighborhood looking for it.

Maybe I should even consider Al a suspect since he drove the van more than I did. But as I'd told Foster, when Al had been on vacation recently, several other people had run the route and I'd given them the extra set of keys from a hook in my office. For that matter, anyone in the plant could have lifted the keys and made a copy. The person would have had to know the code to shut off our burglar alarm, though, and I made a mental note to see that it was changed as soon as the police were gone.

When we got to Capitol Hill near downtown Denver, I pointed out the Victorian house where I lived, and the cop pulled up at the curb. I dragged myself up the stairs to my third-floor apartment, not looking forward to facing my mother. Unfortunately I heard sneezing from behind my door even before I saw her.

"Oh, darn." I'd never told her that I'd brought Spot, the cleaners' resident cat, home with me after Uncle Chet died. I hadn't thought it necessary. My plan had been to take her to a hotel since she didn't like to stay at my place anyway.

She'd be having a fit by now. It wasn't so much that she disliked cats, which she did, as the fact that she was allergic to them and everything else known to mankind—with the possible exception of men themselves.

I opened the door. "Hi, Mom." I took off my coat and went over to give her a hug.

She was sitting at the kitchen table, a box of Kleenex in front of her, a wastebasket beside her, and one of the tissues clutched in her hand.

It was obscene to have a mother who looked as young as she did, but maybe there was something in the gene pool that would make me age well too. I didn't think so. We didn't look alike. Her hair was a much lighter shade of brown than mine, although no one would know it. She dyed it ash blond and fluffed it around her face in the same style she'd worn for years.

Actually she was fluffy all over, favoring feminine clothes with a lot of ruffles and bows. She had a kind of translucent peaches-and-cream skin that I would have thought would wrinkle as she got older, but it didn't. It looked kind of blotchy now, but I was sure it was a temporary condition that would clear up once I got her away from Spot and reunited with Herb.

"Hello, dear," she said, reaching up to kiss me on the cheek. "I'm so glad you're finally home. I didn't know how much longer I could stand it with that cat." She sneezed again and glowered at Spot, the beautiful, long-haired yellow feline with the disposition from hell.

His name had been Uncle Chet's idea of a joke, coming as it did from a cleaner who prided himself on removing spots. The cat was ensconced on a corner of my sofa bed and was washing himself, probably raising dander, which is the thing people are supposed to be allergic to. And in fact he was raising mine because I had a feeling he was doing it on purpose.

"Where's Mack?" I looked around the apartment, but it was easy to see he wasn't here because all I have is one big room.

"I sent him out to get some antihistamine," Mom said. "I should be all right as soon as he gets back."

I was going to owe him big-time for coming over and keeping her company until I could get home.

"As soon as he gets back, we'll take you to a hotel," I said. "You'll be okay when you get out of here."

"No, no, dear." She paused for another round of sneezes. "I think we need to be together at a time like this. I'll be all right as soon as Mack gets back with the pills." Martyrdom had never been one of her strong points, and this surprised me. "If not, maybe Mack can take the cat home with him for a while."

When Spot completed his ritual of grooming, he had the audacity to give a delicate little sneeze himself, probably from the dander floating around him like an aura but maybe just to indicate he was allergic to Mom.

Unfortunately Mack didn't owe me enough favors to take Spot home with him, and even if he did, he lived in a building that didn't allow pets.

"Mack didn't tell me much about what happened," Mom continued, wiping her eyes and throwing the Kleenex away, "so why don't you get us some tea, dear, and tell me the whole story."

"I don't have any tea, Mom. How about a glass of wine?"

I sure could use one, and Mom agreed reluctantly. She always agrees reluctantly on the theory that she doesn't really drink if someone else talks her into it.

"Mack said it was a competitor of yours who was killed," she said as I poured us two glasses of Chablis. "How on earth did it happen?"

"First, you tell me what happened to you and Herb."

She reached for a fresh Kleenex. "I don't want to discuss that man. If I never see him again, it'll be fine with me."

I knew I'd hear the story eventually, but I'd have to coax it out of her. I didn't feel much like coaxing at the moment.

"Let's talk about you right now, dear," she suggested, taking a ladylike sip of wine.

"I don't feel like talking about that right now either." What I felt like doing was slugging down the wine, but I restrained myself.

"Oh, I didn't mean the incident at the cleaners. What about *you*? Are you doing all right? Have you met *someone* yet?"

I thought about making up some creative story about this sexy homicide detective who was about to arrest me, but since I have this problem of itching when I lie, I figured we didn't need two people in the room with allergic reactions.

"No, Mom," I said. "I've been too busy with the business to find some guy."

"Well, I was thinking, dear, maybe you should call Larry. Especially if you need any legal advice about this problem at the cleaners. . . ."

She went on talking, but all I heard was the name Larry.

The reason I called him Larry the Lustful Law Student was that he'd passed a couple of bars while we were married. One allowed him to practice in the state of Colorado and the other one was where he met a lady lawyer whom he'd decided to marry the day our divorce was final.

"I'm not calling Larry." My voice sounded hysterical, and I tried to control it. "Why would I call Larry, for God's sake?" I gulped the wine.

"This wrongful-death problem might be just the thing to get you two back together."

"He's married, Mom, and don't even think about calling him."

Mom started shaking her head. "No, no, don't you remember how I told you that the poor boy wrote me at Christmas and said he and Patricia were separated?" She drank her wine thoughtfully. "I don't think he'd have told me that unless he wanted to get back together with you."

I admit to having had a few gleeful moments when she'd first mentioned that Larry and Pat were having problems. That didn't mean I wanted him back in my life.

I stood up from the table. "If you choose to send Christmas cards to Larry, that's your business, but don't you dare call him and try to get us back together. Do you hear?"

"I just thought he might be able to help in case there's a lawsuit about the man dying in your store. Did he fall or what?"

I couldn't take it anymore. Why try to shield her from the awful truth? "Mom, the man was murdered at the plant. He was hit over the head and hung up on the conveyor to die." I knew the moment the words were out that it was a mistake.

She gasped, but I could almost see the wheels spinning in her head. "All the more reason to call Larry," they seemed to say. It was all I could do to keep from stomping my feet like I was having a teenage temper tantrum. I settled for folding my arms across my chest in a more mature gesture of defiance. "I have serious problems, and I don't want Larry adding to them."

I'm not sure Mom heard me. She was sneezing again, and I went over and pulled out a fresh Kleenex for her to use.

"Oh, dear, I wish McKenzie would get back with that antihistamine," she said.

Mom always did have a way of getting what she wanted. Mack opened the door right then as if she'd willed him to appear.

"Hi, everybody. I got the pills."

To say I was relieved to see him probably isn't an accurate description of how I felt. I was glad it brought a halt to the conversation, but I was left with the unsettling feeling that Mom hadn't paid the slightest bit of attention to what I'd just said.

"Here they are, Cecilia." Mack handed the pills to Mom, and looked over at me sympathetically. "How you doing, Mandy?"

Mom didn't give me a chance to answer. "Thank you, McKenzie, but I wonder if I should take them now that Amanda talked me into having wine. You're not supposed to take the pills with alcohol."

"That does it." I slashed my hands in the air. "You'll have to go to a hotel if you can't take something for your allergy."

Mack looked at me as if I were coming unhinged, and of course I was. It was the image of Larry at my door, combined with all the other problems, that was knocking my whole system out of kilter.

Mom dabbed at her eyes. "I'll take a shower. The steam should help clear up my sinuses."

"Nope, we're going to a hotel."

"But this is the time a mother and daughter need each other."

"I'll stay at the hotel with you tonight. How's that?"

It seemed to satisfy her, and Mack looked relieved that we'd agreed on something. Still, he seemed anxious to leave, and he headed for the door.

"Can you give us a lift, Mack? The police kept the van so they could take a look at it."

"For Christ's sake, why?"

I frowned at him.

"Oh, dear, that's terrible," Mom said. "I really do think you should consult a lawyer."

Mack agreed to drive us to a hotel and helped while we accumulated Mom's luggage. Two suitcases and a cosmetic case. I stuffed a pair of flannel pajamas, a toothbrush, and a change of underwear into a laundry bag, the only thing I could find as a tote bag on such short notice. I grabbed my coat and stopped only long enough to feed Spot and call the downtown Holiday Inn to make a reservation. Lucky for Mack, they had a room.

We went out and got in Mack's pickup. Mom's only concession to fascinating womanhood today was a ruffled blouse under a pink pants suit, and she stepped up easily into the truck. I was still wearing my tight-skirted suit from work, and I had more trouble. Finally I just hiked up the skirt and climbed in after her. Who cared about looking graceful at a time like this?

Mack drove us away from my cat-infested apartment in rush-hour traffic. As soon as we were out in the cold air, Mom's allergies seem to clear up immediately. I was having more trouble getting over my anxiety about Larry and the possible need for a lawyer in my life.

The hotel is right at the edge of downtown Denver and just before the high-rises. On the way, we passed the state capitol, the newly remodeled central library, and Denver's City and County Building. Mom made some comment about the library having too many different architectural styles to suit her, but then she hadn't liked anything but adobe since she'd moved to the Southwest.

Finally Mack pulled into the check-in lane at the hotel, and, gentleman that he was, helped me haul Mom's suitcases to a room on the fourth floor. It didn't make me feel any better that she'd brought enough clothes for a three-month stay.

"Thanks again, McKenzie," Mom said as he started to leave.

I went out into the hall with him and closed the door. "Could you do me a big favor?"

"What do you think this was?" he asked.

"You're right. Well, do you suppose you could do me another big favor?"

"Try me."

"Drive me someplace to rent a car."

I could tell that poor Mack wasn't keen on the idea. "Why don't we do it tomorrow?"

"Because I need to know I can escape if I want to. Also we need to talk, and I can't do it in front of Mom."

As if she'd heard her name being mentioned, she opened the door into the hall. "Which bed do you want, Amanda?"

"I don't care."

"Please, you're being sweet enough to stay here with me. The least I can do is let you pick out the bed you want."

I took a shot. "The one here by the door will be fine."

"Okay," she said. "I just hope it isn't too noisy by the window. . . ."

Now that I'd had a cigarette with Ingrid, I wished I'd

asked for a smoking room. It was going to be a long night, but at least Mack saw my point and agreed to take me out to rent a car.

What he didn't know, of course, was that I had a couple of other things I wanted to do while I was gone.

CHAPTER 5

By the time we broke away from Mom, I was itching so much, it was as if I'd been rolling around in a patch of poison ivy.

I'd told her I needed to go rent a car. It was true, but as she'd so logically pointed out, I could probably rent one on the phone and have the car-rental people bring it to me.

That's when I began to stretch the truth. I'd said I needed to go back to the plant to close out the register for the day, which was a total falsehood because the police probably wouldn't let me near the place. However, I knew Mom wouldn't want to go there. She liked dry cleaning about as much as I liked the thought of Larry coming back into my life.

Mom had finally agreed to let Mack and me go by ourselves. She would take a nap, she'd said, if I wouldn't mind her sleeping on *my* bed away from the window. I gave her my permission and promised to return by eight o'clock so we could have dinner together.

"Thanks, Mack, for helping out." We were in his pickup by then. "Mom's having a bad time right now."

Mack had known her for years, and he looked over at me and grinned as he pulled out of the hotel parking lot and into the rush-hour traffic of downtown Denver. "Right. 'Mother'—what's the phrase?—'isn't quite herself today.' "

I gave him a dirty look as I recognized the line. Anthony Perkins had said it to Janet Leigh in *Psycho*, but I just wasn't up to playing our trivia game today—seeing if we could stump each other with famous movie quotes.

"She and Herb had a fight," I said.

"Oh, God, I'm sorry."

He looked so contrite that I reached over and patted his hand. "It's okay. Don't worry about it."

"She didn't say anything about it to me."

"I probably should have stayed with her, but I just needed a little time to myself to see if I can think of any answers to this mess."

Mack was more than happy to change the subject. "So what's this about the van?"

I told him what I knew.

He was shaking his head by the time I got through. "It sure sounds like someone was trying to set you up. Any ideas?"

I shrugged. "Someone must have had a key to the plant, not to mention the van, and they'd have had to know how to shut off the burglar alarm once they got inside."

"So how many people have keys and know the code to shut off the alarm?" Mack asked finally.

I went through the names I'd given to Foster.

Mack gripped the steering wheel. "I gave the key and the code to Kim that time we were both sick and couldn't open up."

"I'd forgotten about that." I sighed. "But I suppose anyone could have sneaked the key out of my purse and made a copy of it, and the code for the burglar alarm used to be taped in Uncle Chet's desk."

"I guess that means we're all suspects." Mack was quiet for a minute. "So where do you want to go to rent a car?"

"Oh, yeah, the car." I wanted to go to rent the cheapest car possible, but I knew Mom would have a fit if I rented a clunker, seeing as how Herb always drove a brand-new Lincoln. Never mind that he'd been a used-car dealer before he retired. "I think there are some rental places over on Broadway."

"So what are you going to do then?"

"Drive around aimlessly and try to figure out why Farley was out to get me and who could have killed him."

What I really planned to do was go have a talk with my missing employees, but I wasn't about to tell that to Mack. Why involve him in any of my clandestine activities? Especially if he'd ever had a problem with the law.

I cleared my throat nervously and, for the first time in all these years, broached the subject. "You don't have a reason to be afraid of the police, do you? I mean, any more than I do."

There! I'd said it. Something I'd always wanted to ask but been afraid to do because it might jeopardize our friendship.

Mack almost ran a red light. "Why would you ask a crazy question like that?"

"I used to think the name McKenzie Rivers was an alias."

Mack, who usually could come up with an apropos quote he'd memorized even when he couldn't come up with something extemporaneous, was struck speechless.

"It's a river in Oregon, in case you didn't know," I explained. "I learned about it in junior high." I decided not to add that I'd also thought the name might have something to do with being "sent up the river."

"It's also a river in Canada, but spelled with an *a*," Mack pointed out.

"Well, I guess we were taking U.S. geography at the time."

"I'm surprised you didn't think I was some crazed Scotsman—with a name like McKenzie."

"I considered it, but I just couldn't see you in kilts."

He chuckled, perhaps at the mental picture of a big black man in a plaid skirt, and I was glad he was feeling better. "Did it ever occur to you that it might just be a moniker given to me by a very creative mother?"

"No." We'd reached a car-rental agency by then, and I jumped down from the truck. "Please don't be offended. I just always wondered. . . ."

"No offense taken." He shifted into first gear, ready to drive away. "Call me tomorrow."

He was already rolling, so I slammed the door. He had never answered my question, come to think of it, about whether he'd ever been in trouble with the law or had an outstanding warrant for his arrest floating around out there someplace.

It took a while at the rental agency. I picked out a Ford Taurus. It would have been cheaper to rent some economy-size import, but Mom would have had a fit if I didn't get at least a medium-size car.

I looked up the addresses for Juan and Sarah on my roster and decided to visit Juan first. Then I checked everything on the dashboard before I took off, driving carefully out of the downtown area while I became familiar with the car. The sun was already down when I crossed over into North Denver on a bridge that spanned the railroad tracks and the Platte River.

I stopped on Thirty-second Avenue to check a map that the rental people had given me. Juan's address was only a couple of miles farther west, and I spotted the side street easily when I came to the intersection. I had more trouble seeing the house number.

The houses were all brick in this part of town and

looked alike. I stopped and searched for a flashlight in
the glove compartment, but there was nothing there except the instruction manual. However, I got lucky. Surprised but lucky. I recognized the truck parked in front of
one of the houses. It belonged to Mack. I knew because,
as I was almost abreast of it, I spotted the rear license
plate, MAC TRK.

Mack apparently had come up with the same idea I
had. No wonder he'd been anxious to get away from me
and Mom. He, too, had been worried about Juan. I hoped
he'd discovered something that would help us.

There was a parking space just behind the truck, and I
started to back into it, but another car sped up behind me
and zipped into the space before I had a chance. I felt like
giving the driver the finger, but what good would it do in
the dark? I drove up the street a couple of houses and
parked the rental.

When I looked back at the house where Mack's truck
was parked, I saw a thin-looking kid get out of the car,
run up the sidewalk, and take the steps to the porch two at
a time. He was inside the house before I could ask him
if I had the correct address. When I reached the porch,
I could see, from the numbers above the doorbell, that I
was at the right place. I rang the bell and waited, but I
hadn't expected such a quick response.

Someone came running to the door. The kid I'd just
seen enter the house flung open the door and charged
right at me. For a split second I thought he was going to
tackle me. I jumped aside, and he kept running. I would
have fallen if I hadn't grabbed the post that held up the
porch railing.

He leaped down all four stairs to the sidewalk. I disen-
gaged myself from the post and started back to the door.
Mack came tearing out of the house behind the boy but
lost some momentum because I was standing in his path.

"Mandy," he yelled in surprise, "get out of my way."

I stepped off to the side to let him pass, but by that time the kid was in his car, his tires squealing as he pulled away from the curb. Mack was halfway down the steps by then.

I didn't have a clue to what was happening, but I figured if Mack was after the kid, I might as well get involved in the chase. Mack was already in his pickup by the time I managed to open the passenger door, hitch up my skirt, and scramble in beside him.

"What the devil's going on?" I asked, trying to catch my breath as I yanked on the seat belt.

"Tell you later." Mack roared after the kid.

Later was sooner than I expected. We kept the car's taillights in sight until Mack caught the end of a yellow light and accelerated to get through the intersection. Another car, anxious to get a jump on the green, spurted out in front of us from the right, and Mack slammed on the brakes. The truck skidded to a stop, just inches from the car.

"You okay?" Mack asked, glancing at me quickly.

I nodded. "How about you?"

"Just mad." He reversed and pulled away from the car. Meanwhile the driver was screaming at us and giving the same unfriendly gesture I'd thought of using earlier. Mack turned the wheel and steered the truck around the car, continuing in the same direction we'd been going.

Three blocks later he finally stopped. The kid and his car had disappeared. Mack pulled over to the curb and pounded his fist on the steering wheel.

I'd waited long enough for an answer. "Okay, what was this all about?"

"Bobby knows something," Mack said.

"Bobby? Is that one of Juan's kids?"

"Yeah, and according to Mrs. Martinez, his father came home from work this morning and tried to talk to the kid, but Bobby took off, and Juan has been out looking for him all day. So the kid finally comes home, sees me, and takes off again like he's scared to death."

I unhooked the seat belt, which had cut into my neck when it kept me from going through the windshield. "What could Bobby possibly have to do with what happened at the plant?"

"Something maybe, if I understand the boy's mother." Mack started the truck, did a U-turn, and headed back the way we'd come. "He's been working for Farley Mills the last few months."

That threw me for a minute. I couldn't think what to ask.

"Apparently Juan always liked his job at our place," Mack continued, "so when Farley opened his cleaning plant up in this part of town, Juan suggested the kid go in there for a job. Bobby had dropped out of school, and his father wanted him off the streets—"

"That's what I can't figure," I interrupted. "Farley converts an old warehouse up here into a plant and opens all these drop shops all over town. Hauls the cleaning up here to North Denver and undercuts my prices so much he couldn't possibly be making a profit. He hasn't been cutting his prices nearly that much at other locations."

"Do you want to hear the rest of the story or not?" Mack asked.

I stopped talking.

"So Bobby and a friend of his go apply for jobs with Farley. Well, Farley didn't hire the friend, but he jumped at the chance of hiring Bobby."

"Maybe it was because Bobby told him that his dad worked for me." I was getting more paranoid by the minute, but it's really spooky when your friend agrees with your paranoia.

"That's a possibility." Mack had pulled up across the street from Juan's house. "Anyway, Bobby had been doing a lot of after-hours stuff for Farley. . . ."

"I wonder if he's the one who's been sneaking into our

place and marking up the clothes. Do you think Juan would have made a copy of the key and given it to his son?"

"No, I don't." Mack, always loyal to his friends, was adamant. "Anyway last night Bobby told his mother he had another job Farley wanted him to do. He didn't come home until early this morning, and I guess that's why his dad freaked out when he saw the boots. Juan told his wife Farley had been wearing a pair of red boots one day last week when he dropped the kid off at work."

I was lingering in the truck because I wanted to talk this out with Mack, but I knew I'd better get back to Mom.

"So what are you going to do now?" I asked. "Go back inside and wait for Juan to come home?"

"At least tell Mrs. Martinez we lost her kid again." He shut off the engine. "I'll talk to you tomorrow."

"Okay, unless you want to go out to dinner with Mom and me."

"I'll pass," Mack said.

"Do you think you could call the crew and tell people they don't have to come to work tomorrow?"

"That I can do."

I started to give him the roster, but he said he had the phone numbers.

When I returned to my rental, I fumbled around until I found the headlights. The dash lights came on, too, and the car's clock said 8:27. Mom was going to be upset with me for being late.

CHAPTER 6

When I reached the hotel, Mom had changed into a frilly dress in a floral pattern. It might have been all right for Phoenix, but it was a little summery for Denver in March. Her demeanor was as cold as she was going to be in her dress and open-toed shoes.

"You're late," she said with a pout on her lips.

"Sorry." Risking even further ire, I said, "I'll be just a minute. There's something I have to do." I grabbed the phone and tried the number for my other missing employee, but Sarah didn't answer. "Okay, I'm ready."

Mom looked with disapproval at my wrinkled suit. "Are you going to wear that?"

"Yes, I'm going to wear *that*." I couldn't very well change into my flannel pajamas, which was the only item of clothing I'd brought with me to the hotel. Besides, with the exception of one black party dress, this was about as fancy as I got. All my dress-up clothes were suitable for work.

I took her over to the Ship Tavern, a restaurant located in the Brown Palace, the grande dame of Denver hotels. I knew she'd always been impressed with its reputation, and I was hoping it would get her out of her funk about my late arrival, not to mention her problems with Herb.

Her lower lip had receded a little, but she still wasn't talking to me by the time we were seated. However, she began to loosen up after her second glass of wine. I guess she'd decided to forgo the antihistamines altogether, but her allergy seemed to have cleared up anyway.

"So why were you so late?" she asked finally.

I had to think what I'd told her I was going to be doing in the first place. That's the trouble with lying. "It took longer at the plant than I expected," I said, scratching my cheek.

We both ordered New York steak and managed to have a halfway enjoyable meal by not saying much to each other. I tried to think of pleasant chitchat, but with the murder at the plant, Mom's problems with Herb, and her feelings that Larry could help me solve everything, it was kind of hard to find a topic that wouldn't cause tears, anger, or unmitigated fear. I just chewed my way through the meal, ordering an extra basket of rolls to make sure my mouth was always occupied. It was kind of like being on a blind date with someone you had nothing in common with, which as a matter of fact summed up some of the problems between Mom and me.

She was the first one to broach one of the taboo subjects. "About Herb—" she said.

"Why don't we have some dessert and coffee," I interrupted, waving over to our ever-attentive waiter.

I ordered a calorie-laden triple chocolate torte. Mom demurred and settled for coffee, waiting to pounce on me the moment I was through filling my mouth with food. Finally I was too stuffed to eat another bite.

"I'm thinking of moving back to Denver permanently," Mom said.

I almost choked on my coffee, and my stomach churned. I shouldn't have kept eating as a way to avoid the inevitable. What was I to do with Mom while I worked out the other problems in my life?

"Okay," I said in resignation. "Do you want to talk about it?" I sounded like a psychiatrist, but without any solutions to my own, much less anyone else's, concerns.

I was hoping at the very least that Mom wouldn't start crying and making a scene in such an elegant place. This was probably a better environment for talking about Herb, though, than back at the hotel.

"He has been two-timing me, Amanda," she said.

"Herb?" I couldn't picture him having a girlfriend on the side.

He was short, plump, and balding. Who, other than Mom, would want him? And even though he tended to wear garish clothes and have the hail-fellow demeanor of a TV pitchman, he'd built a reputation in his used-car lot in Omaha by always promising "satisfaction or your money back." Either that or he could lie without even twitching, much less itching.

The best part was that he was ever-attentive to Mom's needs, saying often that he'd gotten the Rolls-Royce of women when he'd married her.

"I'm sure there's some misunderstanding, Mom," I said. "Has he told you he has a girlfriend?"

"No." Despite my hope that Mom would rein in her pain, she began to sniffle. "But I know about these things."

Okay, so she'd had six husbands. For all I knew, maybe she'd stolen one of them from some poor, unsuspecting first wife. "So how do you know?" I asked.

"I haven't been connected with dry cleaners all these years for nothing."

"What?" My question came out louder than I intended, and our server glanced over in our direction. I waved him off.

"You heard me, Amanda."

Mom had worked at Dyer's Cleaners in the early days, even after my dad died. However, she'd never liked it and had been happy when Uncle Chet, her brother-in-law, finally bought out her interest in the business. I still didn't see how that had anything to do with Herb's suspected transgressions.

"But Herb's a retired used-car dealer, not a dry cleaner."

She shook her head, presumably at my naiveté about men. "But remember how dry cleaners are always finding things in their customers' clothes?"

I nodded.

"Well, back when your dad and Chester were first in the business, I was working in the store one day and found a diamond necklace in a man's suit pocket. I called to tell him about it, and his wife answered the phone. She let out a bloodcurdling scream when I told her about the necklace. Seems it wasn't hers. She said he'd never given her anything but a plain gold wedding band, and it had made her finger turn green."

"So . . . ," I said, urging her to get to the point. Although her story didn't seem to have anything to do with Herb, I was beginning to have a bad feeling about it.

"Well, I was going through Herbie's clothes, getting ready to take them to our cleaners in Phoenix, and guess what I found?"

I hoped it wasn't a condom, but I waited for her to finish.

"It was a diamond earring, Amanda. Not a pair of earrings, like maybe he was planning to give them to me as a gift. Just one long, dangly earring."

I thought about pointing out that some people wear just one earring these days, but I figured that wasn't a convincing argument.

Mom sniffled and continued, "And when I questioned him, he denied knowing anything about it. Like the Tooth Fairy mysteriously put an earring in his pants pocket."

Unfortunately Mom had too much knowledge about

dry cleaning. As we in the business are painfully aware, where there's a piece of jewelry in the pocket, there may indeed be another woman in the picture.

The two of us had a restless night. When we returned to the hotel, Mom insisted I take the bed nearest the door. I was so exhausted I fell asleep immediately, only to be awakened some time later by a light in my face and Mom pacing back and forth beside me.

"I'm sorry, dear, did I awaken you? I couldn't sleep without Herb to snuggle up to. . . ."

"Uhhh," I groaned, unable to speak, much less say anything coherent that would make her feel better about Herb.

"And of course, those street noises right beside my bed don't help," she said.

Well, I *could* do something about that. I dragged myself to an upright position, staggered between the beds, and crawled under the covers of the one by the window.

"I didn't want you to give up your bed—you were sleeping so soundly over there," Mom protested, "although how you can sleep with all these horrible things going on, I don't know."

I didn't know, either, and now of course I was awake enough to fret about them. I pretended to be asleep, however, and I actually might have fallen back into unconsciousness except for Mom's little aside. "I really think you should consider my suggestion about calling Larry," she said.

I rose up on an elbow. "No, Mom, no, no, no. Do you understand? No, N-O." With that I flopped back down, turned toward the window, and put the pillow over my head. Talk about reverting to childhood.

Her voice sounded muffled, but I could still hear her. "All it would take is one phone call, and he'd be here. . . ."

I'd sounded like a kindergartner with my one-word repetitions. I decided maybe I could get through to her if I gave my reasons, so I lifted the pillow from my head. "Mom, he dumped me, I don't like him, and besides, he practices up in Aspen."

"No, dear, he's here in Denver now. Remember, I said I heard from him at Christmas? He said he was moving down here and has a new job with a law firm right here in downtown Denver."

Oh, damn, Larry was back in Denver. I hated that. I put my head back under the pillow and curled up in a fetal position. I might even have considered sucking my thumb if it hadn't seemed entirely too immature.

"Well, if that's the way you want to be about it . . ." Mom turned off the light and took possession of the coveted bed by the door.

I would never call my ex-husband, I grumbled silently, even if the police locked me up and cemented the cell door shut. Or maybe I should try to get to the bottom of this before I needed a lawyer. I liked that idea better. I would start as soon as I got up in the morning by having one-on-one conversations with all my employees, not just Sarah and Juan. One of them had to know something about Farley Mills.

Somewhere around three o'clock I finally dropped off again. I had a dream that Larry was breaking into the room, carrying a gavel and wearing nothing but a white wig. No, it wasn't a dream. There was someone standing between the bed and the window.

I jumped up, but it was only Mom.

"Did I bother you, dear?" she asked, fanning herself. "I was just trying to get one of these windows open so we could get some air."

"Uhhhh," I said.

"Does it seem stuffy in here to you, or is it just me?"

"It's you." I based that opinion on the fact that she was

in a nightgown and I was in my flannel pajamas, quite comfortable under the blankets and my pillow.

"Well, I still think we'd be more comfortable if we could open a window."

I didn't want to get into a discussion about how a woman who lived in a hermetically sealed and air-conditioned environment in Phoenix could suddenly have this overwhelming urge for fresh air. Instead I went over to the window and gave it a mighty tug.

It refused to budge. "Sorry, it's stuck." I went back to bed and put the pillow over my head.

"Thanks, Amanda, for at least trying. Maybe it's just a hot flash, and it will pass."

It seemed to me that Mom had been having hot flashes for as long as I could remember. God, I hoped I didn't spend as many years going through menopause as she had.

CHAPTER 7

I crept out of the hotel room the next morning, taking time only to brush my teeth and slip into my wrinkled clothes. Mom was sleeping, and I didn't want to waken her in case she might ask the dreaded question: Are you going to work?

Of course I wasn't going to work, but I didn't want to tell her that. She'd made the assumption the night before that I would be working that day, and I wanted to keep it that way. She'd said she would occupy herself by going shopping at the downtown department stores. I hadn't had the heart to tell her that the department stores had fled to more pricey neighborhoods.

But now I was overcome with an uneasy feeling that, not finding anyplace to shop, she might decide to visit Larry's new law firm instead. Just in case she thought about it, I'd call her later and warn her against it. No, maybe it was better not to put the idea in her head. We'd already agreed to meet at the hotel at six o'clock for dinner.

I went by my apartment to call Sarah again and change into fresh clothes. Oh, yes, and to feed Spot. The cat glared at me irritably for abandoning his food bowl for so long. I ignored both him and my blinking answering machine as I dialed Sarah's number.

"Hullo," she said groggily.

Apparently I had gotten her out of bed, but my guilt was overshadowed by relief that I'd finally found her. "This is Mandy. What happened to you yesterday? Are you all right?"

She cleared her throat. "I wasn't feeling well. I called, but all I got was the voice mail."

"Are you feeling better today?" I had a gut feeling that Sarah would normally have come to the plant, sick or not, if she couldn't get me on the phone. In fact I couldn't help wondering if she was lying and if she'd driven by the plant, seen the police, and fled. Sometimes she seemed as skittish about the cops as Mack did.

"Y-yes, I'm better now."

I told her I was glad and that I was calling to tell her we wouldn't be open today.

"I know. A policeman came by last night and told me about it." I could hear a tremor in her voice. "He scared me to death."

"Did he tell you what happened?"

"Yes." The word was so soft I could hardly hear it.

"I wondered if I could stop by your place and get the key to the plant." That seemed a legitimate reason to visit her early in the morning.

She hesitated. "Uh—maybe we could meet someplace, but it'll be awhile. I'm not dressed yet."

I suggested we meet for breakfast, and we settled on a restaurant on Broadway about halfway between our two apartments. She still didn't seem eager about it, but she said she'd be there.

Spot had been digging his claws into the hem of my skirt as we spoke, so I rewound the tape on the answering machine, hit the playback button, and turned my attention to the cat.

The answering machine had registered eleven calls. Why didn't I get that many calls when things were going well in my life? I wasn't sure I wanted to hear the messages, but I listened anyway as I dished up Spot's cat tuna.

"Yo, Mandy," Nat Wilcox said from out of the machine, and I wondered if he was calling as pal or police reporter. "Where are you? I need to talk to you about this guy who was killed in your store." Well, that answered my question. "Foster wouldn't let me near the place all day. Did you finally tell him that I wasn't your live-in lover?"

No, I hadn't told him that Nat's claim last December to be my roommate had been a ploy to get into my apartment so he could get a big story for the *Denver Tribune,* where he works, and I probably never would. Why would Foster want a relationship anyway with someone who was always getting into trouble and whose best friend was a pain-in-the-butt reporter, whether we were lovers or not?

"Call me as soon as you get home," Nat concluded, only to be followed one beep later by another message from the meddling media person. "Damn it, Man. It's eight o'clock. Have you fled the country? Gone on the lam? Decided on a flight to avoid prosecution?"

"A flight to avoid *your* persecution is more like it, Nat," I said to the machine. To show what bad shape I was in, I even stopped dishing out cat food and said it aloud. Spot cocked his head and glowered at me as if I were shirking my responsibility.

"Foster will be royally pissed if you've decided to go AWOL at a time like this," Nat continued.

He might be right, I thought, as I returned to my KP duties. Maybe I should have notified the police as to my whereabouts the night before.

A couple of other media types I didn't even know had called, apparently having gotten my home number from

the IN CASE OF EMERGENCY sign in the front window of
the cleaners. They were followed by more calls from Nat
and then another beep. I'd lost track of how many.

"Hello, Mandy Pie." Oh, yuck. Why had I thought that
Mom's Herb was the kind of guy who wouldn't two-time
his wife? Anyone who would call a stepdaughter a sick-
ening name like that might indeed be out having himself
a fling.

The message continued as I put the kettle on the stove
to boil water for coffee. "This is Herb. I need to talk to
Cecilia. I know she's in Denver because she left me a
note. Will you try to persuade her to call me? We've had
a misunderstanding, but I can explain."

If you could explain, Herbie Baby, why didn't you do
it before Mom came up here to complicate my life? But I
guess I could always hope that Herb had figured out a
good story about the earring by now. It would really help
me a major amount.

Beep. "This is Stan Foster. It's nine-thirty and I need
to talk to you. Please call me at ——" He gave the police
department number. Poor guy. Still at work that late at
night.

Beep. "Nat again. I came by your place to see if you
were not answering your phone *on purpose.* Where the
hell are you? I hope you're not down at the police department being grilled in one of those little rooms they have
for suspects."

I shuddered at the thought.

"Call me no matter what time you get in."

Nat hung up, followed by another call from Foster.
This time he seemed to be getting as irritated as Nat had
predicted. "It's now ten-thirty. I guess I should have mentioned that it would help if you'd keep us advised as to
your whereabouts during the investigation. Please call me
the minute you get in."

It was hard to convince myself that he didn't think I

was a suspect after that request. But maybe he'd removed the crime-scene tape and was calling to tell me we could reopen today.

The last call—at least I hoped I was getting to the end—was from Nat again, and God knows what time it was then. "Mandy, who is this Farley Mills anyway? Where'd he come from, and why was he in your store?"

Good questions. I put a spoonful of instant coffee in the cup, poured water over it, and took a sip before I called Nat to see if he could uncover some answers for me. He was the reporter, after all.

Whoops. There was one more call. It was Foster again. This time he sounded downright riled. "We need to talk. Please meet me at police headquarters at eight-thirty tomorrow morning. Ask for me at the desk."

I glanced at my watch. I'd really have to hustle to make it now. I took a quick shower and put on a pair of jeans, a white cotton blouse, and a brown corduroy jacket. There was no way I was going to wear panty hose when I wasn't going to work today. I ran a comb through my still-damp hair, put on some lipstick, gulped my coffee, and was on my way. Fortunately it had turned sunny, and there was a real promise of spring in the air, the kind of day that might actually go with Mom's wardrobe.

The Police Administration Building is at West Fourteenth Avenue and Cherokee, not far from the hotel where Mom and I were staying. I circled the block once in hopes of finding some on-street parking. I had to watch my pennies, after all, now that my business might be closed for God knows how long.

I got lucky and found a spot in front of a brightly painted row of frame houses that seemed out of place among the more businesslike concrete-and-glass structures. In fact they looked like they belonged in Black Hawk, Colorado's answer to Las Vegas, where Ingrid liked to do her gambling. The buildings could also be mistaken for a cluster of quaint boutique shops, except that I could see they catered to a different clientele.

The businesses had signs that said BAIL BONDSMAN, and were conveniently located by the police department so the owners would be ready with the cash once a person was arrested, providing of course that a judge decided to let him out. I slipped quarters into the meter with the fervent hope that I wouldn't need their services. Perhaps thinking that I'd be out before the time was up on the meter was being even more optimistic.

I walked across the street to the central police building. It's in one of two beige-colored buildings with a wide plaza in front that overlooks the high-rise offices, the dome of the City and County Building, and the turreted, castlelike Denver Art Museum.

One of the buildings said it was a pre-arraignment detention facility, which didn't make me feel any better about my current situation. When I went inside the adjoining police building, I was surprised at its museumlike lobby. There were displays around the sides of the room, and at one end a huge wall hanging that looked like an Oriental tapestry. It seemed out of place.

An information desk was in the center of the room, and I told a man at the desk that I was there to see Detective Foster in Homicide. He announced my arrival over the phone, then told me someone would be down to get me in a minute.

A man who identified himself as Detective Brown appeared before long and escorted me through a gate to the elevators. Were they planning to arrest me, I wondered, since they'd brought a guard? My stomach felt as if it had dropped into my Reeboks by the time the elevator whisked us up to the third floor.

The homicide department turned out to be in a surprisingly small room, but it wasn't as shabby as the ones on the TV cop shows. There were a dozen or so desks in the room, and a hallway leading to rooms where the detectives probably grilled suspects.

I saw Foster at one of the desks. His shirtsleeves were rolled up and his tie was askew. He was on the phone, but he covered the mouthpiece just long enough to tell the other detective to put me in one of the little rooms.

"Where were you last night?" he asked when he finally came in the room. His smile might have been reassuring if only it had reached his incredibly blue eyes.

"My mother's allergic to my cat. We went to a hotel."

Foster and I had already been through the stuff about how Farley Mills had seemed to have a vendetta against my business, distributing his cost-cutting coupons right outside my door. I'm not sure Foster quite saw it as a "vendetta," but I couldn't do anything about that. I'd also told him I didn't have any idea why Farley could have been out to get me.

I tried to be optimistic. "Are we going to be able to get back in business today? Is that why you called last night?"

"I'm afraid not." He folded his tall, lanky frame into a chair across the table from where I was seated. "I'll let you know later if we'll be finished by tomorrow."

"Uh—" I leaned my elbows on the table in what I hoped looked like a relaxed pose. Actually I felt as if I needed the support. "So what *did* you want?"

"We found a can of gasoline in the Dumpster out in back of the cleaners last night."

"Excuse me?"

"A can of gasoline. We're wondering if someone had been planning to set your place on fire."

I swallowed hard. Weren't most arson fires started by business owners in order to collect on the insurance? And hadn't my van been seen at the plant Sunday night when, I assumed, the murder had taken place?

"Do you know anything about that?" Foster asked.

"No, nothing." I was glad my elbows were propping me up or I'm sure I would have slid right off the chair.

Foster asked me a lot of questions about the financial status of my business, and I answered as honestly as I could. The financial picture wasn't great, but things were getting better. Of course why wouldn't they be, what with my chief competitor permanently out of the way?

"Why do you think someone would put Mills's body on the conveyor?" he continued.

"I don't know. Maybe they were trying to hide it?"

"So why go to all that trouble? Why not hide it in one of those laundry carts you have?"

I shook my head, but then I remembered what I'd said to Mom: Mills had been hit over the head and hung up to die. "Maybe . . ." I leaned forward in the chair, excited for the first time. "Maybe the person wasn't sure Mills was dead and hung him from the conveyor to finish the job."

That was the best explanation I could come up with, and it seemed to satisfy Foster. He wrote something in his notebook before he looked up at me. "Give me your phone number at the hotel. I'll let you know if we get through at the plant today."

It wasn't until I was outside that it occurred to me that maybe I'd given too good an answer. He might think I did it. Suddenly I felt shaky, and I gasped for breath in the crisp but smoggy air until the moment passed. I wanted to call Mack and tell him the latest development, but when I found a phone booth, I changed my mind. Better to press forward than to hash over what we did or did not know. In case we reopened tomorrow, this was my one day to get answers. I called Nat at the *Trib,* and surprisingly I got him before he started on his beat.

"It's about time," he said. "Where were you last night?"

I explained about Mom, whom Nat knew because our friendship stretched way back to junior high. He wasn't any more fond of her than she was of him. She'd always thought Nat was a bad influence on me because he'd written bloody stories for comic books, which I illustrated, but I think the final straw was when we made up epitaphs about people we knew. Our next-door neighbor, Mrs. Bell, found one we'd written about her: "Here lies the body of Evelyn Bell . . ." Of course, we rhymed it with hell. Later we revised it to:

> Here lies the body of Evelyn Bell
> Her body's in the ground, but her soul's in——
> Now, don't get excited, folks,
> There's no way of knowing
> When she left here
> Which way she was going.

" 'Nuff said." Nat interrupted my discourse about Mom, anxious to get to the more gory, newsworthy stuff. "Tell me about this Farley Mills and how he got into your plant over the weekend."

"I don't know anything, Nat, except that he was always hassling my customers to try out his cleaners instead." I hurried on before he had a chance to interrupt. "Remember when I told you that you'd owe me big-time if I let you get away with saying we lived together——?"

"You mean you still haven't told Foster the truth about that?"

"No, Nat—"

"Then why wouldn't he let me into your cleaners yesterday to see my lady love?"

"I don't know, but getting back to the favors you owe me, you can start repaying the enormous debt by finding out some background on Farley Mills."

"You honestly don't know anything about him?"

"Nothing." I would have told Nat about the polyester poltergeist that had been marking up clothes and misfiling them on the conveyor, but I didn't want it to become public knowledge.

"Okay, I'll see what I can do, but you must know something about—" I could tell Nat wasn't ready to let me off the hook.

"Look, Nat, I'm at a pay phone, and I gotta go."

"Okay, call you later, alligator." What would I do without Nat and all his clichés that he couldn't use in print?

I got to the restaurant on time, but Sarah wasn't there. I told the waitress I'd have coffee while I waited for a friend. Then I set out to make a to-do list and a suspect list. Unfortunately the list of suspects was a lot shorter than the list of things I needed to do.

The time stretched to three cups of coffee and a lot of doodles before Sarah finally showed up. I waved at her, and she made her way to the booth, where she slid into the seat facing away from the door. She seemed as nervous as a Mafia don who didn't like exposing his backside.

Poor Sarah. She looked terrible. I don't think I'd ever realized the true meaning of the word *wallflower* until then. She moved as far back in the booth as she could get, as if she wanted to fade into the woodwork. In fact her tweed car coat and light brown hair blended into the textured beige wallpaper almost as if she wasn't there. Her shoulder-length hair, which she normally pulled back at the nape of her neck, hung lank and listless around her face. She wasn't wearing makeup, except for lipstick, which she immediately began to chew off her lips.

"I'm sorry I'm late." She handed me the key to the cleaners and took off her coat. "I'd told my baby-sitter I wouldn't be needing her, so I had to find someone else to watch the kids."

I put the key in my purse. "Are you feeling better now?"

She nodded, then fumbled to adjust the neckline of her

white blouse and worry with a strand of hair. "I guess it was just the stomach flu that's been going around, but I'm all right now."

I ordered an omelet, and she said she'd have the same.

As soon as the waitress left, I said, "I need to talk to you about Saturday night. Did you have any trouble closing up?"

"No, everything went fine. I would have called you at home if there'd been any problems."

I guess the thing that bothered me was that she hadn't called me the time there had been trouble. "Did you see Farley Mills or anyone else hanging around the place Saturday night?"

She dropped her hand to the table. "No, everything was fine. Really."

"Did he ever bother you any other time, either before or after that incident last month?"

"No, I swear."

"Do you know if anyone else ever had contact with him?"

"Not that I know of."

"When Mills came in that day just before closing—could you tell me again exactly what happened?"

"I already told you." She clasped her hands together as if trying to keep them away from her hair. "He said he wanted to set up an account to be on our business route, and he wanted any information I had about it. I recognized him, and I said we didn't service other dry cleaners. He—he got mad and said that he had just as much right to the information as any other customer."

"I still wish you'd have pushed our alarm. That's what it's for." I didn't want to call it a panic button. She was edgy enough as it was. "It would have sent a signal to our security company."

"It wasn't really necessary, Mandy. Another customer came in right then and he left."

"But he grabbed you and gave you a bruise."

"I bruise easily."

Yeah, and battered wives run into a lot of doorknobs.

She put her hand to her neck and rubbed it as if it ached. Then she began to torture a strand of her hair again, and I wondered if I'd found the key to tell when she was lying. Some people begin to itch; she twisted a lock of hair.

CHAPTER 8

I took out my to-do list as soon as I got home and added, *Check personnel records*. I was curious about Sarah's background, but I also needed to review the records for the rest of the crew, to see if any of them besides Kim had ever worked for Mills. Once Nat got back to me with some background on Mills, I could see if there was any geographical connection between him and one of my employees.

For now all I could do was make some calls. I phoned the security company to find out how to put a new code into my burglar alarm, since my instruction manual was in the desk drawer in my office at the plant. Then I called Al Pulaski, who'd been with Ingrid the afternoon before.

"What's going on, Mandy?" He sounded so jovial it was hard to believe there'd been a murder at the plant. It was the voice of a natural-born salesman, always ready to make a pitch, no matter what. Not unlike my stepfather Herb's, as a matter of fact, and I think both of them could probably sell kayaks to a wandering tribe of Bedouins if they put their minds to it.

"I was just going to take a run by the plant and see what was up," he said after I finished my capsule version of events.

"Why don't I meet you at Tico Taco's as long as you're going to be down there anyway?" I was curious to know what was going on myself, and we settled on meeting in half an hour.

When I arrived, I took a quick look at the plant. It was still wrapped up in yellow crime-scene tape, like a package that had one of those joke prizes inside—something like a pop-up snake that would scare you to death when it jumped out at you. There were a couple of vehicles pulled up at the back door, and I wondered if one of them belonged to Foster. I decided not to risk his wrath by going over to find out.

I entered Tico Taco's, which usually cheers me up with its sombreros and tin cutouts of parrots on the wall, but not today. Al waved at me from one of the high-backed booths at the rear. Maybe he could lighten my mood.

He's a larger version of my stepfather and would probably grow bald the way Herb had. Right now he had a head of sandy-colored hair that was receding only at the forehead. He also had a set of dimples that seemed to appeal to a lot of women, and in fact Ingrid and he had gone together for a while last fall before she met Warren, the football fanatic.

I didn't see the restaurant's owner, Manuel Ramirez, but Al had been talking to his daughter, Juanita, when I arrived.

"It's terrible what happened, Mandy," she said. "When are you going to get back in business?"

I told her I didn't know and ordered a cup of coffee. After all, I'd just finished breakfast an hour before.

"I'll take the enchilada plate and a large Coke," Al said, then turned to me when Juanita left. "As long as we're not open today, I figured I could go hit some businesses and try to talk them into using our service." I'd wondered why he was all dressed up in the jacket with the Dyer's Cleaners logo on the pocket. He worked on commission, so he was as interested as I was in getting more companies to sign up for our service to pick up and deliver cleaning to their employees.

"Good," I said. "And that's the reason I wanted to talk to you. You have a Blazer, don't you?"

"Uh?"

He touched the logo on his breast pocket, and I realized he must think I was referring to the jacket he had on. "I'm sorry. I mean your car."

"Oh, my car. Well, actually it's a Bronco." He grinned. "You know, like the football team or O.J.'s escape vehicle."

"I stand corrected. Anyway I was wondering if we could use it when we get open. I'll pay you for it." I named a price.

"Sure thing." As long as Al was reimbursed, I'd been sure he would agree to it. "Why do you want it and where's the van anyway? I was going to ask you about that yesterday."

I explained to him that the police had impounded the van, but if Foster hadn't told him about its magical appearance at the plant Sunday night, I wasn't going to. "I guess they're just covering all the bases." I waited while Juanita set down my coffee and Al's order. "And while we're on the subject, I was wondering if you ever talked to Mills when he was hanging around the plant."

"Strange you should bring that up." He put some extra-hot salsa on the enchiladas, but it was as if he'd injected it in my veins.

I perked right up. "What do you mean?"

"I was going to tell you about it before, but I figured you already had enough trouble with that Mills character." Al sounded almost embarrassed, and I had a feeling that very few things made him react that way. "I decided you didn't need to hear that he was trying to start up a competing service to ours."

"You mean he asked you about it?"

"He wanted me to go to work for him, but I told him to take a hike. I said I was happy where I was, and besides, I knew he'd never be able to pay me what he said he would if he was going to undercut your prices the way he'd been doing."

"So that was the end of your conversation?"

Al started shoveling in the salsa-laden enchilada. "Yep, that's the only time I talked to him."

"Do you know if Mills ever talked to anyone else at the plant about the route—or anything else, for that matter?" The question hadn't brought forth any unusual revelations when I'd posed it to Sarah, but hey, you never can tell.

Al thought about it for a minute as he took another big bite. "As a matter of fact, I did see him and Kim having lunch together at that Chinese restaurant, Charlie Chan's. I was wondering if maybe Mills was trying to get Kim to go back to work for him."

"That's interesting. Do you think they saw you that day?"

"No, I was across the room, and I just happened to notice them when I got up to leave."

I picked up the check when Al finished his enchilada plate. Then I walked out with him to take a look at the Bronco in case I thought he should clean it up before we put the clean clothes inside. But he was a man after my stepfather's heart. Like Herb, the retired used-car salesman, Al kept his vehicles spotless.

When I reached my own car, I looked up Kim's name on my work roster. There was no phone number for him, only an address on Colfax Avenue in Aurora, straight east of my apartment. I probably should have gone on home, but when I reached Colfax, I told myself I was so close that I might as well drop by his place and have a talk with him.

Before Interstate 70 was constructed, Colfax had been

the main east-west highway through Denver, and when I crossed Colorado Boulevard, I began to notice the motels that had once served overnight travelers on their cross-country trips. Now the motels had become hangouts for pushers, junkies, prostitutes and their customers, and the hapless tourist who wandered off the freeway. Denver and Aurora were forever launching campaigns to arrest the prostitutes and drug dealers and shut down the motels.

I wondered if they'd been successful, and I guess that's why I was surprised when I found Kim's address. It looked as if it had once been a motel, too, only from an even earlier generation. The kind with cabins and now-rickety carports set back from the street.

I found Kim's number, but when I knocked, no one answered. I decided to hang around and see if he showed up. Besides, everyone needs the experience of going on a stakeout, I thought, just before I fell asleep. I think it was a combination of exhaustion and the sun shining through the windshield that put me out. Some fine detective I would make.

I woke up with a start and decided stakeouts were not a good idea when one had been drinking as much coffee as I had all day. That wasn't what had awakened me, however. I saw that a car had pulled up in front of Kim's place.

Kim climbed out of the passenger's side, but it was the other occupant who surprised me. Sarah appeared from the driver's seat, and two small kids tumbled out after her. I presumed they were her children, and somehow it made me feel as if I'd just slithered out from under a rock. I hadn't really meant to spy, but that's the way it felt. I scooted down in the seat so they wouldn't see me, and as soon as they went inside the unit, I started my car and left.

So much for my stakeout. I'd slept until nearly five

o'clock and managed to feel like pond scum all the same. No more of this covert surveillance for me, but I couldn't discount the fact that I'd found out something interesting all the same. Sarah and Kim were after-hours friends when I hadn't even known they talked to each other. I wondered if she'd called him to tell him about my interrogation of her. That made me feel even worse. I was not cut out for the life of a gumshoe. Any real private eye would have barged right up to the door and asked what she'd come here to find out: What had Kim been discussing with Mills in Charlie Chan's restaurant?

I double-timed it home to my own apartment, went to the bathroom, and checked my machine again. Foster had called to say the crime-scene tape would be coming down late that afternoon. Mack's voice urged me to call him when I got home.

I left word on Foster's voice mail that his message had been received and that I appreciated his efforts to see that we could get back in business the next day. After that I called Mack and told him the good news.

Then I told him the bad news. "The police found a can of gasoline in the Dumpster in back of the plant." Mack was silent for so long I thought maybe we'd been disconnected. "Are you there, Mack?"

"Yeah, I'm here."

"It sounds as if Mills was planning to set the place on fire, doesn't it, and that someone stopped him before he could do it?"

"I don't know. I'll have to think about it."

Mack seemed so upset that I changed the subject. "Have you heard anything from Juan?"

"Nope, he's still out looking for his kid," Mack said. "I'll let you know if I hear anything. Meanwhile do you want me to call the crew and tell them to come to work tomorrow?"

"I'd appreciate it. Or I could call and you could take my mother to dinner for me instead."

"Pass," he said, still not eager for another visit with Mom.

It was six o'clock on the dot when I reached the hotel. I was Ms. Punctuality herself. At least Mom wouldn't be irritated with me for being late, but the surprise was on me. There was no one in the room when I opened the door. I found a note by the telephone: *I've gone to Black Hawk with Evelyn Bell. Back by six. Love, Mom.*

It was like a voice from the past—Mrs. Bell, of the infamous epitaph incident. I didn't know they still kept in touch, but trust Mom to find something fun to do when she couldn't find any shopping opportunities in downtown Denver. I had to hand it to her, she could really take care of herself—and I was relieved that she'd chosen to call her old neighbor instead of looking up her ex-son-in-law, Larry. But Mom and the slots? It was a scary combination.

I cooled my heels for an hour before she finally showed up. And was I mad the way she'd been the night before? Yes, but I didn't show it.

She was wearing a subdued gray pants suit that surprised me, but never fear, it was adorned with enough Indian jewelry to look as if she'd bought out all the stalls on the town square in Santa Fe. She had on several turquoise rings, a squash blossom necklace, a concho belt and a silver bracelet with a big turquoise stone in the middle. In keeping with her feminine tastes, she still had on a ruffled blouse under her jacket, and she was wearing sling pumps in the same turquoise color. High heels weren't the standard attire for gamblers at the mining-town-turned-gambling-mecca, where the outfit of choice tended more to jeans and T-shirts, but Mom lived by her own dress code.

"Look." She shoved a plastic container toward me with the name of one of the casinos on it and a pile of quarters inside. "See what I won. There's forty-five dollars and seventy-five cents in there. I also won over two hundred dollars on the dollar machines."

She was on a gambling high, which was preferable to the low she'd been on the day before. I hustled her to a restaurant in Cherry Creek before the glow was gone. We stopped only long enough for me to check out the cleaners. True to his word, Foster had seen that the crime-scene tape was down. Mom waited in the car while I, armed with my instructions from the security company, reprogrammed the code on the burglar alarm. I took a quick look around the plant but left before I became too depressed. It was going to take a lot of work to get the place back in shape. I could see the evidence of the police search everywhere, from fingerprint powder on various counters to the way the clothes had been gone through as they looked for clues.

Mom and I went to a place called Sfuzzi's in Cherry Creek Mall, and Mom could hardly contain herself. "I'm buying tonight," she said when we were seated. "But I have to tell you something. . . ." She leaned toward me, putting a hand over one side of her mouth as if someone might be listening at the next table. "I'm afraid Evelyn is an addict."

"An addict?" We must be talking about another Evelyn than the one I remembered: a woman who owned a neighborhood restaurant and always wore uniforms and had her hair in a net.

"She has a gambling problem, I'm afraid," Mom whispered. "That's why she didn't want to come in and see you when she dropped me off at the hotel. She lost twelve hundred dollars on the slots today."

"Evelyn Bell?" I still wasn't sure I was hearing right, and I hoped our epitaph hadn't been a prediction of things to come.

Mom nodded. "That's not the worst of it. She told me that she had to take out a second-mortgage on her house to cover her losses and that she finally had to move in with her daughter. On the way up to Black Hawk, she'd been all excited because she said she had a feeling this was going to be her lucky day."

From the glint in Mom's eyes when she'd arrived with her stash of quarters, I wasn't sure but what she might turn out to be another slot-machine maniac. I could just imagine her dropping all of Herb's money in a frenzied stay in Colorado, and I knew I needed to get her home to Phoenix for both my and her well-being.

I decided to bring up the subject after we put in our orders. "By the way, Herb called, and he wants you to call him. He says he can explain about the earring."

"If he wants to talk to me, he can hop on a plane and come up here to see me. I need to be able to look him in the eyes to see if he's telling the truth."

So that's how she'd known when I was lying as a kid—my shifty eyes. I'd always thought it was because of the itching.

"Would you like me to call Herb and tell him to come up here?" I asked.

"No, no." She fanned herself, and I hoped she wasn't getting another hot flash. "Why don't we just let him agitate for a while."

I couldn't help feeling sorry for Herb. She made him sound like dirty laundry slopping around in a washing machine. And I don't know whether it was that image of Herb yearning away for her in Phoenix or her win at Black Hawk, but she continued to be pleasant throughout the meal and on our return to the hotel.

She didn't even mention Larry, and as a reward I

agreed to spend another night with her. I dropped her at the entrance and went to my apartment to check the answering machine—no more messages—and to give Spot enough food to get him through the next day. I also grabbed some fresh clothes so I wouldn't have to go back to the apartment the next morning on the way to work. Since I'd changed the code to shut off the alarm at the plant, I needed to be the first one there.

Once I joined Mom in the hotel room, I started to get ready for bed. The only way I'd said I would stay was if she promised to let me get some sleep that night. Mom had agreed and was continuing with her "girl talk," as she put it, when the phone rang.

"You didn't tell Herb where I was staying, did you?" she asked in a panic.

I was in the bathroom by then, already in my old flannel pajamas and in the midst of brushing my teeth. I shook my head and spit out the toothpaste. "I didn't even talk to him. He left a message on the answering machine. Go ahead and pick up the phone."

She reached for the receiver reluctantly. "It's a Detective Foster," she said, covering the mouthpiece. "He wants to talk to you."

"I'll be right there." I took a gulp of water and swished it around in my mouth. I hoped Foster didn't have any more bad news like the information about the gasoline the police had found in the Dumpster the day before.

"Hold on a minute, please," she said. "Oh, dear." She paused for another minute. "Oh, dear."

I spit out the water and ran to the phone.

Mom covered the mouthpiece again as she handed the phone to me. "He says there's a report of an alarm going off at the plant and the police are checking it out."

CHAPTER
9

Foster didn't know any more about the report than what he'd told Mom, so we didn't linger over good-byes.

I rolled up the legs of my pajamas, slipped into my shoes, and threw on my coat as soon as I hung up. Lucky I'd bought the new full-length coat recently so I didn't have to waste time putting clothes on underneath one of my old jackets.

I refused Mom's offer to go with me because I didn't want to wait for her to "put on her face," which I knew she'd insist on doing.

"Be sure and call me as soon as you find out what's going on," she yelled after me. "I hope it isn't a fire."

I was halfway down the hall by then, and this wasn't what I needed to hear.

"You will call me, won't you?"

"Yes, Mom. I'll call." I shoved open the door to the stairs instead of waiting for the elevator. The last thing I needed right then was a mother to be accountable to.

In the car my mind churned with the terrible scenes of the fire she'd conjured up, the whole place ablaze and the building and its contents destroyed. After all, it appeared someone had been trying to set the place on fire the night

Farley was killed. Maybe they'd come back to finish the job as soon as the crime-scene tape was taken down.

"Oh, God. Oh, God," I kept muttering to myself as I broke a few speed records for crosstown travel.

Dry-cleaning plants have a lot of combustibles in them, and I'd heard of disastrous fires other places. At one southern California cleaners, the owner had to set up shop on card tables outside the charred remains of his plant so he could take insurance claims from customers, one of whom had been Jay Leno, who'd shown up on the *Tonight* show that night without the tuxedo he'd planned to wear. The owner even continued to take in cleaning, but I think he had another plant somewhere that could do the work while he rebuilt.

It was too cold in Denver for a sidewalk location, and I'd have to find a competing cleaner to help me out if anyone still had the nerve to bring me their cleaning.

No, just stop thinking this way, I scolded myself. Wait and see what's wrong before you start making up elaborate scenarios for your doomed business. Maybe someone had gotten inside the plant but fled when he realized he could no longer shut off the alarm.

And why hadn't the security company called me? I answered the question even as I thought of it. Of course they couldn't get me because I was sequestered away in a hotel. This was the last night I was staying with Mom, unless she was ready to provide permanent support for a deadbeat dry-cleaner daughter whose only livelihood might be going up in smoke even as it went down the drain.

And how had Foster found out about the call? I guess it didn't matter. Thank God, I'd been alert enough to change the code for the alarm system earlier that evening. Maybe my action had averted a major disaster.

I turned off First Avenue to the strip center that housed the cleaners. Nothing. The front of the building looked okay. I swung by the side of the plant. Still okay. The tension in my stomach eased a little, but I knew the inside of the plant could be a raging inferno. As I reached the parking area behind the plant, I saw a police car pulled up at the back door.

I parked beside it and headed inside. "Hello," I yelled, and banged on the door. "Is anyone here?" I looked around in relief. I couldn't see any fire or smell any smoke.

A policewoman appeared from around the corner by my office and made me show her some identification to prove that I was the owner. Then she motioned me to follow her. "It appears there was a break-in, but the burglar alarm scared the person away."

"You mean everything's all right?" Maybe my luck was finally changing. I trailed her to the office, but when I got there, I could see I was wrong.

"It looks like someone grabbed some files out of here," another police officer said as he inspected an open drawer in the cabinet.

Okay, I'd done something right and something wrong. By changing the code, the person who'd gotten in undetected over the weekend had set off the alarm tonight. At the same time the burglar had time to grab some files from the cabinet and get away.

Unfortunately I knew what was in that drawer—the personnel records. Maybe if I hadn't been thinking of going through the folders earlier in the day, I wouldn't have been so convinced that's what this was all about. One of my employees didn't want me to find something in the records that would connect him to Mills.

"Do you want to sit down?" the woman asked.

It was only then that I realized I was shaking. "No, I'll be okay. It's not as bad as it could have been."

She nodded. "I assume you have duplicate records on your computer. You can check, but it doesn't look as if they had time to get into that."

"Good." I didn't respond to her first remark, though, because, no, I didn't have backup personnel records in the computer. But why burden the policewoman with that worry? Save it for Foster instead.

And unbeknownst to me, Foster was approaching as we spoke. "Mandy," he said, and I jumped when I heard his voice. Why was he always sneaking up on me like that, especially when I wasn't ready to talk to him yet?

He frowned. "Did they get anything?"

"Some files are missing," the policewoman said, "but it doesn't look as if they took anything else."

Foster glanced around the room. "Thanks for having someone notify me," he said to her, then turned to me. "Now aren't you glad you told me where you were staying?"

"I guess," I said, although as it had turned out, I probably could have done without the bad news until morning.

Foster motioned to the cabinet. "What was in there?"

"Personnel records mostly. I was planning to review them all tomorrow."

"I trust you have backup records."

"No, sorry."

His eyebrows, a shade darker than his blond hair, arched above his blue eyes, but he didn't say anything. He moved out of the room and started talking to the woman cop. I wished I could have heard what they were saying, but I didn't think they'd take kindly to me moving up behind them and eavesdropping. Their conversation was brought to a halt anyway when the phone started ringing.

"You have your answering machine turned on, don't you?" Foster asked. "Just let it pick up."

But it didn't. The caller hung up, rang again, and kept repeating the process until I thought I couldn't stand it. It must be Mom.

Foster grabbed it. "Here, it's for you." He handed the receiver to me. "It's your mother."

"Thank goodness, you're there," she said. "What happened? Was it a fire?"

"No, a break-in, but—"

"That's terrible." I heard her voice droning on, but I wasn't really listening until I caught her final line. "Now maybe you'll take your mother's advice and call Larry. . . ."

Okay, so there hadn't been a fire, but this was just the spark to set me off. It was a wonder I didn't ignite the place myself with my smoldering thoughts. "No, absolutely not, Mom. Do you hear me?"

"Of course, I hear you, Amanda, and probably so does everyone else within fifty feet."

I looked around in embarrassment and lowered my voice. "Look, Mom, it'll probably be a while before I get back to the hotel, so don't wait up for me. Meanwhile the subject's closed. Do you understand?"

Mom didn't answer, which should have given me cause for concern. Unfortunately at the time I had a lot of other things on my mind, like exactly which records had been taken from the filing cabinet.

"I have to go now," I said. "I'll see you later."

I was sweating when I hung up. It was partly because I was overwrought and partly because I was forced to keep my coat on over the pajamas I'd so unwisely decided to wear. I noticed that one leg was coming down, and I reached down and rolled it up again. "Can I look at the files to see which ones are missing?" I asked when I stood up and saw that the cop had finished dusting the filing cabinet for prints.

Foster nodded and accompanied me to the open drawer. It didn't take me more than a few minutes to see that everything had been cleared out from *J* through *R*. When the person heard the alarm go off, he must have grabbed as many files as he could carry—his own among them, I presumed—so that he could get out as fast as possible.

The police had me check the computer, open the safe, and take a trip around the rest of the plant. The tour was getting to be a habit, and it was even more difficult than it had been the day before to see if anything was disturbed, thanks to the search the police had conducted in the building.

"Just call us if you find anything else that's missing," the woman officer said when they finally left.

I nodded and started to leave, too, but Foster was waiting for me at the door. "I need to talk to you about this, Mandy," he said, handing me Mack's key that he'd used during the search. "Want to go someplace for coffee?"

Well, yes and no. I'd wanted to go out with him when we first met. But no, not tonight, not to talk about the case—and especially not in my ratty pajamas, which lacked only a drop seat to look like something I would have worn when I was two.

I agreed anyway. What else could I do?

CHAPTER 10

Foster suggested we go to Tico Taco's.

I imagine he did that because it was close, but I wasn't sure I wanted to be forced to sit melting in my coat in front of a lot of people I knew. On the bright side, it probably was better than going to a well-lighted place like Denny's. At least Tico Taco's was semidark. Customers might miss a flannel pajama leg if it began to roll down again above my sockless feet, which were stuffed into a pair of black flats.

Manuel Ramirez, genial owner and host, came running to the door when he saw us. Normally he had a sign that said, PLEASE WAIT TO BE SEATED, but it was missing tonight. Maybe he thought we'd try to seat ourselves. Instead I realized he wanted to talk about the murder and find out what the police had been doing over at the plant again tonight. "What's wrong now, Mandy? I heard the burglar alarm go off and I called the police. Then I called you at home, but you didn't answer. Is everythin' all right?"

I glanced at Foster before I said, "Someone broke in, but they didn't have time to do much damage."

Manuel wasn't ready to drop the subject. "Have the

police found out who killed that Mills guy? He was one
bad hombre."

"Not yet," I said, and reminded him that Foster and
I needed to be seated. I didn't introduce him to my
handsome companion because I didn't particularly want
Manuel to know that I was being grilled by the police.

"I saw your van over there as I was leavin' work Sunday night," Manuel continued, "but I told the police I
knew you weren't there because I went over and knocked
to see if somethin' was wrong. Didn't you take it home
over the weekend?"

So that's how the police had found out about the van?
Before I could ask Manuel any more about it, Foster interrupted. "We need a place that's private, and we'll only
be having coffee."

Manuel got the idea. Unfortunately it must have
sounded romantic to him. He whisked us to a high-backed
booth in the rear, away from the few other customers, and
winked at me as I slid into the seat. "I'll be back pronto
with the coffee so you can be alone." Manuel's forefathers
probably had been in this country longer than mine, but
he liked to spice up his conversation with Spanish words
as if they were green chilis. He winked again, apparently
having decided this was a hot date that had been interrupted by the break-in at the plant.

Good to his word, he returned almost immediately
with the coffee. I'd barely had a chance to point out to
Foster that my first idea about why the killer put the body
on the conveyor might have been right. He could have
panicked when he heard Manuel's knock on the back
door of the cleaners and put it there in an effort to hide it.
"Why didn't you tell me that your witness had not only
seen the van but went over to my place to see if I was
there?"

Manuel was back again. He set a candle on the table
and lit it with a flourish of his lighter. Actually it took

him several attempts before he managed to get a flame and leave.

"I'm sorry, but we don't make everything we learn available to the public," Foster said, his cool professional tone undoing the restaurant owner's hoped-for effect of coffee by candlelight.

I stiffened. "But I'm *not* the public. I'm the owner of a business that has been seriously jeopardized because someone was murdered there."

"I know, but you should leave the investigating to us."

"You surely wouldn't have objected to my plan to go through the personnel files."

"Even the personnel files."

"Well, it's a moot point now anyway. Half the records are gone. That must mean there was something in them that could have connected someone at the plant to Farley."

"And you really don't have backup records of the files in your computer?" Foster could hardly hide his disbelief.

"No," I explained, "there's a big turnover in the dry-cleaning business, and we have to keep the information for years, just in case someone files for worker's comp, asks for a reference, or decides to sue us for something."

"But wouldn't you still want a computer record?"

"Ideally yes, but we have a whole packet of information for each employee—their W-4 form and eligibility verification to see that they aren't illegal aliens and that sort of thing. We also have to keep statements to show that they've received our policy manual, plus specific training and information about sexual harassment and hazardous-waste procedures that are required by OSHA. Everything requires an original signature by the employees."

Foster still seemed unconvinced, but he took a different tack. "You know, there could have been some other things that were taken too."

Before I could respond, Manuel was back. This time he had some salsa and chips. "Compliments of the house," he said, grinning widely as if he were playing Cupid.

"Thanks, Manuel," I said.

"Yes, thanks," Foster said. "But if you could leave us alone, we'd appreciate it."

"*Sí, sí.*" Manuel backed away from the booth with the silly grin still on his face. I was glad he didn't have musicians, or he probably would have sent them over to serenade us.

The only thing halfway close to what he was visualizing for us was that my heart was racing. Unfortunately it wasn't from love but from an uneasy feeling about the implications of Foster's remark.

"So what are you saying?"—I was halfway out of my seat—"That I feigned a break-in and made it look like someone else stole financial records?"

"Look, I'm just playing devil's advocate here."

"Hi, Mandy." A woman's voice interrupted what Manuel, if he'd been looking at the way I was leaning toward Foster, would probably have perceived as an intimate romantic moment.

"Oh, hi, Winona." It was one of Manuel's waitresses. She had her coat over her arm, apparently ready to leave for the night now that business had slowed.

"I heard the burglar alarm and saw the police cars over at your place. Is everything okay?"

I nodded, and when she gave Foster the eye, I introduced them. Winona's a small, curvaceous brunette, but he didn't pay much attention to her. Too bad he wasn't so captivated by her charms that he would decide to quit asking me questions.

As for Winona, she was in no hurry to leave. "I haven't talked to Ingrid for a while. How's she doing?"

"Fine," I said, glad for any distractions from my problems. "Don't you see her anymore?"

"Not since she fell for that nutty Broncos fan."

I felt sorry for Winona. She and Ingrid were as different as night and day—Winona with her petite perkiness and Ingrid with her statuesque Nordic good looks, but they'd bonded because they were both Kansas City fans. Apparently Ingrid's new husband had put an end to that.

"You mean you don't even go up to Black Hawk together to play the slots?" That had been one of their favorite pastimes last summer, but I suppose the only reason I mentioned it was that I was in no hurry to continue the conversation with Foster. That and because of Mom's recent trip with Mrs. Bell, the gambling "addict."

"Oh, we had to give that up even before she met Warren." Winona's voice was tinged with sarcasm when she said his name. "We'd maxed out our credit cards, and then after she met *Warren* she didn't have time for Sarah and me."

"Sarah McIntyre?" I couldn't imagine Sarah having anything in common with Winona and Ingrid.

Before Winona could say any more, Manuel caught sight of her at our table. He came running over to us. *"¡Vámonos!"* he said, escorting her away. "Didn't I tell you that you could go on home to make up for working late Sunday night? What are you still doin' here? These people want to be alone."

Winona shrugged and gave her boss a dirty look. "When you see Ingrid, tell her to give me a call."

"Scat." Manuel flapped his hands in front of him as if he thought he'd confused her by ordering her to leave in Spanish. "I'm sorry for the interruption," he continued when he returned to our booth. "Winona may look like a Latina, but she isn't." I would never have thought someone named Winona was Hispanic anyway, but I guess Manuel felt he needed to explain. "She just doesn't have the Latin feeling for *amor*." He shook his head sadly, about either Winona or the fact that we hadn't touched our coffee. "Your coffee is cold. I will get you some that's hot." With that he grabbed the cups and returned almost immediately with refills. He then retreated to a position where he could keep a loving eye on us.

Once he left, Foster picked up the conversation where we'd left off. "As I was saying, I was just playing devil's advocate, which is what we detectives do. We have to consider the fact that the burglar might have been after something else."

Well, if Foster was playing devil's advocate, then I was surely feeling the flames of hell. My dark curls were drooping the way they did when I worked at the steam presses. I brushed the hair back from my forehead. That's when I realized that beads of perspiration had popped out on my brow. I grabbed a Kleenex from my purse and swiped it across my face.

Foster gave me a puzzled look.

"It's really hot in here, don't you think?" I remembered that only the night before I'd had nasty thoughts about Mom going through menopause forever. Surely I was too young for hot flashes.

"So why don't you take off your coat?" he asked.

In the heat of the discussion I'd forgotten about the heavy coat. I started to take it off but remembered just in time the reason I'd decided to keep bundled up in the first place. "No, I think I'll just keep it on."

Foster stood up. "There's no need to be uncomfortable. Here, I'll help you with it."

Now, I'm not overly modest, but I didn't feel like revealing my taste in sleeping attire to a cop and an adoring restaurant owner. And I didn't particularly want to tell Foster about it, but as he approached my side of the table, I couldn't see any way out of it. "Please," I said in a whisper that sounded more like a hiss. "If you must know, I have my pajamas on underneath."

"Oh." Foster grinned and returned to his side of the table.

If I'd been wearing something sexy from Frederick's of Hollywood, maybe I'd have considered shedding my outerwear, but not in flannel, especially when I realized that one of the legs had rolled down around my ankle again. No, not even in silk. I was feeling entirely too vulnerable and exposed as it was.

I reached my hands under the table and busied myself with rolling the pajama leg back up as Foster waved his hand at Manuel, who was hovering nearby. "Do you suppose you could turn down the heat? It's kind of warm back here."

His efforts to increase my comfort level, even if he thought I was a suspect, made me feel somewhat more kindly toward him. I guess that's why I felt compelled, in the candlelit intimacy of our booth, to tell him a little of what I'd learned that day, namely that Al had once been approached by Mills to set up a competing route service to mine.

"And when did you find this out?"

"This afternoon."

"You haven't been conducting your own investigation, have you?"

"How could you think I'd do something like that?" Answering a question with a question was a good way to avoid an outright lie, or so I'd heard. So why was I itching? Itching and sweating.

"Mandy . . ." Foster made my name sound like an accusation.

"If you must know," I said, lifting my hair from the back of my neck. "I had to call him to see if we could use his Bronco for deliveries when we reopen, seeing as how you confiscated the van. Any chance we can get it back tomorrow?"

"No, sorry."

I fanned myself. If Manuel had turned down the heat, it sure hadn't done a thing for my personal thermostat. "Excuse me, I need to go to the bathroom." I darted out of the booth and down the hall to the "señoritas" room, as Manuel had identified it on the door.

Inside, I flapped my coat open in front of me like a flasher with a nervous tic. Finally the movement of air began to cool me. I doused cold water on my face, which eased the itching, and once I'd dried my hands and face with a paper towel, I began to feel better. In fact when I finally noticed the sign, I became downright giddy.

The sign that was supposed to be at the entrance to the restaurant must have been stored in the ladies' room earlier in the day and forgotten. It now stood instead in front of the two toilet stalls. It urged customers, PLEASE WAIT TO BE SEATED.

The whole thing probably wasn't that funny, but I laughed until tears ran down my face. Foster must have thought I'd been crying when I returned to the booth, and he didn't ask me any more about my detecting. I decided it was better to have him treat me with pity than to tell him about the sign and have him think I was weird as well as nosy.

When I finally arrived back at the hotel, I tried to let myself into Mom's room as quietly as possible. I was prepared to slip into the darkened room and jump into bed, since I was already in my pajamas.

Instead I was surprised to see that the lights were still on. The first person I saw when I entered the little hallway was Mom. The second person I saw was my ex-husband, Larry.

CHAPTER 11

All sorts of conflicting emotions tumbled around in my head. Well, actually the emotions were all the same; they were just directed at so many people as to be totally ineffective.

I was mad at Mom for calling a man the moment things got dicey for her daughter. It was as if she thought some guy could iron out all my problems with a shot of testosterone. But why of all men did she have to call Larry?

Once I saw him, I was mad at myself for proceeding into the room. Still, I squared my shoulders, raised my head, and went full speed ahead, all the time asking myself why I didn't do the sensible thing and leave. But no, I didn't want Larry to think I'd lost any of my confrontational skills.

But mostly I was mad at Larry. Mad at him for dumping me for a sexy lady lawyer after I'd worked to pay his way through law school. I'd hoped I'd gotten over that. I tried to focus on other things I didn't like about him. I decided I disliked him most of all for his suntan.

He looked like George Hamilton after a week in a tanning salon. Larry had the same sharp chin, dazzling too-white smile, and even his hair was beginning to turn gray gracefully, just at the temples. I bet he'd touched up the rest of it with Grecian Formula, but I figured Larry had probably gotten the tan without benefit of artificial light. He'd acquired it leading the good life, skiing the slopes of Aspen Mountain by day and visiting Planet Hollywood at night.

By comparison, I must have looked like a pale, pinched version of my former self. The only time I wandered outside the cleaners was to be interrogated by the police.

The most pleasant thought that flitted through my mind as I looked at him was that he might get skin cancer if he didn't start taking better care of himself. I immediately felt guilty about it.

"Hi, Mandy," he said, flashing me that 120-watt smile, made even more brilliant by the contrast with his golden tan. "You're looking good."

Yeah, sure, and if I believed that, I'd believe he was Clarence Darrow reincarnated. Here I was with bags under my eyes, no lipstick, no bra, and both pajama legs hanging out from under my coat, and he says I look good.

He, on the other hand, was still tall, dark, and handsome, in jeans and a cableknit sweater that looked handmade. My only consolation was that he might lose his dipped-in-bronze appearance now that he'd supposedly hooked up with a downtown Denver law firm where he'd have to bust his butt in pursuit of the billable hour. I pictured him in a few months—his complexion pasty and his body going to flab as he pored over legal tomes in the firm's law library.

"Mother Cilia called me because she was worried about you and thought maybe I could be of help." Larry said Mom's name as if she were a nun from a contemplative order.

I don't know why that made me mad. "Ex-mom Cilia to you, Larry." I glowered at the woman I'd like to divorce as well. "Why on earth would you think I needed help, Mom, when I'm having the time of my life?"

"Please don't be so stubborn, Amanda. I knew you wouldn't call Larry, so I figured I'd do it for you. And he agrees with me that you need legal counsel, what with all the problems at the plant."

I took a deep breath to keep my head from exploding and turned back to my ex-husband. "Look, Larry, I'm sorry if Cecilia got you up in the middle of the night, but I really don't need your help. If I need legal advice, I'll get it on my own."

Larry was the picture of self-control. He'd always been that way, and it infuriated me. He handed me his business card, of all things. "Well, if you change your mind, you can call me at any of these numbers."

With a flourish I took the card and dropped it in the wastebasket. It was not my finest hour, but then neither was much of what had transpired that night. That included my decision to stay at the hotel for the few remaining hours until morning. I should have gone back to my apartment, where I could pout in private, but I was just too tired to make the trip.

I shook my index finger at Mom after Larry left. "I absolutely do *not* want to talk about this now."

With that I took off my coat, pulled back the covers, flopped down on the bed nearest the door, and pulled the sheet and blanket over my head.

It was a long time before I fell asleep, and the last thing I remember thinking was, So Mom doesn't want me to call her husband, Herbie, huh? She wants to let him agitate for a while. Well, we'll see about that!

By the time Mack arrived at work, I'd already turned up the boiler and was in my office, going through the files.

"Mandy," he yelled from the back door. "What you doing at work already?"

"In here," I called back. "I'm in my office."

As soon as he reached the door, I motioned to the drawer I'd been going through. "Someone broke in last night and ransacked the files."

Mack shook his head as if he couldn't believe what he was hearing. "How'd they get in and what did they take?"

"Same as before—with a key. Luckily I'd changed the combination, so it set off the burglar alarm, but they still had time to grab a lot of the personnel records." I handed him the new code. "Memorize this. It will self-destruct in thirty seconds."

He didn't even react to my attempt at humor.

"I'm having the locks changed today, and I'll give you a new set of keys later."

"That's all they took?" Mack asked as if he hadn't heard the intervening conversation.

"Yep, it looks like they grabbed all the files from *J* through *R*."

"Why?"

"That's a good question, Mack. Maybe when they realized they couldn't shut off the alarm, they decided that's all they could get before the police got here."

"I mean, why *J* through *R*?"

"I'm guessing there was something in them that one of our employees didn't want me to see, and I'm assuming it had something to do with Farley Mills. Otherwise why take them at all?"

"So what do we do now?"

"I guess you might as well get to work on that mountain of clothes we have to clean, and maybe you could have a couple of people start cleaning the plant. I'm going to see if anything else is missing from the files. Then maybe we can eliminate some of the employees as suspects."

"*J* through *R,* huh, as in *R* for *McKenzie Rivers*?"

I nodded.

Mack looked dejected as he started to leave. Then he stopped, but he didn't say anything more. It wasn't like him to be at a loss for words.

I returned to the files. "Any news about Juan or his missing son?"

"I talked to Juan last night, and he said he was about to resort to desperate measures."

I looked up. "What'd that mean?"

"He wouldn't tell me, but he wanted to know if he still had a job."

"Of course he does."

Mack seemed to make up his mind about something, and he came back into the room. "We need to talk, Mandy. Maybe now would be a good time, seeing that none of the other people are here yet."

I motioned him to follow me to the break room. "Let's go have a cup of coffee. I've already made a pot."

I poured us both a mug and brought the sugar and creamer to the table for Mack. "What's going on?"

Mack was still hesitant. "You know how you asked me about my name the other night? You said you'd wondered when you were a kid if it were an alias—and if I had a dark, mysterious past."

I had this sick feeling in the pit of my stomach. "You mean it *is* an alias?"

"No, it's my real name."

"But—" I moved my hands in a circular motion for him to continue. I sensed this wasn't the end of the story.

"But I was under suspicion once years ago for starting a fire at a cleaners where I worked down south. The owner and I had a fight, and that night his place went up in flames."

I sucked in my breath.

"I didn't do it, but the police arrested me because the

owner was convinced I started the fire. One of my friends swore I was playing chess with him that night, but a lot of people didn't believe him."

I let the air out in such a rush that I hardly had enough left in my lungs to speak. "Were you?" I squeaked. "Playing chess, I mean?"

"Yes, and the police finally let me go, but as soon as I walked out that jailhouse door, I beat it out of town and never looked back."

"So what's wrong with that?"

Mack dropped his head. "Well, they told me not to leave town, but the owner was having a fit about them releasing me. He kept telling them that my friend was lying. I was afraid they'd arrest me again, and a black man wasn't apt to get a fair trial in Alabama back in those days."

"Damn it, Mack." I looked away, not able to watch my proud friend reduced to telling me this story.

"Your uncle knew about it, if that's any help, and he gave me a job anyway when I came to Denver."

I looked back at him. "I didn't mean damn it about that. I meant damn it, I hope the police don't find out and think maybe you were trying to start a fire the night Farley was killed."

"I swear I didn't have anything to do with the fire in Alabama, much less Farley's death."

"I know that."

He drew himself up in the chair, more like the Mack I'd always known. "Think maybe I should tell the cops about it?"

I hated our sudden role reversal. In the past I'd always been the one who'd gone to Mack with my problems. "No charges were ever filed against you, were they?"

"Not that I know of."

"Well, then I don't see why you should. Besides, maybe Juan's son will show up soon and he'll be able to tell us about Sunday night, since he was apparently doing a job for Farley."

"That's another thing. I'm afraid the police may think Juan had something to do with Farley's death, the way he's been acting," Mack said. "I can see a father trying to protect his son if Juan thought Farley was leading the kid astray."

I couldn't think of any words to ease Mack's worry, and I hoped the police wouldn't wonder how far Mack would go to protect me if he'd believed Farley was trying to ruin my business. Mack and I had always had that kind of relationship where he looked out for me, especially after Uncle Chet's death.

I jumped up from the chair because I couldn't stand to think about it anymore. "It'll be all right, Mack," I said, more confident-sounding than I felt. "Let's get to work. We'll talk about it later." When I got to my office door, I stopped. "Would you send Kim in here when he gets to work?"

"You going to talk to him about working for Mills?"

"It's as good a place to start as any."

"Just don't scare him," Mack said. "He's the best assistant I ever had."

"I promise."

I called a locksmith to change our locks, called our distributor to fix the conveyor, and went back to sorting through the files. Mack's file was definitely gone, as was Kim's. So were the files for Ingrid, Juan, Al, and the timid Sarah. I was so preoccupied I didn't even hear Kim when he came into the room.

"Big Mack say you want to see me." The young Korean loved everything about America, which is why he always referred to Mack as if he were a hamburger.

"Why don't you have a seat, Kim."

He came over to the chair in front of my desk. With his slight frame, the chair seemed too big for him, and he sat on the edge as if his feet might not touch the floor otherwise.

I tried to put him at ease. "We're really happy with the way you're doing your job, Kim. The only reason I wanted to talk to you was to see if you could tell me anything about Farley Mills. I remember you worked for him before you came here."

Kim didn't respond, maybe because I hadn't really asked a question. "Did you like Farley?" I continued.

"No." Kim looked at a space above my head. "He was a—a cheeseball."

"A cheeseball?" Since Kim's nickname for Mack made me think of hamburgers, I was trying to picture Farley as one of those round cheeses covered with nuts that you buy at the grocery store.

"*You* know . . . ," Kim explained. "A cheeseball— that's what Ingrid calls him."

By the time I decided he meant *sleazeball,* I didn't have the heart to correct him. "So you thought he was a cheeseball too?"

"He wants that"—Kim struggled for a word, then grinned—"he wants me to play James Bond for him. But I don't do it. No sir."

I wondered if Mack should tell Kim to quit watching so many movies. "Why do you think he wanted you to spy for him?"

Kim shrugged, but the way he ducked his head made me wonder if he knew more than he was saying.

"How did Mills even know you had a job here?"

"He's the one say I should come."

From what I could tell from Kim's broken English, he'd worked for a dry cleaners in California, and when he moved to Denver, he'd gotten a job at Farley's plant on the other side of town. Only thing was he had trouble getting there because he didn't have a car. Farley had suggested he come here because it would be easier for him to get back and forth to work on the bus.

"Why did he suggest Dyer's Cleaners in particular?"

"Don't know, but when I got the job, that's when he takes me out to lunch and says he pay me to spy for him. I say, 'No way.' "

I had one more question to ask before I let him go, only because I'd seen him and Sarah together. "I was out on Colfax yesterday afternoon, and I thought I saw Sarah McIntyre's car. Was that you with her?"

"I baby-sit for her—" he said, and I had the guilty feeling that he knew I'd been playing James Bond too. "So she could meet you for breakfast. Okay?"

CHAPTER 12

I followed Kim out of my office to talk to Ingrid. He detoured to the rest room, and Mack hailed me from the spotting board. "Is he okay? I hope you didn't scare him to death."

"When have I ever scared anyone?" I asked.

Mack managed a grin. "You scare me all the time." He finished spotting a stain and held the dark wool jacket up to inspect it. "So did you learn anything?"

Out of my peripheral vision I saw Kim coming back to work. "I'll tell you later." I waved at Al, who was picking up orders for the business route. Then I went on over to Ingrid's press station and asked her if she'd come in my office.

"You wouldn't want to go have a smoke instead?" she asked hopefully.

"Don't tempt me." I'd be darned if I'd get hooked again, no matter how bad things got.

Ingrid was wearing a short red skirt and a tight white sweater with red piping around the neck. She and Warren must be going out on the town tonight. That's the way she used to dress when she and Winona would hit the singles' bars after work, and for the life of me, I couldn't see Sarah making that scene with them.

I closed the door, and Ingrid sat down in my yellow chair and crossed her legs.

I sat down behind my desk. "I was just wondering if you ever had any more run-ins with Farley Mills except for that one time I saw you back in the parking lot."

"No, why do you ask?" She chewed her gum but seemed to be making an effort not to blow any bubbles.

"You're the one who started calling him sleazeball," I said. "I got so I thought of him that way, too, and I wondered how you figured him out so quickly if you saw him only that one time in the parking lot." She'd also called him Hitler, but I didn't think of that as a nickname.

"Believe me, I know when men are sleazeballs. If you'd heard what he said, you'd have called him a sleazeball too."

I grinned. "Kim thought you said 'cheeseball.' "

"Actually I think I did. That's what I used to call the guys in Wisconsin. That's a sleazeball with a hole in his head."

So much for thinking Kim had misunderstood her. "What did Farley say to you, if you don't mind my asking?"

"Oh, you know, something dirty about jumping my bones. I told him to get lost."

I leaned back in my chair, trying to act casual. "Did Warren ever find out about it? I remember you said he would have killed Mills if he'd heard him."

She looked angry. "Hey, you aren't implying that Warren killed him, are you?" She shook her head until her ponytail began to prance. "I was just kidding when I said that. Warren would never hurt a fly."

That wasn't the impression I'd had of Warren. He probably weighed over 250 pounds and looked as if he could hold his own on the football field or in a tag-team wrestling match. The only time I'd actually met him was one memorable night last fall when he'd roared into

the parking lot in his pickup truck to take Ingrid to a
Monday-night Broncos game. His face was covered with
orange and blue paint in honor of the Broncos, so I
probably wouldn't recognize him if I ever saw him again.
All I remembered was that he looked like a ferocious
mask of comedy and tragedy, only in Technicolor.

Ingrid had introduced us, and I'd asked him why they
weren't driving her little red convertible.

"You've got to be kidding," Warren said. "It's bad
enough going to a game with someone who always wears
red and carries a Kansas City pennant. I'm not taking
her car."

Frankly I was glad to see that even after she'd married
Warren, she retained her maiden name and steadfastly refused to give up her red ensembles and her jazzy car.

She stood up, ready to terminate the discussion. "I'm
not having anyone spread rumors about Warren. He's a
pussycat."

Yep, Warren and Spot. From what I'd seen of him, at
least he had a better disposition than my feline friend.

"Look," I said, "I didn't mean to imply that Warren
killed anyone. I was just quoting what you said." The last
thing I needed was to have her get mad and quit, especially with the backlog of work we had to do.

"Okay." She seemed to calm down.

"I'm just trying to find out if you knew anyone who
had a grudge against him."

She returned to the chair and crossed her legs. "No, no
one except maybe Sarah."

"What did she say about him?"

"Nothing really. I just heard about the fight she had up
in the call office."

"Had you ever seen Farley before that day in the parking lot?"

She shook her head, and popped her gum in spite of
herself.

"And Farley never approached you again?" I asked.

"I avoided him like the plague after that."

There was a knock on the door, and before I could say anything, Ann Marie came into the room.

"It's like a zoo out front." The teenager sounded disgusted that I was loafing. "We're in need of some major help."

"I'll be right there." Any other questions I had for Ingrid would have to wait.

She seemed happy to drop the conversation, except for one final word. "Just so you know, Warren's been on the road with his rig since last Friday."

We all went back to work, and Ann Marie was right. When I got to the call office, it was a mob scene. Maybe it was the same as with celebrities who get a bad press— the notoriety increases their popularity. I didn't think a similar phenomenon applied to dry cleaners. The customers more likely were trying to get their clothes out of a place where a murder had occurred.

I had to sidestep Joe from our shirt laundry, who was vacuuming the rug. Apparently Mack had put him to work cleaning the place. Ann Marie and her older coworker, Julia, were both explaining to customers that it would be at least another day before their clothes were ready. I couldn't in good conscience return some of the clothes on the conveyor without recleaning them—and I had to get them down first.

I'd left instructions for the women to explain the situation to our customers and, if the customers were unhappy, to offer to clean the orders for free. Apparently the explanation was taking longer than our usual two-minute in-and-out policy.

I went through the door to the plant and motioned to Lucille, who was putting tags on the clothes she'd had to quit marking in on Monday. "Can you give us a hand out front?"

I would have preferred to stay off the counter in case any reporters came in asking for me. One had already dropped by this morning, and several more had called. I wanted to keep a low profile if I could.

But Lucille shook her tight dishwater-blond curls at me and put her arms around a dirty-clothes bag. "I still have work to mark in if it's ever going to get cleaned. And furthermore you need to tell your other employees to quit hanging around my table and bothering me, or I'll never get anything done. Everybody and their brother has been skulking around up here to see where that man was killed—like there's anything left to see once the police got through."

"Okay, what if I work the counter until you get things under control?" I said. "Then I'll go back and tell people to leave you alone."

But she was never satisfied. "I wish you'd talk to them now. Especially that Ingrid." Lucille had always taken a dim view of Ingrid and her boisterous ways. "She and her buddies were all up here poking around first thing this morning."

I tried to remember the book I'd read about developing good management skills. Nothing brilliant came to me. "If Ingrid or anyone else bothers you, tell them I said to get back to their jobs."

The rest of the morning was a blur as pick-up customers left empty-handed and very few drop-off customers took their place. Sarah arrived for her shift at eleven o'clock, but she didn't look much better than she had the day before. There were dark circles under her eyes, but at least her hair was pulled back at the nape of her neck and she was neatly dressed in a white blouse and a tan wrap-around skirt.

I told Julia and Ann Marie to take their lunch breaks and I'd keep working through the noon hour. It didn't turn out that way, however.

Mack poked his head out from the back of the plant. "Can I talk to you for a minute?"

I finished waiting on a customer and ducked back to the mark-in table, where Lucille glowered at us.

"Can you get away right now?" Mack asked.

I knew it must be important or he wouldn't suggest my leaving. I looked over at Lucille, who was deliberately avoiding eye contact. "I'm afraid you're going to have to help on the counter for a little while. Just until Julia gets back from lunch."

She slammed down an unopened bag of dirty clothes, but at least she went out front.

"What's the matter?" I asked Mack.

"Juan came by, and he wants us to meet him at the juvenile detention center. Bobby was just arrested."

CHAPTER 13

I didn't ask Mack for details. I probably should have. By the time I grabbed my coat and reached his truck, I had developed this entire scenario for how Juan's son, Bobby, had been arrested for the murder of Farley Mills. Maybe Farley had pushed the kid too far with the dirty tricks and the boy had killed him. It didn't play quite right, but somehow it was easier to accept than some of the other suspicions I'd had lately. After all, I didn't even know the kid.

But why were we going to be allowed to see him, and why wasn't he in an adult facility if he'd been arrested for murder? Besides, how could he have gotten the keys to the plant and figured out the combinations to shut off the alarm?

I voiced my concerns as soon as I was in the truck. "Why do the police think Juan's son killed Farley?"

Mack's truck roared out of the parking lot. "Did I say that?" he asked, glancing over at me from beneath a black knit cap that hid his salt-and-pepper hair. "Did I say that?"

"No, but you said they arrested him."

"For stealing a car, that's all. I guess that's what Juan meant by taking desperate measures. It seems the kid had been planning to buy the car from his aunt, but he didn't have title to it yet, so Juan had the aunt file a report of a stolen car when he couldn't locate the boy any other way. A deputy arrested Bobby a little while ago."

I fidgeted under my seat belt, which I'd harnessed around me tightly. "You mean we're going to see him because of a trumped-up charge of auto theft?"

"Seems like."

"So why does Juan want us to go to the jail anyway?"

"He thinks maybe we can get something out of Bobby about what he was doing for Mills the night of the murder."

When we reached the jail, Mack pulled the truck into the parking lot. "Juan said he'd meet us out here."

We waited, but he didn't appear.

"Maybe we ought to go inside and look for him," I said.

Mack gripped the steering wheel. "God, Mandy, I don't know if I can do this. I've stayed clear of jails and the police for so many years."

"Hey, you're an actor, Mack. You can do it. Just pretend you're a lawyer on your way to see your client."

He started doing some deep breathing exercises. Either that or he was hyperventilating. "I don't know," he said finally. "I can't get over the feeling that if I go in there, they're going to lock me up and throw away the key."

"It'll be okay." I grinned. "They wouldn't put you in here. You're too old."

He smiled in spite of himself. "I'm glad I told you about Alabama. It would have been a lot harder if you hadn't started asking questions about it the other day."

"Come on," I said, urging him out of the truck. "Let's go."

Inside, there was a lobby with a few chairs and sofas. A guard sat behind a glass-enclosed cage. It reminded me of one of those booths where you pay your bill at a self-service gas station. I'm never sure they can hear me, and I'm tempted to bend down and speak through the tray at the bottom where they pass the money back and forth.

"We're here to see Bobby Martinez. I'm his father's employer. . . ." I hesitated, wondering what I should say next. "We have the money in case he needs to post bail." And of course I would if it became necessary.

The guard made a call, gave us a pass with a key attached, and told us to store our belongings in a locker in a small room off to the side of the lobby. When we'd done that, he pointed to a door. "Go through there and turn right. Wait for the other door to open and then go into the next room and wait."

Mack tensed as we went through a metal detector and an electronic door slammed shut behind us, and I couldn't help picking up on his anxiety. I felt as if this was just a preview for when they would arrest Mack or me for Farley's murder.

Sweat had broken out on Mack's forehead so that it glistened like polished ebony. His hands were doubled up in fists.

I grabbed his arm and gave it a squeeze, hoping it would bolster his spirits. "This is another fine fix we've gotten ourselves into, eh, Ollie?" I whispered as we waited by the second door.

Mack seemed to relax a little at my mention of the old Laurel and Hardy movie quote. We hadn't played our trivia game nearly enough in recent days.

" 'It's a fine *mess*— another fine mess you've got us in, Stanley,' " he corrected as the second door slid open. "And thanks, I needed that."

Inside we saw Juan and Bobby, although I wouldn't have recognized the boy from our brief encounter on Juan's front porch. After all, that other time I'd seen him, he'd almost knocked me down with his quick exit from the house, and I'd been busy trying to keep from falling off the porch.

The boy had one of those haircuts where his neck was shaved halfway up his head. Dark hair sprouted on top like one of those Chia plants they always advertise at Christmas that grow out of a ceramic dog's back.

A man in uniform was with them, and they were just finishing some paperwork. "They release Bobby to me," Juan said, sounding relieved. "We can go soon."

Mack and I could hardly wait. Once the paperwork was completed, the four of us were able to return through the clanking doors to the main lobby. Juan said something to Mack in Spanish and left.

"He's going to wait in the car," Mack said. Then he turned to Bobby. "He says you don't want to talk to him, so he wants to see if you'll talk to us. Let's go outside."

Bobby shrugged as only a teenager can do, but he went with us. His strut seemed like an attempt at bravado that didn't match the rest of him. Maybe it was because of his eyes, which still seemed bright with fear, the irises so dark that you couldn't even see his pupils.

"Okay, what was this all about?" Mack asked.

The boy looked away.

"Remember when I coached you in Little League? You were having a problem with some of the other kids on the team, and you talked to me about it. We managed to work it out, didn't we?"

I glanced over at Mack. He was full of surprises. A Little League coach on the side. I couldn't believe it.

Suddenly Bobby's face contorted in anger. "He had Aunt Marie turn me in for stealing her car, but she was letting me buy it from her."

"He was desperate to find you. Why'd you run away?"

"You wouldn't understand."

"Try me."

The kid shook his head, setting his thatch of black hair quivering.

"This is Mandy Dyer, your dad's boss." Mack motioned to me. "We're both in a lot of trouble because Farley Mills was murdered in Dyer's Cleaners. You heard about that, didn't you?"

He nodded.

"Your mom said you told her that Farley asked you to do something for him Sunday night."

Bobby made a face. "Dad's the one who suggested I get a job with him."

"We know, and he's sorry about that." Mack had managed to establish eye contact with the boy. "But Mandy or I may be arrested for his murder if we can't find out what happened that night. Do you know anything about it?"

The kid lowered his eyes.

"So what were you doing for Mills that night?" Mack asked.

"Nothin' bad."

I couldn't keep out of the conversation any longer. "What was it, Bobby? If it wasn't anything bad, why not tell us?"

"Dad always thinks everything I do is bad."

"So what was it? Tell us, and we'll square it with him."

The kid walked away, then back to us. "Mr. Mills called Sunday night and said his car wouldn't start and he needed someone to give him a lift, so I gave him one, but Dad came home Monday and started accusing me of all kinds of stuff."

"Where did you take Mills?"

"Down on Colfax Avenue someplace."

"Where on Colfax?"

The kid shrugged. "Somewhere near the capitol. That's all I know."

That was also near where Mack and I both lived, and I

had this sinking feeling that the police would think he was meeting one of us in a plan to torch my place.

"Did he say what he was going to do after you dropped him off?" I asked.

"No."

"Did he want you to pick him up later?"

"No, he said he was meeting someone, and they'd give him a ride home."

They? Maybe there was a whole gang of people out to torch my plant. "Are you sure he didn't mention a name or at least say *he* or *she*?"

"No."

"Let's go find your father." Mack started walking toward the parking lot, apparently satisfied that we had found out everything, but I had another thought.

"Was he carrying anything with him?"

The kid didn't hesitate. "He had a can of gasoline. Said his friend's car ran out of gas."

Yeah, right! It was undoubtedly the can of gasoline the police had found in the Dumpster outside the plant.

We left Juan to make amends to his son for jumping to conclusions, and he said he'd have Bobby call the police and tell them what he'd just told us.

"I'm feeling shaky," I said to Mack as he drove back to work. "Want to stop and grab something to eat?"

Mack seemed preoccupied. "Yeah, that might be a good idea."

We stopped at a bar called Down Under. It sure fit my mood these days, especially when we discovered that it had boomerangs on the walls for decoration. Every idea I had for getting to the bottom of the murder came back and slapped me in the face.

Mack ordered a beer and a steak sandwich. I ordered a cheeseburger and a glass of milk. I don't normally drink milk, but I figured it might act as a nonmedicinal form of Maalox.

"Do you believe he told us everything?" I asked Mack as we waited for our orders.

"Yeah, I do."

"So why do you think Farley wanted to go down to Colfax?"

"Probably the same reason you think he did: to steal the van, set fire to your place, and make it look like you did it for the insurance money."

I agreed. "But Mack, what I can't understand is, why me? What on earth could Farley Mills have against me? Like I've said before, I'd never even seen the man before he showed up with his cut-rate coupons at our front door."

Mack didn't say anything.

"I just don't understand it."

The waitress brought our orders, and I gulped the milk in hopes it would soothe my queasy stomach. It didn't do much good. The more I thought about why Farley Mills had been out to get me, the more confused I was. I put some catsup on the burger and bit into it. It was only then that I noticed Mack hadn't touched his sandwich or even his beer.

"I guess I'd better tell you the rest of the story," he said.

I stopped with the cheeseburger halfway to my mouth. "You mean there's more? Isn't it enough that you never told me you were a Little League coach?"

Mack frowned. "You know what I mean."

"I'm not sure I do."

He tapped his fingers on the table. "Remember how I told you about that fire at a cleaners where I worked in Alabama, and how the owner was sure I set it?"

I nodded.

"He swore to get even, not just with me but with the

guy who backed me up about my whereabouts the night of the fire."

I put the cheeseburger back on my plate. "Are you saying the owner was Farley Mills?"

Mack shook his head. "No, Mills was too young for that, and besides, the owner's name was Dewey Harper. But I've been doing a lot of thinking about it lately, and Harper had a son who would have been about the same age as Mills. . . ."

Now Mack was getting as paranoid as I was.

"It just doesn't wash, Mack," I said. "Even if someone was out to get you, why would he have a grudge against me and Dyer's Cleaners?" I picked up the burger again, satisfied that I'd successfully deflected this particular concern of Mack's.

He waved his hand in the air. "Will you let me finish, Mandy?"

I held the burger in midair.

"Remember how I said this other guy provided me with an alibi, but a lot of people in town didn't believe him?"

I nodded. "You said he confirmed your story that you'd been playing chess that night, so the police finally let you go."

"Just listen, will you?" Mack took a gulp of his beer. "I wasn't going to tell you this till later, but the man who provided me with the alibi was your Uncle Chet."

I squeezed the cheeseburger so hard the catsup squirted onto my plate like blood from an open wound. Now here was a reason someone might have a vendetta against Dyer's Cleaners if I'd ever heard of one.

CHAPTER 14

"Uncle Chet?" I yelled so loud that the bartender and the few patrons in the bar turned around and stared at us. I lowered my voice. "I didn't know the two of you could even play chess. I never saw you do it." I don't know why I focused on something so innocuous to be accusatory about.

Mack gave a sad half smile. "You might say we kind of lost the spirit for it after that."

I waved my hand at him. "Forget I even said that. What I really meant was that I didn't know you and Chet ever knew each other except here in Denver."

"Yep, Chet was down in Alabama in the service, and when he was discharged, he got a job at the same cleaners where I worked. I'd been helping him fix up this old car he bought, and afterward he'd invite me in for a beer and a game of chess. He was teaching me how to play, but we kept it kind of quiet because blacks and whites didn't socialize much back in those days. Good old Chet was color-blind, though, and he couldn't see anything wrong with us getting together."

"So what happened after he provided you with an alibi?"

"I guess it was bad for Chet, too, and there were

all sorts of innuendoes about us. Our boss had a fit and threatened to file suit against the police for letting me go. He swore to get even with both of us and claimed Chet had probably planned the fire himself and hired me to set it. Chet left town under a cloud the same as I did."

I felt as if that cloud, thick and black like smoke, had descended on our table, giving both of us a motive for killing Farley if he had somehow been connected to that long-ago fire.

"So what happened to the owner?"

Mack twisted his glass of beer in his hands. "Like I said, the owner's name was Dewey Harper, and it turns out he had a bad heart. He was over at the police station raving and ranting about them letting me go, and he had a heart attack and died right there in the police station the day after I left town. At least that's what Chet told me when I finally looked him up here in Denver."

I pushed the cheeseburger away from me. "The important thing here seems to be: Was Farley Mills somehow connected to the fire in Alabama?"

"I've been doing a lot of wondering about that myself."

"Okay, you said Harper had a son. Do you seriously think he could have been out to get even after all this time?"

"He was only a little kid when I was there, and I can't remember his name. I'm not even sure I ever knew it, but he'd be about the same age Farley was, somewhere in his forties."

I reached out to my plate, grabbed the burger, and took a bite out of it as I considered the possibilities. "The owner's wife could have remarried, I suppose, and the child could have taken the stepfather's name. But isn't it hard to believe that Farley Mills could have been the son?"

"It's a stretch, but I guess anything's possible— especially when it does seem like this Farley fellow had some personal grudge against Dyer's Cleaners."

The burger tasted like sawdust, and Mack didn't seem interested in his food either. I grabbed the check and started to scoot out of the booth. "This is on me today," I said so Mack wouldn't fight me for it. "I need to get back to the office and call Nat down at the paper. He was going to get me some background information on Farley."

Mack nodded and took a last swallow of his beer while I put money on the table for our bill. "So how'd you ever reconnect with Uncle Chet?" I asked.

"Well, I knew that his brother—that was your dad—had a cleaners here in Denver, so I wandered around the country for a while and I finally wound up in Colorado. I called the cleaners, and damned if Chet wasn't running the place, and he offered me a job." Mack got up to leave. "Be sure to tell me what you find out from Nat."

I followed Mack to the truck, thinking how powerful he looked for a man who must be in his early sixties. What was I going to do when he retired—or, God forbid, got arrested? "If I don't get Nat before you leave, I'll call you at home," I promised.

He nodded. "I'll be waiting."

I hoped maybe Nat could ease my mind. If Farley didn't appear to have a connection to what happened in Alabama, it would eliminate any motives Mack and I would have had for killing him.

Unfortunately Ingrid had already left for the day when we got back to the plant, which meant we couldn't finish our conversation. I had a pile of "While You Were Out" calls to return, and I skimmed through them before I did anything else. Several calls were from Nat, but he wasn't at the *Trib* when I phoned him there. I left a message for him to call me at work or later at home, no matter what time it was.

Another message was from Mom, and I called the hotel. "I'm sorry," I said peevishly when she answered, "but I'm not going to be able to have dinner with you or spend the night tonight. I have a lot of things I need to catch up on at home."

"That's all right, dear. I just called to tell you I was going out for dinner tonight with Evelyn." So much for me spurning her so she'd know I was still mad about Larry. "I told Evelyn I'd pay with my winnings from Black Hawk yesterday."

I wondered if they were planning another foray to the casinos that night and she didn't want to tell me.

"She's here with me now," Mom continued. "We've just been reminiscing about old times. Would you like to talk to her?"

I was protesting that no, I would not like to talk to her when I realized that Evelyn was on the phone. "Oh, hi, Mrs. Bell," I said to our former next-door neighbor. "I didn't mean I didn't want to talk to you. It's just that I have to run. Oh, so Mom told you I was divorced. . . ." I refused to agree with Evelyn that it was too bad, but I had to listen to her tell me how sorry she was all the same. "I have to go now, but it was good talking to you," I said at the first opportunity. "Will you tell Mom I'll talk to her tomorrow? Oh, hi, Mom. Yes, I'll call you tomorrow, but I really have to go now."

When I went to the call office, the locksmith had finished putting new locks on the front door and had gone around to start on the back. A mechanic had the conveyor up and running, and Lucille began complaining about working overtime to take down the clothes that needed to be recleaned. I pitched in to help.

"I don't think all this rushing is really necessary." She sniffed. "After what happened, it wouldn't hurt people if they had to wait a couple of days for their clothes."

"I'll get Sarah to help me. Why don't you go on home?"

"Oh, and that's another thing. Sarah's as bad as the

others." I noticed that Lucille was getting ready to leave even as she complained. "She's been hiding back here every chance she gets as if she's afraid to be out front."

I wished I could figure out what was going on with her, but Sarah wasn't in the call office when I went to get her. Theresa said she was on her break.

"Hi, Sarah, mind if I join you?" I grabbed a cup of coffee when I got to the break room and slipped into a chair across the Formica-topped table from her.

Something from that book on acquiring management skills was coming back to me. It said to try to put an employee at ease before you talked business with her. I gave it a shot. "I was thinking about your children," I said. "I was wondering if it's working out all right for you to come in on the late shift or would you prefer to work mornings?"

She ran her finger around the rim of her cup but didn't drink from it. "Afternoons are okay, I guess."

"How old are your kids anyway?"

"They're six and four. Why?"

"Do you have a picture of them? I'd like to see them."

"I don't have any pictures with me." Her hands went to her throat. She fidgeted with the collar of her blouse, rubbed her neck, and finally yanked a strand of hair out from the clasp that held it back from her face. If this was a tip-off that she was lying, I couldn't figure out what she had to lie about right now. I thought everyone liked to talk about their children, but this wasn't helping either one of us. "I don't know if anyone mentioned it," I continued, "but someone broke in here last night and stole our personnel records. I'll need you to fill out another resume."

She nodded.

"Where was it you said you worked before you came here?"

She continued to twist her hair. "Sunnyvale—Sunnyvale, California."

"That's right. Sunshine Cleaners, wasn't it? I remember thinking that sounded like a good name for a cleaners." I took a sip of coffee. "Oh, by the way, Winona over at Tico Taco's said you used to go out with her and Ingrid sometimes."

Sarah let go of her hair and dropped her hand to the table. "Not very often, and I always had a baby-sitter." It occurred to me that she might think I was questioning her about Kim or that I was insinuating that she left the kids alone at night.

I needed to get to the point. "Look, Sarah, I hope you'll treat this in confidence, but did you and Ingrid ever talk about Farley Mills when you were together?"

"No." Now her eyes began to tear up. "Just about men in general. We'd both had some bad experiences."

I could relate to that—as recently as last night, as a matter of fact, and it sure wasn't my intention to make her cry. I was trying to think of something cheerful to say, when Mack appeared at the door. He looked in surprise from Sarah to me. I felt like the type of boss I never wanted to be.

"The locksmith wanted me to tell you that he's finished and needs to settle the bill," he said.

"I'll be right there." As much as I wanted to say something to raise her spirits, all I could think of was, "Did Kim ever talk about Mills with you?"

Her face seemed to get even paler than usual. "No, he baby-sat for me sometimes, that's all."

"Well, if you ever think of anything, let me know." I wanted to reach over and give her a hug of reassurance, but I didn't think that would work.

She nodded, but at least she wasn't twisting her hair.

I followed Mack to the back door. I was grateful he didn't tell me that I needed more work on my people skills.

I settled up with the locksmith and took possession of the new keys. I gave a set to Mack, but none of the other keys was getting out of my possession until Farley's killer was found. I didn't even give one to Al, who'd returned from his route and said he'd be out the next day trying to sign up new business customers. Later I asked Sarah if she'd bag clothes and mark in the few orders that had come in that afternoon. I removed the garments from the conveyor to be recleaned, then joined Theresa on the counter and waited until the CLOSED sign was on the door before I left.

On the way home I tried to analyze Sarah's behavior. Why did she always get so upset when I talked to her? What was I missing? Even when I talked about her children, she acted as if there was something wrong.

What I needed, I decided as I climbed the stairs to my apartment, was a nap to see if I could restore a few of my brain cells. Sometimes I did my best thinking when I was trying to fall asleep.

The phone began to ring just as I put my key in the door. No rest for the terminally curious, I realized, as I rushed to answer it. I should have let the answering machine pick up.

"Hello," I said as my recorded voice began to speak. "If you have something pressing on your mind or if you want to come clean about something . . ." I really should change that message, but at the same time, a confession would be nice about now.

Spot came and jumped up on the counter by the phone, offended that I'd left him alone for another whole day to fend for himself. I would have tried to shoo him off, but I was afraid he'd take some sort of retaliatory action with his claws.

"Hello," I said again over the tail end of the recording. "This is Mandy."

"Mandy Pie," said the voice on the other end, a sure

tip-off that it was my stepfather from Phoenix. It didn't take much detecting to figure that out.

"Oh, hi, Herb."

"I've been trying to get you two girls ever since Cecilia went up there Monday. What'd you do—go to some fancy condo up in the mountains or something?" Unfortunately I could only wish for a vacation at some remote wilderness retreat.

"I'm sorry. I got your messages and told Mom about them, but she said she didn't want to talk to you."

"Mandy Pie, you have to help me get my sweet Cecilia back."

Yuck, and double yuck, as Ann Marie would say.

"We had a little misunderstanding," Herb continued, "and I'm desperate to get it cleared up. You have to help me on this. I miss her something fierce."

I thought about Mom not wanting to talk to Herb until he'd had time to agitate for a while, and I thought about how she'd ignored my wishes about Larry. It didn't take me more than a nanosecond to make up my mind on what to do. I'd show her how it felt for someone to meddle in your life.

"Mom's staying at a hotel," I said, and gave Herb the number. "And when you talk to her, I'd suggest you tell her you're coming up here. She says she has to be able to look you in the eye before she'll know if you're telling the truth."

Spot's tail swished across the numbers on the phone, and if he had known how to break the connection, I'm sure he would have.

"Thanks, Mandy Pie. I'll do that, and I appreciate your helping me out."

Mom would probably be mad at me, but I didn't care. Maybe this would teach her to stay out of my life.

CHAPTER 15

When I hung up from Herb, I checked the answering machine. No messages. Nat hadn't called while I was on the way home. I got off the stool by the phone and headed for the refrigerator. Spot thumped to the floor and trotted beside me.

Once I fed him, we went back to our normal relationship, which was to ignore each other. I changed out of my work clothes and into the sloppiest, most comfortable pair of sweats I had. Then I fell on the Hide-A-Bed, which was in its sofa mode. I would try to think from a prone position, I decided, staring at the half-finished painting I'd started Sunday that was supposed to reflect summer and wildflowers blooming by a mountain stream.

Uncle Chet had always loved the mountains. I'd gone up to Estes Park with him and his wife when I was a child, but I never went there anymore. Too busy wrestling with my inheritance. I wondered what he'd been like when he was in Alabama. I'd have to ask Mack about it when this was over. What about my dad? Had Mack known him too? Mom never talked about him much, and I wondered if they'd have stayed together if he lived or if I'd still have had such an endless procession of stepfathers.

The next thing I knew the phone was waking me out of a deep sleep. It was all I could do to struggle to my feet, stagger to the counter, and answer it. My voice sounded thick and groggy.

"Yo, Mandy. It's Nat." I'd have known who it was even without him giving him his name. "Yo" was as much a signature greeting for Nat as "Mandy Pie" was for Herb.

I grunted my response.

"Sorry we've been playing telephone tag all day," he said. "I wanted to touch base with you on what's been going on. So why don't you start by giving me all the inside poop that the police aren't releasing?" When I didn't answer, he continued, "Come on. What's the scuttlebutt on that break-in at the plant last night?"

"Nat, you were the one who was going to find out some information for me."

"I was getting to that." I could hear him shuffling through his notes.

"So what'd you find out?"

"Nothing that's going to break the case open. Farley Mills had a chain of cleaners in Missouri before he moved to Denver last year. Before that he lived someplace in Alabama."

Alabama! My heart began pounding so hard I could feel it pulsing in the ear pressed against the receiver. If Farley was from Alabama, there might very well be a connection to that fire years ago. "Find out where in Alabama, will you?" I asked.

"Why? What's so important about Alabama?"

"Nothing, really. I just want to know." My nose began to itch.

"You're holding out on me, Mandy. I can always tell."

I didn't think he really could, since this conversation was taking place over the phone. Still, I stopped rubbing my nose and dropped my hand to the counter, where I ripped open a bag of potato chips. Unfortunately I always eat under pressure.

"Well, never mind," Nat said impatiently. "So tell me, who do you think broke into the cleaners?"

"I don't know anything, Nat." Suddenly I was rubbing my face again and eating potato chips at the same time. But itch or not, I wasn't about to tell him about Mack and Uncle Chet and the fire in Alabama. Much as I liked Nat, he was a human tape recorder, ready to repeat verbatim everything I said for the early edition.

"The only thing that was stolen was some of the personnel files, so it probably was an inside job," I said, dangling a morsel for him so that he'd go away.

"That's it, isn't it?" I could almost see him fidgeting in his chair as he pressed down with his No. 1 pencil on his ever-present notebook. "You think one of your employees has a connection to Alabama."

"Yeah, that's right, Nat, but the trouble is I don't know who because half the personnel records are gone."

"I still think you're holding out on me."

I grabbed another handful of potato chips, stuck them in my mouth, and then rubbed my eye.

"I really have to go now, Nat. My cat needs me." Actually Spot was nowhere to seen, probably having disappeared into the dark recesses of my walk-in closet, but I wanted desperately to get off the phone so I could call Mack.

"You're a liar, Dyer," Nat said.

"You're a brat, Nat." I hung up the phone.

I'd gotten some salt in my eye, so I had to go run water on my face and hands before I called Mack. He didn't answer. His answering machine didn't answer. I sat there using the redial button every thirty seconds as I stuffed my face with chips.

Where was he? He said he'd be home tonight waiting

for my call. I'd thought he was as anxious as I was to find out something about Farley.

"Come on, Mack," I whispered as I hit the redial again. "Answer, will you?"

Someone knocked at the door as I hung up the phone for the fifteenth time. It had to be Mack. He'd gotten so nervous that he'd driven over to my place to await the information.

"Coming," I yelled as I tried to swallow some more chips before I opened the door. "Mom, what are you doing here?"

She'd probably come to chew me out, but she practically waltzed into the room with a triumphant look on her face. Spot materialized from the closet as if by magic, and he had the same satisfied look as Mom did now that he had a person in the room with allergies.

"Amanda, I just had to come over and tell you the good news." Mom fluffed her blond hair and then the ruffles at the neckline of a dress with yellow flowers on it. She looked like a field of daffodils that had somehow bloomed a month early. "Evelyn dropped me off on her way home from dinner."

And who, pray tell, was going to get her back to the hotel? "You really shouldn't have come, Mom, what with your allergy to—" I motioned to Spot, who was heading for her legs as if they were a scratching pole.

"Oh, this was too good to wait. Herb's coming up tomorrow, and he swears he's going to clear everything up about—well, you know. He said I'm the only woman in the world for him and he can't live without me." Spot wound himself around her legs, and she had to do a little two-step out of his way. "And since you gave him my number at the hotel, I wanted to thank you, dear. I just couldn't bring myself to call him until he'd apologized."

So much for getting even with Mom for calling Larry.

So much for showing her how it felt when someone else tried to mess in your personal life.

"Come on in," I said. "We'll have a cup of coffee. You ought to be able to stay that long before you have a reaction to Spot." Or before I had one to her, for that matter.

This time she didn't demand tea. She followed me to the kitchen, where I turned on a burner under my kettle. She hovered over me as if she were watching a master chef at work. It made me nervous, since all I intended to do was put my usual spoonful of instant coffee into two mugs and wait.

"Herb said he has a surprise for me, something I'm going to love, and then I'll understand what all that mixup with the earring was about." She fluffed her hair again. "Oh, dear, I need to get to the beauty shop tomorrow morning. Do you suppose you could drop me off at one on your way to work?"

Never mind that I'd be going to work long before any of the high-priced beauty salons opened.

She began to pace, her high-heeled shoes sounding like castanets as she circled the small kitchen. "I wonder what the surprise is."

I thought about suggesting that maybe it was the matching earring to the one she'd found in his pants pocket, but that seemed unnecessarily cruel. Besides, she hadn't been insulted by my earlier effort to interfere in her life, so why bother. I was saved from the temptation to find a more devious way to irritate her when the phone rang again.

This had to Mack. I grabbed the receiver. Maybe I could drop by his place after I took Mom back to the hotel. That would give me an excuse to get her out of here as soon as possible.

"Mandy." It was a man's voice on the line. "It's Manuel at Tico Taco's."

I was immediately on the alert. "What's the matter?"

I heard Mom sneeze in the background. "Can't you do something about that cat, Amanda. Why does he always want to rub against people's legs?"

The background at Tico Taco's was noisy too. I heard Manuel order someone to be quiet. "Mandy," he said again. "I was looking outside a minute ago, and I saw somebody sneaking around the back of your place. It's probably just kids, but I thought I should let you know."

My heart started pounding again, this time in sync with the tap of Mom's heels. I guess she was trying to elude Spot.

"Thanks, Manuel. I'll be right down."

I hung up the phone and headed for the door. "Call Nine-one-one and tell them to come to the plant, that I received a report that someone was hanging around the back door." I stopped only long enough to put on a pair of Reeboks and grab my coat. I was only slightly more presentable than I'd been the night before, but at least I wasn't wearing flannel. "I'll meet them there."

Mom started to protest.

"I'll be okay. Just call a taxi and have the driver take you back to the hotel."

"But you shouldn't go there alone," Mom said.

At the time, I was relieved to get out of there before she decided to ride shotgun for me, but later her words came back to haunt me.

CHAPTER 16

I couldn't believe this was happening again. Me racing off in the dark of night because of another disaster at the plant. Oh, please, don't let there be another break-in.

A cold front was moving through, and it felt like snow. Maybe we'd have one of those messy spring storms tonight. I tried to think of something amusing. Something like Mom in her flowery dress and open-toed shoes in the middle of a blizzard, but it wasn't funny.

Damn it, where was Mack? It nagged at me that I hadn't been able to reach him. Why hadn't he answered his phone when he said he'd be home all evening? Since Farley must have been in partnership with someone who worked for me, maybe that person had lured Mack to the plant for a confrontation.

Obviously someone had been Farley's partner. My competitor couldn't have gotten inside my locked building without the help of someone who worked for me.

When I reached Cherry Creek, I made a left turn off First and swung into our parking lot. When I got to the back of the plant, there was nothing there. No police cars. No shadowy figure by the door. Only the light from Tico Taco's across the lot in the strip shopping center behind the cleaners. It was like a beacon shining at me and easing my fears, promising me that there were friends nearby if anything went wrong. I looked over at the restaurant and thought I saw Manuel standing at a window. I waved at him and gave a shrug to indicate that I couldn't see anything. He probably couldn't see my gesture, but I'd take a quick look around and then go over to Tico Taco's and have myself a good strong drink. I deserved it.

I grabbed a flashlight out of the glove compartment. I'd wisely put it there because I'd discovered these loaners don't come with amenities for people who lead dangerous lives.

The first thing I needed to do was check the back door. I climbed out of the car and crept to the door, checking to see if it had been tampered with. It looked okay. I tried the knob, careful not to jiggle the door and set off the burglar alarm. Actually a few windstorms had done that in the past, and I hoped the one blowing through tonight didn't activate it. I didn't need any more false alarms.

I went over to the Dumpster and shot a beam of light up onto the window above my office. I couldn't help remembering a time just before Christmas when someone had broken into the cleaners through the window, my Achilles' heel when it came to security. The window hadn't been wired into our alarm system then because Uncle Chet with his be-kind-to-small-animals philosophy had left the window unprotected so that Spot, when he was in residence at the cleaners, could go in and out of the locked office at will.

After Uncle Chet died, I'd taken Spot home with me, hoping it would help the cat's disposition to have company at night. I'd also hoped it would decrease Lucille's complaints about finding cat hairs on the clothes when she inspected the freshly pressed garments. Unfortunately the move had been in vain; both Spot and Lucille still found things to complain about.

The window, which was now hooked into our system,

was intact. I listened carefully for scary night sounds. I didn't hear anything but the wind, which whooshed through the lot and chilled me, even through my coat. I pulled up the collar and returned to the back door, fumbling in my purse for the set of keys. Just as I found it, I thought I heard a noise that wasn't the wind.

With the key halfway to the door, I stopped and listened. Damn, where were the cops? They should be here by now. I'd have to complain to Foster about their response time.

The noise seemed to come from the vicinity of the Dumpster. I went over to it, trying to sneak quietly in my white Reeboks, which glowed in the dark like they were phosphorescent. If I was going to do much of this night work, I'd have to get an all-black outfit.

My Reeboks crunched on some gravel, but it was the only sound I heard. When I reached the Dumpster, I flashed my light behind it. There was nothing there but some loose trash, odds and ends of papers that had blown across the lot.

I made a circle around the Dumpster, but I didn't see anything. Not unless someone was circling around in front of me. No, I'd hear them if they were doing that, just as I was sure someone could hear me as I circled on the other side.

There was a door on the front so people didn't have to open the heavy lid to throw trash inside, but it was closed. I stopped in front of it, satisfied that no one was hiding in the area. I tried to give Manuel an all-clear signal, but before I could be sure he saw me, something slammed against my back, smacking me in the head. The impact knocked me forward. My arms flailed out in front of me, and I landed on my right knee and then bounced forward and hit my chin.

I turned my head back toward whatever had hit me. I half expected to be hit again. All I could see was the open door on the Dumpster and someone in burglar-black running away from me. He must have been hiding in the Dumpster, and he faded in and out of my still-blurred vision as he raced across the street to a nearby parking lot.

I tried to get up, but my head hurt too much. I heard footsteps coming from the opposite direction, and I rolled over toward the sound. Someone was yelling at me in a flood of words I didn't understand. *"¿Qué pasó? ¿Qué pasó?"* It was Manuel.

"What happened?" I asked groggily.

"¿Sí, qué pasó?" he said.

I staggered to my feet. My leg almost buckled under me. I could see a pickup backing up in the parking lot across the street. The taillights came on when the driver put on his brakes to shift gears. It was the person from the Dumpster. I was sure of that. It probably was the killer as well.

I headed for my car, but Manuel tried to stop me. I shook him off. "Let go, Manuel. Call the police and tell them I'm going after the guy."

Surely the cops were on their way by now and could pick up the chase so that I could drop out.

At first the ignition wouldn't turn on. I finally remembered that you had to have your foot on the brake when you started these cars. I hit the brake. Pain shot to my head from my wounded knee, but the key turned and the engine caught.

I backed up, put the Ford in drive, and stepped on the accelerator. The car jerked forward as I headed for the street. I'd lost sight of the truck, and just as I reached the curb, a low-slung sports car nearly cut me off as it turned into the driveway. It glinted like aluminum foil in the glow of my headlights. I honked the horn and kept moving.

Who was the smart-ass in the fancy car anyway? The driver had looked as if he'd deliberately been trying to block my way. It sure wasn't the cops. I came within inches of clipping the other car before I swung the wheel, bumped over the curb, and made a sharp right turn into the street. I stopped to get my bearings when I reached First Avenue. I looked both ways and took another right. The only taillights I could see that looked as if they belonged on a pickup were heading west several blocks ahead of me.

I wrestled to put on my seat belt as I took off in pursuit. I was closing on the truck when it turned south onto University Boulevard at the edge of the original Cherry Creek Shopping Center. I pushed down on the gas in the hope of getting close enough to see the back license plate.

I don't know when I became aware that I'd picked up a tail. Well, maybe it wasn't a tail, but someone was definitely riding my back bumper. And it wasn't the cops with a comforting light on top of their car. In fact it looked like a sports car, so low to the ground that I could hardly see it in my rearview mirror. It had to be the one that had tried to cut me off at the curb as I pulled out of the parking lot. I'd have taken a quick turn up a side street to see if it would follow me, but I didn't dare lose the pickup. It was slipping away from me in the distance as I tried to figure out who the person was in the car behind me.

There were several vehicles between me and the pickup, and I had to concentrate to keep the truck's taillights in view. Fortunately they were a little higher off the pavement than the rest of the traffic. But where were the police? Why weren't they at least pulling the truck over for speeding?

The pickup made a right on a green light at Alameda Avenue and disappeared around the corner. The light turned yellow, but I blasted toward the intersection and made the turn. The sports car followed me through on a red light.

I tried to remember what the car had looked like that had been in the parking lot. A silver bullet, I decided, as I caught the glimmer behind me from a passing streetlight.

Maybe there'd been a second person who'd been working for Farley before he was killed. Someone who was now trying to see that I didn't catch up to the truck. I gripped the steering wheel in case he tried to ram the rear end of my car or pull up beside me and take a potshot at me.

The sports car swung into the inside lane. I shot ahead and veered to the left so he couldn't move up beside me. Meanwhile the truck was almost out of view as it dipped under a railroad overpass just as we were approaching Interstate 25. I thought I'd lost it for a minute, but I finally spotted the truck as it headed south just before the freeway.

I followed, losing ground all the time. The truck swung around to grab the northbound entrance to I-25. I circled around and merged into the freeway traffic, the sports car still following in my wake as if trying to ride the wave I created. Still no police, but I tried not to think about it. I'd given up any hope of stopping the truck, seeing that I'd never picked up my hoped-for police escort. I only wanted to get close enough to get a look at the license plate.

I saw the truck take the ramp that looped around to the Sixth Avenue Freeway heading west toward the mountains. The ramp soared up to the other road in a circle, and I soared with it, trying to keep my eye on the truck as I did so. I should have been watching the car just ahead of me. It was creeping up the ramp at well under the speed limit, and I was on it before I knew it. I slammed on the brakes, which sent pain radiating out from my knee. The sports car that had been playing tailgate tag with me plowed into the rental's backside. My foot slipped off the brake, and I went crashing off the ramp and down a sharp embankment at the side of the road. I was heading for a huge pylon that supported one of the swirling roadways that converged in the area.

I tried to find the brake pedal again, but by then the car had a mind of its own. It skidded down the steep incline and didn't stop until it hit the pylon. Metal crunched. I slammed forward and then back in the seat. Thank God for the seat belt, but where was the air bag?

I half rose in the seat to look for the truck. It had disappeared. So had the doddering driver on the ramp. I was left with nothing to do but check for wounds. I seemed to be okay. No noticeable cuts or bruises that I hadn't had before. I also discovered a hole in the knee of my sweats, but I was pretty sure I'd done that in the fall.

Still, I wanted vengeance on the driver of the sports car who had wrecked my rental. Probably totaled it. It didn't take much these days to demolish a car. I hoped the police would see it my way and at least ticket the driver of the other car in absentia for following too close. I was assuming that he'd be a hit-and-run, now that he'd knocked me out of commission.

I had never seen the sports car swing onto Sixth Avenue, but I hadn't been looking. I checked the shoulder of the ramp high above me, and there it was. I'd been sure the driver would keep going after he hit me. For the first time, I felt fear instead of anger. Why hadn't he moved on once he'd eliminated me from the chase? Wasn't that what he'd been after the whole time?

I tried to start the car. If I could get the engine going, I could back up and try for a running start to get myself up the embankment by the side of the road. The dead grass underneath should give me traction. I even remembered to put my foot on the brake. The engine spat at me and died. I tried again. It growled but wouldn't start.

I thought about getting out and trying to flee on foot to the freeway so I could hail down some passing motorist to take me to the nearest police station. But no way was I getting out until the sports car left. I checked to see if the doors were locked, and I hunkered down behind the wheel.

Surely the driver would leave once he'd seen that my car was incapable of going anywhere. I waited for the car to move, but it just perched there and waited. What if the driver decided to come down and check on my condition? I couldn't believe he'd take a chance on revealing himself to me, since he was apparently working in tandem with the person in the pickup.

I took a quick look up the hill. Horrified, I saw the driver getting out of the car. I scooted down in my seat. If he came down to my wrecked car, I'd pretend to be unconscious. Maybe he'd think I was dead.

To my relief I saw another vehicle pull up to the side of the road behind the sports car. Other traffic was moving around them and merging onto the divided highway as if nothing had happened. At least there was a witness up there if the guy tried to do anything to me. That's assuming there wasn't a whole convoy of people out to get me.

The guy looked familiar as I saw his shadowy silhouette start down the hill. Well, why wouldn't he? He was probably one of my employees, and he couldn't let me live once I could ID him.

I shut my eyes and slumped forward against the wheel. The man tapped on the window, and I expected a shotgun blast to follow. There was no exploding glass. The man tapped again. I opened one eye just enough to take a peek at him. I recognized him, all right, and for the life of me, I couldn't figure out why he would have been following me.

I rolled down the window. "Damn it, Larry. What the devil are you doing here?"

CHAPTER 17

Why, of all people, would my ex-husband be pursuing me through Denver when I thought I'd made it perfectly clear the night before that I wanted to purge him permanently from my life?

Surely he wasn't part of the vendetta against me. If anything, I should be the one with a vendetta against him.

The wind ruffled his short dark hair, which had a far better cut than mine. "Are you all right?" he asked.

"Never mind that. Why are you here?"

"I was trying to see what was the matter with you. You were driving like a madwoman."

"Not as mad as I'm going to be." I yanked off my seat belt, opened the door, and got out of the car. I stomped my feet before I remembered the pain in my right knee. I shook my leg and limped away, first to the front of the car and then to the back to survey the damage. The rental place wasn't going to like this one bit.

I bent down to check the crumpled rear end. No one would be able to stuff a body in the trunk for a while, and at the moment I'd have liked to do just that to my former husband.

Meanwhile the driver of the other car that had pulled up behind Larry was standing at the edge of the ramp.

"Anything I can do?" he yelled. "I have a phone, and I can call the police."

I scrambled up the hill to the Good Samaritan, limping as I went, and took a look at Larry's silver car—a Jaguar, according to the logo that peeked through the front of what's euphemistically called the bra. I noticed that the bumper had a few scratches, but the hood cover, which looked more like leather than vinyl, hid whatever damage there was to his car. It wasn't fair.

"Yes, call the police," I said to the other driver.

Larry had followed me up the embankment. "I'll bet we can get your car out of the ditch ourselves and pull it back up onto the pavement. I'll pay for the damages."

What was with Larry? Did he have a bundle of outstanding speeding tickets or something? "Oh, please," I said. "You know we can't do that. If I don't call the police, how can I sue for damages?" I grabbed my neck. "Ouch, I think I may have whiplash."

Larry looked as if he were the one in pain, and I wondered if he'd gotten so many speeding tickets in his fancy car that he was at risk of losing his driver's license. The other man had trotted back to his car to make the emergency call.

I limped away from Larry's car to the edge of the embankment. No sense being a target for another crazed driver.

"Did you hurt your leg?" Larry asked anxiously.

"No, I'm limping because I want sympathy." I took my weight off it and put my arms on my hips. "Now, if you don't mind telling me, why were you even in a position to follow me? And please don't tell me it had something to do with Mom."

"Your mother called me on my cell phone and said you were in some sort of trouble and were on your way to the cleaners."

Was there no way of getting through to that woman? I

thumped my hand to my head and realized it ached from the clip I'd taken on the chin. I quickly dropped my arm.

Wasn't it enough that Mom had called Larry the night before? Now she'd apparently decided to repay me for setting up her reunion with Herbie. Frankly I didn't think Mom and I would ever understand each other.

"Fortunately I was having dinner at the Rattlesnake Grille right across the street," Larry continued.

Naturally. It was one of the "in" places to eat in Denver at the moment.

"So you just dropped everything and came running to my aid," I said sarcastically.

"I told Mother Cilia to call me if she ever needed anything, and I'm happy to say she did."

"And so here we are. . . ." I swept my hands around our cold, windy perch at the side of the interstate with its commanding view of my car down below. "Yep, I sure needed your help, all right."

"She called me again when I was in the car a few minutes later and said it was a false alarm. By then I was on my way."

Everyone but me seemed to have a cell phone. So why wasn't Larry in his car calling the police at this very moment? As for Mom, I hadn't a clue as to why she'd decided to sic Larry on me, much less call him off, but I guess I'd find out later. "Then why didn't you just go back to your dinner and leave me alone?"

"That's what I was going to do after I told you everything was okay. Then I saw you tearing out of the parking lot as if the devil himself were after you. I thought maybe you did need some assistance after all."

I put my hands on my hips again. "I was trying to get the license plate off a pickup that had been hanging around the plant." All of a sudden I felt like crying in frustration. I'd be damned if I'd cry in front of Larry. I took a deep breath of the cold night air. It pierced my lungs but cleared my head enough that I could continue. "Thanks to you, I lost any chance of getting it."

"I'm sorry. When the police get here, I'll see to your car, and then I'll give you a ride home."

"Damned right you will. But not home. You're taking me back to the plant."

It was nearly an hour before we actually started back to the cleaners. Meanwhile there was some justice in this world, even for lawyers. Larry had received a ticket for following too close. I felt a little guilty about my part in the accident. I should have seen the slow-moving vehicle on the ramp ahead of me, but the point was that I'd had enough room, so I didn't hit the other car. What's more, when I remembered my fear as Larry came down the incline toward me, my feelings of guilt about the accident vanished.

A policeman finally finished his questioning and said we could leave. Larry was full of concern for my welfare as we reached his car, but he wasn't fooling me for a minute. He just wanted to make sure I wasn't going to sue his socks off for injuries sustained in the accident.

"How does your neck feel now?"

I moved my head from side to side. "It feels okay, but don't these injuries sometimes take days to show up?"

His suntanned face seemed to pale as he held the car door open for me. His normally bronzed good looks went well with the glitzy car, which had the rich leather-smell of a new vehicle. I'm sure that as it aged, he'd used one of those leather sprays to sustain the odor, just the same way he'd probably go to a tanning salon to keep his Aspen tan.

He touched my chin gently with his finger. "It looks bruised," he said. "Are you sure you're all right?"

I jerked my head back. "I'm okay. Now can we just go?"

I bent down and climbed into the passenger's seat. It was like I'd always imagined it would be to try to squeeze into one of those race cars at the Indy 500.

I felt as if I were lying down when I got inside, but I managed to lean forward and move the rearview mirror so I could see my face. There was just enough light that I could see that my chin was scraped and beginning to swell. I looked a little like Jay Leno except that my hair wasn't as gray.

"Are you sure you don't want to go to the emergency room?" Larry asked as he climbed inside, much more gracefully than I had done. But of course, he'd had more practice.

I moved the mirror back into its original position. "No, I want to go to the plant, and besides, you can quit worrying. I was hit by a door earlier tonight."

Larry might have been puzzled, but he couldn't hide his relief.

I waited until he started the car. "The driver of the truck had been hiding in the Dumpster at the back of the plant," I said. "He knocked me down when he escaped."

Why was I being so forthcoming with Larry, I wondered, when he'd never been that way with me? I guess I just didn't have the energy to lie—and besides, I didn't want to start itching.

"So why do you want to go back there now?" Larry asked once he managed to merge into the westbound traffic on the Sixth Avenue Freeway.

I took one last wistful look back at the tow truck that was hauling my rental car out of the ditch. "I got a report that someone was hanging around the back of the cleaners. He must have hidden inside the Dumpster when he heard me coming, and I want to see what he'd been up to."

Eventually Larry managed to get turned around so

that we were heading back on Sixth Avenue in the right direction. "I'm really sorry this is happening to you," he said. "You know I want only the best for you."

"Sure."

"It was a big mistake, you know, my leaving you for Patty. We need to talk about it sometime."

Good grief. I hoped he wasn't going to suggest a reconciliation. I didn't respond, and Larry didn't pursue the subject. It was silent in the car, and I was happy about that. It had been a long time since Larry and I had been around each other when the air hadn't been filled with vitriolic conversation.

Larry turned south on York, and soon we were back at the plant. The wind had died down, so maybe the cold front had moved through Denver. There wasn't much traffic on the street anymore. It must be after midnight by now, and most people probably were home in bed.

As we reached the side street where the plant is located, I glanced up the block. All was calm. Larry slid the Jaguar around the side of the building, and all hell broke loose. Behind the plant the parking lot was jammed with vehicles. Police cars. An ambulance. Other vehicles I couldn't identify. My first thought was that the person I'd followed had come back and done his damage. Broken in and did God knows what.

Just then a light flashed from the top of the open Dumpster. Someone was perched on the edge taking flash pictures of whatever was inside. I grabbed for the handle of the door before the car came to a stop.

A crowd of people stood in a semicircle back from the Dumpster. They were prevented from moving forward by the all-too-familiar crime-scene tape. Where had all the spectators come from in the middle of the night? Other people milled about inside the cordoned-off area. I didn't see anyone I knew, but I didn't think the police blocked off an area like this unless there was a serious crime.

The potato chips I'd eaten hours earlier lurched into my throat as Larry finally came to a stop. For a minute I thought I was going to throw up on his leather upholstery. It would have served him right, but I couldn't afford to take the time. I had to find out what had happened. My fear about Mack returned. Had someone tricked him into coming here, and now they'd found his body? If they had, I'd never be able to forgive myself.

I opened the door, but then I had trouble getting out of the car. It was like trying to get out of a bed that was six inches off the floor. I finally crawled out and managed to stand up.

Larry was right behind me as I took off through the crowd. At the barricade a cop stopped us. "You can't come in here," he yelled. "Stay back behind the tape."

"This is my dry cleaners, and that's my—my Dumpster." Actually I didn't know who owned the Dumpster, but that was beside the point.

"Are you Mandy Dyer?" the man asked.

I nodded.

"The detective's been trying to get ahold of you. He told me to get him if you showed up. I'll tell him you're here."

I don't think the man intended for me to follow him, but I started to slip under the tape.

The uniformed officer turned around. "Both of you. Stay where you are."

We stopped.

"I'll find him and bring him over to you."

I looked back at Larry, who'd almost run me down again when I came to such an abrupt halt. "Would you just go on home, Larry? This doesn't concern you, and I'll find a ride later."

Larry shook his head. "No, this is the time for legal counsel if I ever saw one."

I couldn't figure out how to stop him if he really wanted to hang around, so I decided to ignore him. I looked for someone else I knew. Finally I spotted Manuel. He was talking to another policeman.

I yelled at him.

He looked over at me with horror in his eyes. "Mandy, Mandy, Mandy." The cop he'd been talking to tried to hold him back, but he came to me with outstretched arms.

"It's one of my girls," he said as he hugged me. "I can't believe it."

"Who? What girl?"

He was holding me so tight I could hardly breathe. "She's dead. I found her body in the Dumpster with a belt around her neck."

I pushed him back so I could look at him. He had his eyes squeezed shut.

"What girl, Manuel? Tell me."

"She asked to leave work early tonight. She said she had something she needed to do."

"Please, Manuel, tell me who it is."

"My waitress, the one who was talking to you and your boyfriend last night. You know—Winona."

CHAPTER 18

Winona. Ingrid's friend. The one who'd told me she was a friend of Sarah's as well.

I stood there in a daze as the policeman hauled Manuel away so he could finish making his statement. I couldn't deal with the news. All I could think about was how I'd tried to talk to Sarah this afternoon about Winona and Ingrid and her connection to them.

Had I somehow put Winona in danger with my inquiry about the three women? It had all seemed so innocuous at the time, but now Winona was dead in what I had unfortunately called *my* Dumpster.

But surely Winona's death didn't have anything to do with Farley's murder. Her only connection to the cleaners was her friendship with a few of my crew. Her death could be totally unrelated, the killer a guy she'd picked up at a singles' bar. Somehow I couldn't convince myself that was the case.

I searched the crowd behind the crime-scene tape for someone else to give me information. None of the other shopping-center tenants were around. They had all closed their stores much earlier and gone home.

"Do you know the dead woman?" Larry asked. He'd followed me over to where I'd talked to Manuel.

Before I could answer, I saw Foster coming toward me. He loomed over the policeman I'd talked to originally. He was even taller than Larry.

"I understand Mr. Ramirez called you earlier because he thought he saw something at the Dumpster," Foster said.

I nodded.

"He said he called you a few minutes later because he couldn't see anyone and decided it had just been kids. By then you were already gone."

Maybe that explained why Mom never called the cops. But it sure didn't explain why she'd called Larry.

"Anyway we need to get a statement from you about what happened."

Larry cleared his throat. "Excuse me, Detective, but I'm Lawrence Landry. I'm Ms. Dyer's attorney."

Foster looked surprised. "You hired a lawyer?"

My face probably turned as red as the welt on my chin, but I wasn't blushing. I was angry. "You are *not* my lawyer, and I'd thank you to stay out of this, Larry."

"So who is he?" Foster motioned toward my companion.

"He's *not* my lawyer," I said again.

"I'm her ex-husband," Larry said.

"Well, Mr. Landry, would you please step back behind that tape over there while I talk to Ms. Dyer?"

"Detective Foster," someone shouted from near the Dumpster. "We need you to take a look at this."

What had they found? I wanted to demand an explanation, but I stood there like the law-abiding citizen I was and didn't say anything.

"Okay." Foster waved at the person at the Dumpster. Then he motioned to the policeman I'd first talked to. "I'm going to have Officer Burns take a statement from you right now. Then I want him to accompany you through your building to see if everything's all right." I nodded cooperatively. "But I'll need to talk to you later. Be at the police station at eight o'clock tomorrow morning."

I started to say I'd wait around so we could talk tonight.

"Just be there. Okay?" Foster walked away.

By the time I got through giving my statement and going through the apparently undisturbed building with Officer Burns, I couldn't see Foster anywhere. The person I did see was Larry standing on the other side of the yellow tape with none other than my buddy, Nat, the nosiest newspaper reporter in the world. It was a scene to make even the most fearless person blanch, not to mention one who'd had about all she could take for one night.

This was probably the first time I'd seen the two of them be civil to each other since they'd first met back when I'd started dating Larry. Nat had warned me that Larry was a ladies' man who would never be happy with just one woman, and Larry had said Nat was nothing but a pint-sized gossip monger who was always sticking his nose in where it didn't belong.

Larry was a good four inches taller than Nat, who was only about five seven. I hadn't paid any attention to what Larry was wearing before, but I noticed now that he had on dark brown slacks and a tan sweater, probably cashmere, while Nat was in jeans and an open-necked plaid shirt. What really struck me, though, was that they both had on similar brown tweed jackets with patches on the sleeves. Larry's jacket probably had been purchased that way, but I was pretty sure the patches on Nat's jacket were there because he'd worn out the elbows. Even so, the matching jackets made the two men look like the best of buddies.

Nat was writing something in his ever-present spiral

notebook, and it made my skin crawl. Surely Larry had enough sense not to spill his guts to Nat.

There were some TV cameras up closer to the crime scene, and I wanted to stay away from the lot of them. Still I scooted under the tape and hurried toward Nat, fearful of what he and Larry were talking about.

"There you are," Larry said. "We've been wondering where you were."

Nat gave me one of those sardonic John Lennon looks that he cultivated and pushed his wire-rimmed glasses back up on his nose. "You didn't tell me Larry was back in town."

"I've had a lot of other things on my mind."

"So what's the scoop? Do the police think the waitress from over there"—he motioned to Tico Taco's—"saw someone trying to break into your plant, and the person killed her?"

"I don't know. Everything inside the building is okay."

"I hear you may know this woman—" He flipped back through his notes. "—Winona Morris."

"I didn't even know her last name."

"Do the cops think she had some connection to Farley Mills's death?"

"Look, Nat, I don't know anything. I've had a hard night, and the police said I could go home. Why don't you talk to Detective Foster if you want information? Maybe you could share it with me if you find out anything."

"I'm ready to take you home whenever you want," Larry said.

"Hey, you probably should hang around, don't you think, Mandy?" Nat asked. "I'll give you a ride later."

I didn't want a ride with either one, but since my rental was now out of commission, Nat's motorcycle probably had less appeal than Larry's Jaguar. And if I didn't go with either Larry or Nat, I'd have to find Foster and ask him if one of the cops could escort me home in a police car. Somehow that didn't sound good to me either.

"I'll go with you, Larry, as long as you go right now."

Larry gave Nat a self-satisfied smile, and Nat looked hurt. "Okay, if that's the way you want to be about it."

That's all I needed was to be part of a jealous triangle between an ex-husband and a good friend, neither one of whom I had the least romantic interest in.

"Look, Nat, I have to be down at the police station at eight o'clock, and I have to get some sleep before then." Larry turned to leave, and I started to follow him.

"Psst." Nat motioned me back with his head. "I need to ask you something, Man."

I returned to where he was standing, pencil still at the ready. "What's with Mack?" he asked.

"What do you mean?" I remembered my earlier fears about my production manager, not to mention his confession to me about the fire at the cleaners where he and my uncle had both worked years ago. What was Nat getting at?

He shrugged. "I was just wondering what his connection was to all this."

"There's no connection." I sounded defensive, even to myself. "And if you know something I don't know, spit it out."

He put up his hands as if to ward off my verbal blows. "Hey, I don't know anything. I was asking you." Unlike me, Nat could lie with no outward signs of guilt. I was pretty sure he knew something, and I wanted to strangle his skinny neck until he told me.

Larry had come back to where we were standing. "Are you ready to go or not?"

I turned away from Nat, still upset by his strange inquiry.

"I'll talk to you tomorrow," Nat said. Before we'd even gotten to the car, he was off trying to find someone else to interview.

I squeezed into the Jaguar, which had only a slight bit more to recommend it, as far as I could see, than Nat's Harley.

"What did the police want to know from you?" Larry asked.

I leaned back in the seat and closed my eyes. "I don't want to talk about it right now. Okay?"

Surprisingly he abided by my wishes until he pulled up in front of my apartment. He started to get out to open my door.

"Don't bother." I made my ungainly exit from the car. All I wanted to do was get to my apartment and call Mack.

I gave the door a shove to close it, and as I did, I heard Larry's parting words. "I'll give you a lift to the police station tomorrow. . . ."

I tried to yank the door open to protest, but by then the Jaguar was in motion. I was left standing at the curb, shaking my head back and forth and yelling into the darkness, "No, no, no. I do not want you to go to the police station with me."

Mom had left a note inside my apartment: "Call me as soon as you get home."

Damned right I would, but it wasn't my first priority. I checked the messages on my answering machine. Mack had called and said he needed to talk to me. Then he'd called again and said he was going to bed and he'd talk to me in the morning.

I was relieved that he was okay, but I still had the feeling something was wrong. Why else would Nat have been questioning me about him? Even as a reporter, Nat shouldn't have known that Mack might have a connection to Farley Mills.

To heck with waiting until morning to talk to Mack. I

dialed his number. Unfortunately when he's asleep, it would take a nuclear explosion to raise him. I tried his number three different times. His answering machine kicked on each time after only two rings. I left messages for him to call me, and I asked him if he'd open for me the next morning. I didn't want to tell him there'd been another murder and that I had an appointment with Foster at eight o'clock.

Finally I dialed the hotel and asked the desk clerk to connect me with Mom's room. He let the phone ring four times and then came back on the line and asked if I wanted to leave a message. I said no, to keep ringing. At least this was something I had control over.

When Mom answered, she sounded as groggy as I do when I'm awakened. "I'm glad you called. I've been waiting to hear from you." Sure she had. "Was everything all right at the plant, dear?"

"No, it was not all right." She was stronger than I was in the emotional department, so I continued, "There's been another murder."

She gasped. "But the man at the restaurant called back and said it must have been kids hanging around the plant. He said he couldn't see any sign of them."

"I gather that's why you didn't call the police."

"Of course."

"So why did you call Larry?"

"I'd already called him by then. I thought you needed some moral support."

If she thought I needed moral support, I wished she would have called Mack.

"When the restaurant man phoned back," Mom continued, "I told Larry just to let you know everything was okay, seeing that he was already on his way."

I sighed. "Okay, we'll let it go, but what I need from you right now is Larry's phone number."

"See, you never should have thrown away his business card."

The woman had a memory like an elephant, even when she was half asleep. Me, I couldn't remember my own name without two cups of coffee when I first woke up.

"You're just too impetuous, dear."

"The phone number, Mom . . ."

"Hold on a minute."

I drummed my fingers on the counter while I waited.

She finally came back on the line. "Here it is." There was a long pause. "I can't make it out. You'll have to wait until I put in my contacts."

Oh, vanity, thy name is Mom. Didn't she even have a pair of glasses to slip on in an emergency?

I waited some more. When she returned, she gave me the numbers of his home phone, his beeper, and his cell phone. I told her to stop when she started to give me his office number.

"Don't forget about taking me to the beauty shop tomorrow morning. I have an appointment at eleven."

"Yeah, yeah." Maybe I'd have another rental car by then or maybe she'd have to take a taxi. I'd deal with that later.

As soon as we hung up, I called Larry.

When he answered, I didn't even bother to identify myself. "Don't pick me up tomorrow morning, Larry. I repeat, do not pick me up. I can get to the police station by myself."

"But you don't have a car."

"I'll walk."

"But you have a bad leg. . . ."

"I'll rent another car. I just don't want an escort."

"All right. Whatever you say, Mandy, but as a lawyer, I feel I should advise you to get a good criminal attorney. Maybe someone like Brad Samuels."

I remembered Brad "The Cad" Samuels all too

well from Larry's law school days. A chubby little guy whom I'd always thought compensated for his weight problem by being obnoxious. Maybe that's why he'd persuaded Larry to go with him to the singles' bar to pick up women.

"I don't have the energy to think about it now." I hung up.

CHAPTER 19

I guess that's what I get for being irritated with Mack for sleeping through a ringing telephone. The next morning I slept through a phone call, my alarm clock, and very nearly my appointment at police headquarters.

I'd had a horrible night. Even though I hadn't seen Winona's body, I kept having nightmares in which her face appeared on top of Farley Mills's body.

Sometime around five in the morning I must have fallen asleep. The only thing that awakened me at all was Spot walking on me and giving me a swat across the face.

"Damn it, Spot, don't do that. I'm trying to sleep." I rolled over and pulled the covers over my head. That's when it hit me. I had an appointment with Foster at eight o'clock. It was already light outside. I checked the clock. It said seven twenty-five.

I jumped up before I knew what was happening. I didn't realize how stiff my leg had become until it almost buckled under me. At least my chin didn't hurt, but of course I hadn't tried to talk yet. I moved my jaw. Yep, it was sore too.

Spot followed me to the kitchen and made it known that his needs came first. One of his claws snagged a thread on the sweats I hadn't bothered to change out of the night before. I had a hard time disengaging his paw from my pants leg, and to keep him from launching another attack, I fed him. Then I put water on to boil and took a look at my answering machine. One call. Mack had left a message at six-thirty on his way to work. Whatever was happening with him, I'd have to wait for an explanation. No time to call him now.

Too bad I'd been so quick to reject Larry's offer for a ride to the police station. I called a taxi and asked the dispatcher to have it in front of my building in fifteen minutes.

I took a shower, and when I finally got around to looking at my chin, I decided cosmetic surgery was the only thing that would help. Not being anywhere near a doctor's knife, I slathered on some cover-up cosmetics and proceeded to dress.

I put on a burnt-orange suit with a slightly lighter shade of blouse underneath. Something bright and cheery to indicate to Foster that I had complete confidence in his ability to solve these crimes without involving me in them.

But maybe orange indicated hostility. If I'd had one of those charts that tells what different colors mean, I'd have consulted it. Lacking that, I slipped into my shoes and went into the kitchen to get my mandatory shot of caffeine. The water was barely warm, but I couldn't afford to wait. I sure didn't have time for a second cup this morning. Instead I put two spoonfuls of instant coffee in the cup, poured in the tepid water, and slugged it down.

I grabbed my coat and purse and went down to the sidewalk in front of my apartment building to wait for the taxi. I was left cooling the heels of my black pumps as the second hand of my watch kept circling until it was ten minutes to eight. It flitted through my mind that perhaps I looked too much like Halloween in my orange-and-black ensemble. I didn't have time to do anything about it now. I saw the taxi turn the corner and waved it down.

"The Police Administration Building at Fourteenth and Cherokee," I said when I climbed inside. "I'm in a hurry."

The cabbie didn't respond. I wondered if he could speak English, but when he headed off in the right direction, I decided to forget it. He didn't say anything until he pulled up in front of the police building.

"You in trouble, lady?" he asked as I handed him the fare. He could speak English as well as I could.

"No," I said a tad too sharply. "Keep the change."

He shrugged and took off as soon as I handed him the money. I glanced at my watch and ran across the plaza to the entrance.

"I'm here to see Detective Foster in Homicide," I said when I reached the information desk. "I have an appointment at eight o'clock."

The man called on a phone, then said, "Just have a seat over there." He motioned to the chairs where I'd waited on Tuesday.

I was too nervous to sit. I looked at the displays of guns, handcuffs, and badges. I went over to take a closer look at the tapestry. It turned out to be made up of Japanese coins stuck to a wine-colored background. In an alcove around the corner were more coins under a sign that said THE HISTORY OF JAPANESE CURRENCY. I felt as if I were losing touch with reality, and I was still puzzling over the reason a Japanese numismatic display would be in police headquarters, when someone tapped me on the shoulder. I figured it was Foster sneaking up on me again.

"Ever have a yen to escape to Japan?" someone asked, but I had to lower my eyes when I turned around. It was Brad "The Cad," Larry's old law school buddy.

"I think the display is a gift from our sister city in Japan," he continued.

It was bad enough that he'd read my distracted mind; it was even worse that Larry apparently had sent him to me.

Brad still looked like Woody Allen with a weight problem. He had thick black horn-rimmed glasses that matched his hair and his dark view of life. And despite the fact that he might be a good criminal attorney, I should have known better than to leave Larry with the idea I might even consider his suggestion.

"Please tell me this is just a coincidence," I said.

Brad gave out a laugh that belonged on a much taller, though perhaps not heavier man. "Never could pull the wool over your eyes, could we?"

"Not since I became a dry cleaner," I said.

He laughed again. "Larry called me last night and told me a little about your problem. It so happened I was going to be down here this morning anyway."

"I think it's premature to be talking to a lawyer."

"Just consider for the moment that you're talking to an old friend."

I would never consider him that, even in my wildest dreams. Not after he used to lure Larry away on a regular basis, supposedly to study at the law library.

I saw Foster making his way across the lobby toward us.

"I have to go now." I started to walk away from Brad.

"Sorry I'm late," Foster said. He looked as if he'd overslept, too, and he ran his hands through his curly blond hair. The effort only made him look rumpled to start the day. "So what are you doing here, Samuels?"

Brad shoved his chin out toward Foster's chest belligerently. "Just advising Ms. Dyer that she has the right to have an attorney present."

"I'll advise her if she needs to have an attorney present," Foster said.

Brady thrust a business card in my hand. "Call me the minute he does that, Mandy." He turned and walked away.

"Where did you ever meet him?" Foster asked.

Unfortunately I didn't need to stick my chin out defiantly. It was already jutting out. "He was a classmate of Larry's."

Foster led me through the security gate to the elevators.

"What did you find out about Winona?" I could have used one of his off-center smiles about then, but he looked grim.

He led me to one of the little rooms where we'd talked before. "McKenzie Rivers, your production manager, came to see me last night," he said.

I let out a gasp. "I thought you were going to be talking about the murder of the waitress from Tico Taco's."

"We'll get to that. Mr. Rivers wanted to tell me about his background in Alabama. He said he'd already told you about it."

I nodded, bobbing my head as if it were one of those decorations that people with bad taste put in the back window of their cars. I wished Mack hadn't come to visit Foster without talking to me first. It made me wonder when he'd left the message for me last night. Before or after his trip to see Foster? After, I decided, because Foster must have talked to him before the police and I both got called to the cleaners by Manuel.

"Rivers said you had never known anything about the incident until this week. He also said you hadn't known that he and your uncle had been acquainted in Alabama."

"That's right." I felt dumb for not knowing more about my friends and family.

"We checked out his story about the fire at the dry cleaners where they both worked, and it does seem to be the missing link to Farley Mills. Mills was the son of Dewey Harper."

So Mack and I had been right in our speculations about a connection. "But Mack and my uncle didn't have anything to do with what happened there," I said.

"We're checking into that with the local authorities down there right now."

"Mack would never start a fire. He said he didn't, and I believe him."

Foster nodded. "Still, your friend seems to have a very protective attitude toward you."

I didn't know whether to say yes or no. Since I didn't know where the conversation was going, I decided to say nothing.

"What if he decided to put an end to Farley Mills's dirty tricks, as you called them, because he wanted to protect you?"

Now my head was wobbling back and forth the other way. "No, he would never do that."

"So who other than Rivers had a connection to Farley, either here or in Missouri or Alabama?"

"I've already told you everything I know." And I desperately wanted to change the subject. "While I'm here, I was wondering when we'll be able to get our van back."

"We're still checking it out."

I supposed that meant they'd found something suspicious in it, but why wouldn't they? The person who'd killed Mills had obviously driven it back to my place after the murder.

Foster switched back to what he wanted to talk about. "The owner of the Mexican restaurant where the murdered waitress worked says she was friends with a couple of your employees." He looked at a sheet of paper and gave me the names of Ingrid and Sarah. "I'll need to talk to them again."

"Of course."

"Are they both working today?"

"Yes, but Sarah won't be in until eleven o'clock. She works the late shift. Ingrid is generally there until four."

"Where did they work before they came to work for you?"

"That's what would have been in their personnel records, but they're gone. I remember Ingrid saying she learned to be a silk finisher in Wisconsin, and when I hired Sarah, she said she'd worked at Sunshine Cleaners in Sunnyvale, California."

None of this information lifted the cloud in the interrogation room. "Now why don't we review the statement you gave to Officer Burns?" Foster asked.

We went over it twice, and from what he said, I could tell he thought the murders were connected.

"But aren't you looking into other aspects of Winona's life?" I asked finally.

"Of course we are, but we have to look at all the possibilities."

"But Winona wasn't even killed the same way. Someone strangled her with a belt."

Foster jumped all over me. "How do you know that?"

"Manuel said he found her body. . . ."

"You talk to too many people. You know that?" Foster closed his notebook and jammed his pen in his shirt pocket.

"You forgot to retract the point," I said.

He gave me a withering look, but he took out the pen and pushed on the top.

"So what if the murders aren't connected? Surely you're checking out her boyfriends and ex-husbands, aren't you?"

"Well, no, but thanks for the suggestion." I knew he was being sarcastic, but at least a smile flickered across his face. "And speaking of ex-husbands . . ."

I didn't let my guard down. "I'm sorry about Larry. My mother called him because she thought I needed help."

"I was wondering about that. I was also wondering about the name. Lawrence Landry."

For a second I thought Foster might have found

something in the police files about Larry. Something more than the speeding tickets I'd visualized when he'd seemed reluctant to call the cops last night.

"Mandy . . . ," Foster said, and now he had a wide grin on his face. "Mandy Landry. No wonder you went back to your maiden name."

CHAPTER 20

Why couldn't I have thought of a smart retort when Foster made the comment about my name? Maybe I should have told him I went back to Mandy Dyer because I hadn't wanted to change the name of Dyer's Cleaners and Dyers to Mandy Landry's Laundry. I groaned, and the cab driver turned around and gave me a puzzled look. Perhaps it was better that I'd had no comeback at all.

I'd called the taxi once I left the police building. No time to go pick up another rental. The company would have to bring one to me, and Mom could fend for herself about getting to her hair appointment.

I wondered if I should talk to Ingrid and Sarah and check out their backgrounds a little more when I got back to the plant. No, I decided, I'd just tell them I expected their full cooperation when Foster talked to them.

But I definitely was going to talk to Mack. For the life of me, I couldn't figure out why he'd decided to tell the police about the fire in Alabama after all this time. He wasn't wanted on any outstanding warrants or anything. But what if he was? What if the police had brought charges against him after he left Alabama years ago?

He was at his accustomed place at the spotting board

when the taxi driver dropped me at the back door. "Where you been?" he asked as I walked in.

"I had a command performance at the police station."

"Are you okay?"

"As okay as possible under the circumstances."

Mack nodded. "I heard about Winona."

I shuddered. "Can we talk about it later?" I didn't give him a chance to answer. "Right now I want to know why you decided to go have a talk with Foster."

"So he told you about that, huh? I was hoping to explain it to you after I got home last night."

"Why didn't you tell me about it before you went to see the police? At least I could have gone with you."

"If I'd told you, you probably would have tried to talk me out of it."

I couldn't deny that. "But you've made the police suspicious of you for no reason."

"It's been on my mind for a long time, Mandy, and I decided it was time to tell someone about it. Besides, it may explain why Farley Mills seemed to be out to get you, and I think the police needed to know that."

"But—but—" I didn't want to tell him what Foster had said about Mack being protective of me and how that could have been a motive for murder. Mack and I should have thought about things like that before he went blabbing to the police.

He shook his head. "Look, Mandy, a man's gotta do what a man's gotta do."

I gave him a dirty look. "What is that? A quote from some old John Wayne movie or something?"

He had the audacity to grin. "Beats me, but if he didn't say it, he should have."

There was no use talking to this man. "Okay, what's done is done," I said. Surely John Wayne or some other stalwart of the silver screen had said that, too, at one time or another.

Near Mack, Kim was dividing clothes into cartloads of lights and darks, and he'd given me several nervous looks as Mack and I were talking. It was almost as if he'd heard what we were saying and had a guilty conscience about something.

I started to leave, but Mack called me back. "Ingrid took the day off. When she came in and heard about her friend being killed, she was so upset she asked if she could go home."

Actually I wasn't surprised. If Winona had been my good friend, I would have done the same thing. Only trouble was it meant more work for our other pressers on a day when we were already overloaded. I'd have to pitch in and help.

First, though, I called Mom and told her she'd have to get to her hair appointment by herself. She didn't even argue about it; she was too excited about the imminent arrival of Herb on an afternoon flight from Phoenix. Then I called the rental company about providing me with another car. An employee said someone would bring a loaner out to me at noon but that I'd have to drive the person back downtown to the rental agency. I agreed, even though I'd be squeezed for time.

I'd have to let my counter people fend for themselves without any help from me. Under normal circumstances I tried to be on the counter as much as possible so I could keep in touch with my customers and they'd know who I was. Nothing was normal anymore, so I set to work at the silk press, trying hard to ignore Ingrid's clutter around me. There was an empty Coke can at the end of the press, along with a lipstick and a few other sundry cosmetics, a pack of cigarettes, a lighter, and the inevitable bubble gum. I'd have to have another talk with her about keeping her work station clean, but for the time being, I decided to ignore it.

I don't know how long I'd been working when Ann Marie came and got me. "It's twelve-fifteen, and Sarah's over an hour late," she said. "She didn't even call, and

I'm absolutely going to die of hunger if someone doesn't relieve me on the counter so I can get something to eat."

"Go ahead." After all, Ann Marie was still a teenager with a voracious appetite for junk food. Maybe she burned up calories with her cheerleader tendency for overexaggeration. "I'll get Lucille to help on the counter."

Lucille of course was her usual pugnacious self. "I don't know what's got into Sarah lately," she grumbled as she prepared to do battle with the customers. "She's been acting like her girdle's on too tight ever since the troubles Monday."

Lucille didn't need to remind me, although I don't know if a girdle's quite the analogy I would have used for Sarah. Who needs a girdle when you're already rail-thin?

I went back to my office and called Sarah's home number. No answer. Then I called Ingrid, who was one of the people I figured might know about her. Maybe the two were grieving for their old friend together.

There was none of the usual gum-popping bravado when Ingrid answered the phone. "I'm sorry, Mandy, I'm just so shook up about everything."

"I know. We all are, but I was wondering if you called Sarah this morning and told her about Winona?"

"Nooo. . . ." Her voice trailed off. "Why?"

"I thought maybe you talked to her, and she decided not to come to work today too."

"I don't even have her phone number. She was a better friend to Winona than she was to me. After I got married, I didn't see that much of either one."

That gibed with what Winona had told me but not with what Sarah had said in our conversation the day before.

After we hung up, I went looking for Kim. After all, he'd told me he baby-sat for her. He was at the spotting board working on a man's suit, and Mack was nowhere to be seen. That was good. He wouldn't want me disturbing the best assistant he'd ever had.

"Kim," I said as I approached. You'd think I'd bellowed as loud as Mack did sometimes when he assumed his stage voice so he could be heard above the rumble of the equipment.

Kim jumped guiltily and looked at me.

"I'm sorry if I startled you. Sarah hasn't come to work, and she didn't even call in about it. Do you know where she is?"

Kim's eyes dropped to what he was working on. "No, I not see her."

"But you said you baby-sat for her sometimes."

He looked up from his work. "Yes, and then she gives me English lessons. It's called the *barter* system." He smiled proudly, and I could tell it was a new word he'd learned.

"So when's the last time you saw her?"

"She was going to help me last night, but she not home. I wait for her, but she never come."

Why did I feel as if he'd landed a karate blow in my midsection. Had something happened to her too? No, I tried to reassure myself, more likely one of her children was sick and she'd had to rush him to a doctor.

Just then Mack came in the back door. "There's someone out there with a car for you. What's that about?"

I decided not to give him the full story. "The other car wasn't satisfactory." Mack would have a fit if I mentioned how I'd gone off on a wild-goose chase across Denver the night before and wound up totaling the car. I'd tell him the story later, especially the part about how Larry was involved. Mack didn't like Larry any better than Nat did.

He looked at me as if he knew I was holding back, but I guess he decided it wasn't worth fussing about right now. "I told the guy I'd get you," he said, shrugging his broad shoulders out of his old pea jacket and going to the break room, where we had lockers for the employees' personal belongings.

I went to my office to get my coat and purse. As I returned to the cleaning machines, I stopped. "Is it okay if I borrow Kim for a little while? I have an errand, and I could use his help."

Mack wasn't about to okay the request without an argument. "Maybe I can help instead."

"No, I need Kim. Sarah didn't come to work today, and I want him to show me where she lives so we can make sure everything's okay." Never mind that I had her address and could find the place by myself.

"I could do that," Mack said. "I gave her a ride home once when her car was in the garage."

I turned away from Kim and tried to whisper, but it was hard to do when I was irritated. "I want to talk to Kim, Mack, so will you drop it."

Mack gave in.

"Kim, would you come with me?" I asked.

The young Korean looked nervous.

When we were outside, he touched my arm before we climbed in the car with the rental-company driver. "I'm sorry I not tell you about Sarah right away. Maybe something bad happen to her."

My fears exactly, especially after her friend Winona was murdered.

Once we dropped off the rental employee, we headed south on Broadway to where Kim said Sarah lived in an apartment. We were close to the police station where I'd been earlier this morning.

The sun was shining, and lots of people were out walking and bicycling on the bike path along Cherry Creek when we went over the bridge above the creek bed. It wasn't until we passed the Gates Rubber plant and the old Samsonite plant, now moved to a new location in town, that I finally brought up the subject Kim had mentioned earlier. "When Farley Mills asked you to spy for him, you said you told him you wouldn't do it."

I could see him shaking his head, but I kept my eyes on the road. "I think he found someone else to spy on me for him. Who do you think it could have been?"

I took a quick glance at him. He was staring at me. "Oh, no, Miss Dyer, he didn't want me to spy on you. . . ."

"I don't mean on me personally, Kim. I mean on the cleaners." I was about to explain about the dirty tricks, but he wouldn't let me.

"No, he didn't want me to spy on the cleaners. He wanted me to spy on Ingrid."

I nearly jerked the steering wheel into a parked car. "Ingrid?" I croaked as I straightened the wheel.

"Yes, Mr. Mills says she's one—how he say?—one hot tomato."

"Hot tomato?" I was beginning to sound like a human replay on the television's remote control.

"That's right." Kim nodded. "He say he would like to get her in the sack with him."

Surely this whole thing wasn't about sex.

"Why doesn't he say 'hot potato'?" Kim asked. "Tomatoes don't come in sacks."

It made sense to me. The only thing that didn't was why Farley would have wanted someone to keep an eye on Ingrid.

"Right here," Kim shouted. He was pointing to the left.

I was in the right-hand lane of traffic, and I had to veer into the other lane and make a sharp turn in front of oncoming traffic to catch the street. Another driver slammed on his brakes and honked his horn. If I didn't watch out, I'd wind up destroying a second loaner, and I'd be permanently blackballed as a car-rental risk.

Kim told me to turn right two blocks later. "She lives there."

He pointed to a three-story apartment building about

as wide as it was high. It looked like a child's block that should have had letters on the side instead of windows.

The apartment building was wedged in beside old brick houses on either side, and there was only a tiny patch of lawn in front. Where did Sarah's kids play when they wanted to go outside? There didn't appear to be any parks in the neighborhood, and I doubted if there was room for playground equipment in back. Did the kids just stay indoors all the time?

When we reached the entry to the building, there was a panel of buttons on the wall. Kim knew which one was hers. He went to the panel and buzzed her apartment. There was no responding buzz to let us in.

"See, she still not home."

Just in case, I tried the door to the building. It was locked, which relieved my mind about someone sneaking in and doing her bodily harm. Still, I knew it was easy to slip inside a building as another person went in or out. No one was coming or going right then, however, and Kim wanted to leave.

"Is there a button for the manager?" I asked.

He checked the panel and nodded.

"Buzz him, please."

He backed away.

I went over and pushed the button.

On the second ring a woman answered.

"Is this the manager?" I asked.

"Yeah, what do you want?"

"We need to go up and check Sarah McIntyre's apartment," I said. "She didn't show up for work today, and she isn't answering her door or her phone. We need to make sure she's okay."

"She's fine," the manager said, sounding miffed. "She moved out in the middle of the night last night."

CHAPTER 21

I wasn't about to accept such a curt response about Sarah's departure without further information.

"Why did she say she was moving?" I asked.

The manager of the apartment building had apparently thought it was explanation enough. She had shut off her end of the connection.

I buzzed her again. She acted irritated when she answered on the third buzz.

"This is Sarah's employer. Could you let us into her apartment?"

"I told you. She moved out."

This wasn't getting anywhere. "Please, could I talk to you face-to-face? I'm worried about her."

There was a pause. "Oh, all right."

I heard the lock on the door release, and I ran over and grabbed it before it locked again. When I looked back at Kim, he hadn't moved. "Come on, Kim. Let's go."

Frankly I felt as reluctant to go inside as he did. Nothing good was going to come out of this, I was sure, except that we could reassure ourselves that Sarah hadn't been the victim of foul play.

Maybe she'd gotten behind in her rent and had left

without paying. That would explain the manager's apparent irritation. But why hadn't Sarah come to me if she were having money problems? It wouldn't have been the first time I'd made advances to employees on their salaries. And she'd never even approached me for a raise, although after that episode with Mills at closing time, she'd said she'd like to learn inspection and mark-in when I had an opening. She was tired of working on the counter.

Kim followed me into the hallway, but now that we were inside, I realized I hadn't noticed the number of the manager's apartment. Fortunately a woman came out of a door at the end of the hall.

I hurried toward her. "Are you the manager?"

The woman nodded. Actually she didn't look as unfriendly as she'd sounded on the intercom. She was slender with long dark hair that seemed to droop with weariness. She was bouncing a baby up and down in her arms. The child, which I deducted was a girl from the bow in her wisp of blond hair, looked to be about eight or nine months old, and she was very unhappy.

"I'm sorry, but we're really worried about Sarah. Did she tell you she was leaving?"

The child let out a howl, and the woman hoisted the baby to her shoulder. "No. She just left in the middle of the night, like I said. I looked out the window, and she was putting suitcases in the trunk of her car."

"You mean, she was skipping out on her rent?"

The child was still crying, and the woman put a pacifier in her mouth before answering. "That was the funny thing. She was paid up through the end of the month."

"Maybe she was called away on an emergency and she's planning to come back."

"I thought that too. She was a nice tenant, and I thought she'd probably slipped a note under my door, but there was nothing there this morning."

"So how do you know she moved?"

The pacifier slipped out of the baby's mouth, which set off a loud cry of complaint. The woman poked it back in and shook her head. "I took a look at her apartment this morning. Everything's gone."

"You mean even her furniture?"

"It was a furnished apartment. When she moved in, she had only a few suitcases and her kids. That was all."

I took a deep breath. "Do you suppose we could see the apartment? I'm afraid she's in some sort of trouble and I need to locate her."

The woman seemed to be trying to make up her mind. "She was so quiet. Always kept to herself. I sure wouldn't want something to happen to her."

"You could go with us," I said. "We wouldn't take anything."

The baby spit out the pacifier again, apparently no longer satisfied with a stupid rubber nipple instead of food. Before it hit the floor, the woman swooped down and grabbed it so fast that I was surprised the bow in the child's hair didn't fall off.

"How do you do that?" I asked.

"Do what?"

"Keep that bow on her head?"

The woman smiled for the first time. "Karo syrup," she said. "It washes off when I bathe her, and so far she hasn't been attacked by ants."

I laughed. If people used safety pins and masking tape to fix hems on some of the clothes they brought us, who was to say that Karo syrup wouldn't work for bows on top of heads?

Maybe it was the fact that for a minute we'd related on a different level, but it seemed to make up the woman's mind. "Okay, I'll take you up, but I got to get back and feed Jessica. You can just lock the door when you leave."

The baby stopped crying as the woman jostled her up to the second floor. I guess little Jessica had wanted Mom to walk with her all the time. At Apartment 208 the manager stopped and pulled a ring of keys out of her back pocket. The baby grabbed for the shiny, jingling ring, but the woman managed to unlock the door despite Jessica's outstretched arms.

Once the door swung open, she stepped aside to let us pass. The baby started to cry again as she stretched for the keys.

"You know," the woman said as she gave them to the child in a gesture that said "anything to keep her quiet," "maybe you should talk to Mrs. O'Neal in Apartment 130. She baby-sat the kids when Sarah was at work."

The baby started to put the keys in her mouth, and her mother grabbed them away. "I gotta go." She gave a tired shrug as she started back down the hall. "Just remember to lock the door as you go out."

I checked the lock. It was just a button in the doorknob. No dead bolt or chain. If Sarah was as scared as she'd seemed sometimes, I'd have thought she'd have had better fortification.

I turned and looked at the room. A sofa with torn Naugahyde cushions, a coffee table of veneer instead of wood, and a kitchen table with stainless steel legs and a green vinyl top. It looked like she'd led a monastic life here, but before I made too severe a judgment, I had to admit that it didn't look a whole lot different from my studio apartment. Only difference was that all the personal stuff was missing.

The manager was right. Everything was gone. I went into a bedroom. It had a double bed, stripped now of everything but the mattress. I glanced into a second bedroom. It had the same empty look.

When I returned to the living room, Kim was standing in the middle of the floor, a tear running down his cheek. He quickly wiped it away when he saw me.

I tried to reassure him. "It's okay, Kim. There's no evidence that she was forced to leave or anything."

"But why would she go and not tell us?"

"I don't know. Why don't we look around and see if we can find anything that could tell us why she left?"

I didn't hold out any hope. It was just something to do. I could already see that her kitchen cupboards were bare, except for a few dishes. I wondered if they came with the apartment or if she'd left them behind. I went over and looked in her refrigerator. Empty. A crushed carton of milk and the crumpled remains of a box of cereal were in a large wastebasket along with some of the other discards of Sarah's life in the apartment. I opened the drawers in the kitchen cabinets and found a few pieces of silverware.

Kim was still standing in the middle of the floor. "Check the bathroom," I told him as I went back into the first bedroom. I searched a chest of drawers and finally bent down and looked under the bed. All I found were dustbunnies.

The second bedroom yielded a small stuffed animal, forgotten under the bed. It was a lamb with a missing eye. Somehow a lamb seemed a fitting image for Sarah's vulnerability, but was Sarah the lamb or the wolf in sheep's clothing?

The lamb's fleece was no longer white, handled by too many kids until it was a dirty gray. Too bad Sarah hadn't brought it to work with her. We cleaned stuffed animals for customers, and we could have made it look like new—except for the missing eye of course. But now that Sarah and her kids were gone, it didn't matter.

Kim came to the door of the bedroom. "This was in the bathroom." He held out an empty bottle of children's aspirin. So much for finding something that would tell us why she had fled in the middle of the night. He retreated to the living room while I wrestled to open the drawers of another chest, this one more dilapidated than the first. When I finally assured myself there was nothing of Sarah's inside, I moved back to the living room myself. Kim was standing by the wastebasket this time.

"Guess we aren't going to find anything," I said.

He jumped guiltily and stuffed something in his pocket.

"What did you find, Kim?"

"Nothing."

"But you put something in your pocket."

Reluctantly he pulled it out and looked at it before he showed it to me. "It's for a pizza. Half price."

He tucked it back in his pants before I could examine the slip of paper, but it was a pizza coupon all right. If Kim liked pizza, it was news to me.

I had a feeling he was hiding something, but short of strip searching him, I didn't know what to do about it. Maybe he'd plucked something from the trash as a memento of Sarah and was too embarrassed to show it to me. After all, I'd retrieved the one-eyed lamb from among the dustbunnies.

"Can we go now?" Kim asked.

"Sure." I put the stuffed animal under my arm, figuring I could clean it just in case Sarah ever returned. Then I depressed the lock on the door and joined Kim in the hallway. "I want to go talk to her baby-sitter anyway."

When we descended to the first floor, I found Apartment 130 and knocked on the door. A woman who looked like Mrs. Santa Claus opened it.

"Are you Mrs. O'Neal?" I asked.

"Yes." She looked disappointed, as if she'd been expecting someone else.

"The manager told me you baby-sit Sarah McIntyre's children."

"Yes, did she send you to tell me she wouldn't be coming today?"

I shook my head.

"Oh." Mrs. O'Neal looked disappointed. "She didn't show up this morning, and I was just wondering about her. She must have gotten another day off from work and forgot to tell me."

"Could we come in?"

There was no reluctance on her part the way there had been with the manager. She held the door open to let us enter. Maybe she was lonely and welcomed the company, but I almost felt as if I should warn her about letting strangers into her apartment.

All the personal touches that had been missing from Sarah's apartment were here in profusion. There were doilies on the arms of every chair and little ceramic figures on the tables. Framed pictures covered the walls as if she'd set out to turn the room into a giant photo album. Most of the pictures were of children.

"Are any of these Sarah's children?" I asked.

"No, they're mostly the grandchildren and my kids when they were young." She took one of the photos off its nail and showed it to me. "This is my youngest grandson, Nicky."

I was glad to know Mrs. O'Neal had family, but it would take all day if she planned to show me every one of the pictures. "Do you have any pictures of Sarah's children by any chance?"

Mrs. O'Neal cocked her head. "You know, that's interesting you should ask. I went to the park one day with Sarah and her kids. I wanted to get some pictures, but Sarah said no."

"I wonder why."

Mrs. O'Neal replaced Nicky's photograph on its hook, stopping to make sure the frame was straight. "I guess it must have been a religious thing," she said.

That satisfied her, but it didn't satisfy me. Of course she didn't have any information, and I explained, "I'm Mandy Dyer, Sarah's employer, and Sarah didn't come to work this morning. The manager said she moved out last night."

"Oh, my." Mrs. O'Neal put her hand to her mouth.

"Did Sarah say anything to you about planning to move?"

"No, nothing, and the money I earned from baby-sitting helped out a lot with my Social Security."

"I'm sorry." I waited for her to adjust to the news. "Was there anything else about Sarah that seemed unusual? I mean, except that she didn't want you to take pictures of her kids."

"No, she seemed like a very good mother."

"Well, if she gets in touch with you, will you let me know?" I took a business card out of my purse and handed it to her.

"Oh, yes, and will you call me if you hear from her?"

She gave me her phone number, and I started to leave. Kim, who hadn't said anything, was already in the hall.

"Oh, there was one thing," Mrs. O'Neal said. "Sarah was a blonde when she first moved in here. She dyed her hair that mousy brown color, and I kept telling her she should go back to being a blonde." She smiled a grandmotherly smile, but there was a twinkle in her eye. "Aren't they supposed to have more fun?"

"Maybe she just went back to her natural color," I said. "Some people dye their hair when they want to get it back to the original shade."

"I don't think so." Mrs. O'Neal curled her finger to motion me to bend over toward her. "I saw some brown Clairol one day in her apartment when I baby-sat the kids up there." Maybe she thought hair dyeing was not an appropriate subject in mixed company. "The little girl, Jennifer, said Mommy used it on her hair, too, so they'd look alike. Now why on earth would anyone dye a child's hair?"

I had to agree. A little Karo syrup to secure a bow, maybe, but dyeing a child's hair. Now that was a whole different matter.

CHAPTER 22

Kim and I returned to the car in silence, and I placed the stuffed toy on the armrest between us.

"Did you hear what Mrs. O'Neal said?" I asked.

He nodded and picked up the lamb as if it were a security blanket. I hoped one of the kids wouldn't be missing it at nap time.

"Did Sarah ever say anything to you about her ex-husband or what she'd done before she came to Denver?"

He clasped the lamb to his thin chest and shook his head.

"You came from California, didn't you?" I continued. "Sarah said she'd lived there too. Did you ever talk about that?"

"All I know is she's a nice person." He stared out the window as he hugged the lamb. "I don't want to get her in trouble."

"You're not going to get her in trouble, Kim. If she's in trouble, it has nothing to do with you, and we need to find her."

We'd headed back to the cleaners on Alameda, the same street I'd been on when I chased the pickup the night before.

It was a while before Kim spoke. "She didn't know

much about San Francisco," he said. "She didn't even know where the Forty-niners play football."

At first I was amused. She wasn't Ingrid, after all, who probably knew all the teams in the NFL and every quarterback's throwing stats. But it wasn't that surprising to me that Sarah didn't know those things.

"They play right down on the way to where she say she lives, in Sunnyvale," Kim continued. "When I poke fun at her for not knowing, she say she doesn't want to talk about it. It was a bad time in her life."

"So you didn't ask her any more about it?"

"I have bad times, too, that I don't want to talk about."

And did Sarah's bad times have anything to do with Farley, I wondered, or was her fast getaway totally unconnected? Her disappearance seemed to make the first possibility a lot more likely—if Farley had been blackmailing her about something in her past. Something so bad that she'd had duplicates made of our keys to aid him in his dirty tricks, at least until they escalated to the point where she'd killed him? She didn't seem the killer type, but who knew what that type was?

I took a quick look at Kim and wondered if she could have persuaded him to help her kill Mills. I couldn't believe it, not with the innocent, hurt look on his face as he held the lamb.

Mack was waiting for us when we returned to the cleaners.

"See, I brought Kim back safe and sound," I said.

"Good."

Kim looked down at his hands where he still clutched the stuffed animal. He shoved it at me and darted to the rest room.

"So what's that?" Mack asked.

"I don't know—a sacrificial lamb maybe."

Mack gave me one of his disgusted looks. "What'd you find out about Sarah? Is she all right?"

"She's gone. Apparently she packed her bags last night and took off. No one seems to know why."

"You're kidding." Mack followed me to my office and sat down. "Want to talk about it?"

I would, but I had too much to do. "Maybe later. Want to grab a drink about six?"

"You're on. I've got plenty of work to do until then." Mack left, shutting the door behind him. I guess he figured this wasn't the time for my open-door policy with the crew.

I glanced at the forms I'd asked employees to complete to replace the missing personnel records. So far only a few had turned in the information. Sarah wasn't one of them, but Ingrid had completed one of the forms in an almost illegible scrawl. She said she'd learned her pressing skills at a cleaners in Wisconsin, but there was a gap in her work record right before she came to work for Uncle Chet.

At the moment I was more interested in Sarah, though. I picked up the phone book and thumbed through it until I found the page with area codes for California. I dialed the area code for Sunnyvale and asked for a number for Sunshine Cleaners.

A real live operator told me there was no Sunshine Cleaners in Sunnyvale, California. So Sarah had lied about her last place of employment. Why wasn't I surprised?

I dialed Foster's number at police headquarters and reached his voice mail. Frankly it was one of those times I was glad just to leave a message. "I wanted to let you know that neither of the people you wanted to talk to are here today. Ingrid took the day off, and Sarah moved out of her apartment last night and didn't leave a forwarding address." I didn't tell him we'd already searched her apartment.

Then I took off my jacket and went out to the press line again, where Ingrid's clutter continued to irritate me.

Why couldn't she stick her junk in her locker? That's why we provided them in the break room for our employees.

Although my other three pressers had been trying to handle part of Ingrid's work, it had really stacked up while I was gone. As I pressed, perspiration broke out on my forehead and stained my blouse, but I didn't care. It was as if the sweat was pulling out the stress that had been my constant companion since Monday. Nothing like hard work to reduce the pressure. Maybe I'd be so tired tonight that I could sleep without having nightmares.

At four o'clock I told the other pressers to go on home, and I decided to grab a cup of coffee to keep me going. Fortunately Julia from my morning counter crew had said she'd come back this evening and help Theresa with the after-work crowd in place of the missing Sarah. I hoped Ingrid would be at work tomorrow and want to get in some overtime for the time she missed today. We'd be in big trouble otherwise, maybe have to pull an all-nighter, what with the Easter weekend coming up and all those customers desperate to get their Sunday finery out of the plant. Fortunately the Easter parade wasn't what it used to be, but we were still way behind because of our crime-scene status. I started for the break room, then came back and collected Ingrid's clutter so I could toss it in her locker out of sight.

The lockers, half the size of old school lockers and without combination locks, are on one wall of the break room. Employees can put locks on the doors if they want, but most don't bother. I liked to think it was because we trusted one another, but at the moment I didn't think that was such a wise idea.

I went over to Ingrid's locker. I knew which one it was because it had a Kansas City Chiefs decal on the front. I started to open the door, then thought better of it. It was because of that "trust" thing.

Clasping Ingrid's stuff in my hands, I stared at the rest

of the lockers. Tomorrow I'd have to start looking for a replacement for Sarah on the counter. And I needed to clear out her locker, make certain it was empty before I assigned it to a new hire. Sure I did. What I really wanted to do was check out the locker to see if she'd left anything inside that would tell us where she'd gone. I didn't figure she had, but now that I'd thought about it, I couldn't let it rest.

I went to my office, put down Ingrid's things, and rifled through my desk until I found the sheet with locker assignments on it. Luckily it hadn't been in the filing cabinet with all the papers that had been stolen.

It turned out that she had the locker next to Ingrid's, and there was no lock on it either. I yanked it open, expecting it to be as empty as her apartment had been. Instead I found a big paper bag inside, and I reached down to get it.

"Mandy, you're wanted on the phone."

I jumped guiltily.

Lucille had her hands on her hips, clearly disgusted with having to come clear back here to get me. "I wish you'd get an intercom if you expect me to work the counter." She made a production out of sighing deeply.

"Thanks, Lucille. I'll be right there." I wished I hadn't given the impression that I'd been caught with my hand in the cookie jar. I tried to undo my guilty reaction. I picked up the sack, checked to see that it was the only thing inside, and closed the door slowly. After all, I had every right to remove things from the lockers of people who were no longer here, especially people who had disappeared without a trace.

"Julia's here now," Lucille continued, patting her tight curls as if all that work on the counter had surely gotten them in disarray. "Can I go home?"

"Sure, that's fine."

She'd watched me suspiciously as I made my way to

my office with the loot from Sarah's locker. Maybe she was wondering if I searched her locker too. For a woman who took delight in what she found in other people's pockets, Lucille was very proprietary about her own things. Of course I couldn't really blame her after everything had been knocked off her worktable, apparently by Farley Mills's killer.

When I got to the office, I grabbed the phone.

"Mandy Pie." Herb again, arrived from Phoenix to try to mend things with Mom.

"I'm at the hotel, and Cecilia and I want to thank you for getting us back together."

I didn't know if I could take any of the credit, but I wasn't going to argue about it. "Believe me," I said, feeling that a great weight had been lifted off my shoulders, "it was my pleasure."

"So we want to take you out to dinner tonight to celebrate."

Oh, darn, I'd walked right into that, taking credit where none belonged. "Wouldn't you rather just spend your first night alone? Maybe we could go out tomorrow night?"

"Nope, we've already had time for a little whoop-dee-do, if you know what I mean." Herb chuckled.

I could hear Mom in the background. "Oh, shush, Herb."

I wanted to throw up. Instead I fumbled with the bag I'd carried in from Sarah's locker.

"We have a little surprise we want to share with you, and we won't take no for an answer."

I opened the bag and looked inside. Talk about a disappointment.

"So what do you say? Why don't we come down and pick you up about seven?"

The only thing inside was stuff for Sarah's children: a package of dye to color Easter eggs, a couple of chocolate bunnies, a box of Crayolas, two wrapped baskets with a mix of chocolate and hard candies inside.

"Mandy, are you still there?"

"Uh, yeah, sure."

"So what about it—we'll pick you up at seven?"

I came to my senses long enough to reject being picked up. "Why don't I meet you at the restaurant? I might be a little late."

"Okay, Mandy Pie, whatever you say. We have a reservation at Baby Doe's at seven-thirty. I love that place."

Herb always did like theme restaurants, and Baby Doe's was built like an old abandoned mine.

I told him I'd be there, and hung up. Then I sorted through the items in the bag more thoroughly. I couldn't help but wonder if Sarah and her kids would have time to color Easter eggs now that they were on the run.

I turned the familiar-looking yellow box of Crayolas over in my hand, but they weren't the usual crayons. Instead they were identified on the front as nontoxic washable crayons. I flipped the box over to the back. "Normal laundering should remove stains from cotton, polyester, acrylic, nylon fabric, and their blends," it said.

Some of the slashes of color that had started appearing mysteriously on our finished garments a few months ago had been made by markers as well as lipstick. I wondered if Sarah's purchases had been innocent gifts for her children or if she'd been trying to tell me something.

It sounded like a stretch to me. I put the items back in the sack and stared at Ingrid's work record again. She'd had experience in several cleaners in Wisconsin before she came to Colorado. So why wasn't she a Green Bay Packers fan or a Denver Broncos booster? Why a Kansas City Chiefs fan?

And hadn't Nat told me that before Farley Mills had come to Denver, he'd had a cleaners in Missouri, home of the Kansas City Chiefs? I'd have to check that out with the roving reporter. Maybe there was a connection.

I guess it was that thought that made me say, To hell with trust. I grabbed Ingrid's stuff off my desk, stomped to the break room, and jerked open Ingrid's locker. It was empty.

I placed her cosmetics, her cigarettes and lighter, and the packages of bubble gum inside and slammed the door shut. I couldn't help feeling guilty for my invasion of her private space, but I left a note at her pressing station telling her where to find her stuff and reminding her to keep her work area clean in the future.

CHAPTER 23

Mack and I crossed the parking lot to Tico Taco's, Mack looming over me like my guardian angel. It always helped to talk to him, and once when he'd played a psychiatrist in a community theater production, I'd thought of it as typecasting. He'd always been a good sounding board, if you could put up with an occasional bit of unsolicited advice.

I hadn't even bothered to change my clothes before we went for drinks. I'd do that just before my dinner date with Mom and Herb, but I had taken the time to run up to the front counter to tell Theresa where I'd be and to reassure myself that Julia actually had arrived to help with the customers. I didn't really trust Lucille to tell it to me straight, not when she hated working the counter so much. But then I didn't trust anyone right now except Mack. My invasion of Ingrid's locker surely proved that.

The restaurant was beginning to fill up with the dinner crowd, but Juanita found us a booth at the back. I didn't see her father, but she must have told him we were there.

Manuel came out of the kitchen and over to our table. "It's terrible," he said. "I can't get over poor Winona being murdered right behind your store."

I slid to the back of the booth so he could sit down with us. "Have the police said anything more to you?"

He shook his head and slumped in the seat.

"We thought you might not even be open today."

"Saturday. We're gonna close for her funeral." He told me the time and place of the service and seemed to be debating about whether to say something else. Finally he made up his mind. "One of my other girls"—I winced at the term *girls,* but this wasn't the time to give Manuel a lesson in political correctness—"she says Winona did have a new boyfriend." My hopes that this would divert the police's attention from the cleaners didn't last. "She's been going out with your driver, Al. You know about that?"

I shook my head, and my insides started knotting up. I'd been hoping for a boyfriend or an ex-husband as a suspect. So here was the suspect, and he led right back to the cleaners.

And Al had even told me that he'd been approached by Farley to jump ship and set up a competing delivery route for him. He'd said he nixed the offer, but what if he'd accepted a more subtle form of assistance, like destroying my business from within? After all, he had keys to the building and the van.

He'd said he was going to be out visiting prospective new clients today so he probably wouldn't come in to work at all. Now I wondered where he was. Had he heard about Winona and, like Ingrid, decided not to work today or was he out drumming up business, unaware that his girlfriend was dead?

Or maybe he'd been the one who'd been doing the dirty tricks after hours and then decided to "off" Farley, as he put it, when the game got serious. What if Winona had known about his extracurricular activities and been killed because of that knowledge? Or had he disappeared the way Sarah had?

"You think I should tell the police?" Manuel asked.

I nodded. I needed this whole thing over with so I could

quit being so paranoid about my employees. "You have the detective's phone number, don't you?"

"*Sí*. I didn't know he was a policeman when he came in here with you." He seemed irritated, maybe because all his romantic efforts had been in vain.

A few minutes later he got up to seat four customers, and when his daughter saw that we were through talking, she brought us a menu and some salsa and chips. Mack and I both asked for beers, but I added an order of nachos. I realized I hadn't had anything to eat all day, and the beer would probably knock me off my feet unless I had some sustenance to get me through till my dinner with Mom and Herb.

"Geez, Mack," I said when Juanita left, "it just keeps getting worse and worse."

His face mirrored my pessimism. "I know. So tell me about last night."

I went over every detail—Manuel's call, the incident at the Dumpster when I was blindsided by the metal door, the chase through Denver in pursuit of a possible killer, and the return to the cleaners to discover that Manuel had found Winona's body.

At some point Juanita returned with the nachos and the beers, but I hardly noticed. I even told Mack about the car that followed me and how I got rear-ended and wound up going down an embankment.

"God Almighty, Mandy, you could have been killed doing something crazy like that."

"Oh, I haven't told you the worst part yet." I grabbed a handful of chips and began dipping them in the cheese mixture. "The person who was following me turned out to be Larry."

Mack did a double take. "Not Larry the Lecher."

I smiled at Mack's name for him. "Yes, he's back in Denver, and Mom seems determined to get us back together again. She called him because she thought I might be in trouble and need some help last night."

Mack snorted. "That's all you need—Larry back in your life."

It felt good getting everything off my chest, not unlike arriving home and removing a too-tight bra.

"What I really wanted to talk about was Sarah." I told him about my conversation with the grandmotherly baby-sitter and how Mrs. O'Neal said Sarah dyed not only her own hair but her daughter's as well. "It sounds as if she was trying to hide her identity, so I just checked out the place she said she worked in California. It doesn't exist. So what I'm wondering is if Farley could have recognized her from some other place and blackmailed her into helping him in his nefarious schemes."

"Nefarious?" Mack asked with a grin that faded as quickly as it came.

"You know what I mean. Anyway, maybe she couldn't take it anymore and killed him."

"She was such a little thing. I can't imagine her hitting Farley on the head and then lifting his body on the conveyor."

"But, Mack, what if she talked Kim into helping her?"

"No." Mack's denial was so loud several people looked over at us.

"I saw them together Tuesday. Kim said he'd been baby-sitting, but when we went over there today, he acted strange. He found something in her wastebasket, and when I asked him what it was, he said it was a pizza coupon. He even showed me the coupon, but there must have been something else in his pocket."

Mack still wasn't willing to suspect his assistant. "I think he had a crush on Sarah. He's probably brokenhearted that she's gone, and he took something to remind him of her."

I still couldn't let it go. "Okay, but remember the problems we were having with the markings on the clean clothes? When I went through Sarah's locker this afternoon, I found some Easter stuff she'd bought for her kids, and Mack, there was a box of Crayola markers like the ones we thought might have been used on the clothes."

"Anybody can buy markers. Besides, some of the stains were lipstick."

I thought about telling him of Ingrid's ample supply of cosmetics, but I was sure he'd say anyone could buy them, too, even Al. And he certainly fit my profile better for a polyester poltergeist with the strength to kill Farley. At least better than Sarah or Kim did.

Mack pounded his hand on the table so hard that it startled me. "You gotta stay out of it, Mandy. Just dump all this on your friend, the detective, and let him figure it out."

I nodded and dug into the nachos container for another chip. They were gone. I wondered if I'd eaten them all or if Mack had snatched some while I wasn't looking.

I also looked at my watch. It was almost seven.

"Oh, damn." Theresa and Julia would be waiting to close the call office, and I needed to change and get to Baby Doe's.

"I have to get over to the plant and lock up, Mack."

"Want to come back later and have something to eat?"

"I'm having dinner with Mom and Herb. They've reconciled, and we're having a celebration dinner. Why don't you come too?"

"I think I'll just have something here."

"Okay, if that's the way you want to be about it." I slid to the edge of the booth.

He shook his index finger at me. "Just remember what I said about staying out of trouble."

I grinned. "Yeah, sure, Mack, but a woman's gotta do what a woman's gotta do."

Mack obviously hadn't forgotten our John Wayne conversation earlier. "What's that?" he asked. "Something Gloria Steinem said?"

"I don't know, but if she didn't, she should have."

CHAPTER 24

Baby Doe's Restaurant is named in honor of one of Colorado's most famous women. She was a divorcée who stole the richest man in the state away from his straitlaced wife back in the late 1800s.

H.A.W. Tabor had been the Silver King of Leadville when the beautiful Baby Doe caught his eye. He dumped his wife, Augusta, to the horror of everyone in Denver whose wealth and social status went back more than a couple of years. Denver's Social Register snubbed them, and Tabor and his young lover were married in the nation's capital with only politicians in attendance.

A few years later the couple lost everything in the Panic of 1893. Everything, that is, except his Matchless Mine. "Hold on to the Matchless," he'd told Baby Doe on his deathbed in 1899, and she heeded his advice. She moved into a shack beside the Matchless and died there in 1935, starved and frozen, her feet wrapped in gunnysacks.

The restaurant was a quasi-ramshackled tribute to Baby Doe, and it perched on a hill that overlooked Interstate 25 with a view of the Denver skyline. The theme of its dilapidated exterior was carried out on the inside by a dark entryway and tracks that looked as if they led down into the bowels of the earth.

I fumbled my way through the sudden darkness from the brightly lit parking lot and hoped Herb wasn't going to give Mom her walking papers as Tabor had given poor Augusta. No. Mom was more the Baby Doe type with her ash-blond hair and peaches-and-cream complexion. And I was the one who felt as if I were getting the shaft, not by Herbie of course but by the person who was killing off the people at and around my cleaners.

I found the happy couple in the bar, where they were toasting each other with glasses of champagne. Herb stood up when he saw me and gave me a big bear hug. I would have expected nothing less from the retired King of Used-Car Salesmen. However, right now, in his plaid pants, red polo shirt, and forest-green blazer, he looked like an aging golfer just off the links in Sun City. It clashed a little with Mom's fluffy look, her ruffled pastel dress and open-toed shoes, but I had to admit they were a matched set who surely belonged in the warmer climes of Phoenix.

"Mandy Pie," Herb said, clamping an arm around me and knocking the shoulder pad askew in the freshly pressed basic-black dress I'd changed into at the cleaners. Somehow I felt like the Augusta in this picture with my high-necked dress and only a splash of color at the neck, thanks to a silk scarf I'd paid an outrageous amount of money for.

"We were afraid you weren't going to make it." Herb's voice boomed through the bar as he grabbed a chair for me from another table. "Let's all have a toast, and then I'll go tell the gal at the desk that we're ready to go to the dining room."

"Here's to a long and happy marriage for the two of you," I toasted, and the three of us drank the champagne, which my buddy Mack always called "nothing but decadent beer." Then I adjusted my shoulder pad so I wouldn't look lopsided.

"You'll have to see what Herbie gave me." Mom beamed and opened a jewelry box that held a silver locket, two hearts entwined, on a silver chain.

It wasn't quite as ostentatious as the ninety-thousand-dollar necklace Baby Doe reportedly wore on her wedding day, but Mom seemed happy with it, and the silver was appropriate.

"Look inside," she said.

I expected to see a smiling picture of the happy couple. I was surprised because I couldn't even make out what the tiny photo was. It looked like a microdot with wings. I moved my face down to within a few inches of the open locket and leaned over toward the candle in the center of the table.

"It looks like a building of some kind," I said finally.

"It is." Mom laughed in delight. "It's our new house. Herbie bought it for me. That's what he was doing with the real estate agent when she lost her earring."

Herb's head nodded as if it were coming unhinged, which seemed a little suspicious to me.

"And of course, jealous me, I jumped to the wrong conclusion," Mom said.

Not a jump of Olympic proportions, as far as I could see.

"I always loved that house, and when I saw that it was on the market, I told Herb we ought to take a look at it, but he wanted to surprise me."

Herbie was still nodding. "I wish my sweet Cecilia here had never worked in that dry cleaners of Chet's and seen the stuff in your lost-and-found drawer. It made her too suspicious of people—"

Mom interrupted. "When I found that earring in his pants pocket, I couldn't help thinking of the time I found a man's wedding band in his pants at the cleaners." This was a different story than the one she'd told me earlier, and she continued, "When I called his wife, she started screaming, 'I knew that son of a *B*'"—Mom seldom swore, but she did use first initials a lot— "'was taking off his wedding ring so that he could step out on me.' It was as if the wife thought I was the other woman."

"That's why we quit calling people about most items," I said. "Now we put them in little envelopes to be attached to the orders when they're finished."

Herb bent over toward me. "And I bet most of the stuff that winds up in those envelopes is just as innocent as this." Yeah, and I bet Herb had told people that the cars he used to sell had been owned by little old men who only drove them to the golf course on Sundays.

"The real estate lady lost her earring in my car when we were out looking at the house," he continued. "I put it in my pocket, figuring to give it back to her the next day when I was going to put in a bid on the place, but I forgot about it."

It was Mom's turn to nod as she looked adoringly at Herb. The only thing that seemed wrong to me about this picture was, Didn't real estate agents usually take clients out in *their* cars? I wouldn't for the world have said anything about it.

I closed the locket with the microdot of a house in it and handed the jewelry case back to Mom. There was something about this whole conversation that bothered me, but I couldn't put my finger on it. I had a feeling it was something about the murder, but maybe it was just my nasty suspicions about poor Herb.

"I can hardly wait to get back home and see our new house." She reached over and squeezed Herb's hand before she looked back at me. "I hate to leave you with all this trouble, but we have to go back tomorrow to sign the contract."

Eureka, I thought. Isn't that what someone was supposed to have said when they struck the mother lode?

Eureka. Mom was going back to Phoenix tomorrow, and whatever was bothering me flitted away into the cluttered recesses of my mind.

We had a nice dinner overlooking the interstate and the skeletal shapes of the rides at the Elitch's Amusement Park, which had moved a few years ago from North Denver to its new location in the Platte Valley near downtown. The park wouldn't reopen until later in the spring and neither would Coors Field where the Colorado Rockies played baseball.

We could barely see the stadium in the distance to the north of the downtown skyline, and Herb raved enthusiastically about how he and Cilia would have to come back in June on "a second honeymoon" so they could visit both.

"That'd give us a chance for a longer visit, Mandy Pie," he said, wiping his forehead with a handkerchief and mussing up the swirl of hair he had combed across his almost bald pate.

He seemed to be sweating profusely for a hot-weather person in a cold climate, even more than I had at the steam press this afternoon. I figured it was because of his relief that Mom and I had bought his story, but maybe it was because of having to listen to Mom talk all through dinner about the murders at the plant.

"I wish there was something we could do to help," he said as he and Mom shared a piece of chocolate cheesecake that looked far more decadent than the champagne.

"There's nothing you can do," I said hastily, just in case they decided to cancel their return to Phoenix the next day. "Believe me. It's in the hands of the police, and they don't want any help."

We said our good-byes in the parking lot since they would be leaving before I got off work the next day.

"As soon as we get moved, I want you to come down and see our new house, Amanda," Mom said.

"Yessiree," Herb added. "As soon as this trouble at the cleaners gets cleared up, Mandy Pie, you come on down." He sounded like the announcer on *The Price Is Right*. "You need to get away from this cold weather once in a while."

Actually it was a surprisingly warm night for March, but Herb was right. I needed a vacation, and maybe I would take one when and if the murders were ever solved. I wasn't sure I'd go to Phoenix, though.

We hugged, and I started to climb into my rental car, which was dwarfed by Herb's deluxe model nearby.

"Mandy," Herb yelled. "I mean it. If we can help with anything, you let us know. You hear?"

"Thanks for the offer, but there's nothing you can do." I waved and climbed into my car.

I tried to convince myself that they couldn't do much from Phoenix. Or could they? I pushed the thought from my mind and drew out my list of employees' phone numbers and addresses. I ran my finger down the page until I got to Al.

I'd even tried to call him before I left work, but there wasn't any answer. Not even a recording saying he'd get back to me later. That bothered me because I knew he had an answering machine, and I think I headed south on I-25 to Hampton just to reassure myself that he hadn't disappeared the way Sarah had.

He lived near Englewood, on the south boundary of Denver. I hauled out the Denver-area map thoughtfully provided by the car-rental people and found his address. It turned out to be a small house with a detached garage that was set back from the street. The windows were dark and the sidewalk leading up to the front door was almost invisible under a webbed overhang of trees and the dark sky.

I hadn't intended to stop if there were any lights on inside. It was the absence of light that made me worry. What if he really had disappeared the way Sarah had or, like Winona, met with foul play? I climbed out of the car and went up to the porch. The sidewalk was uneven, apparently cracked by the roots of the trees, and I had to feel my way along it. When I reached the porch, I couldn't hear any sound from inside, not even a TV running in some back room.

I looked for a doorbell, but it was too dark for me to see one, even if it was there. I knocked and waited, then knocked again. At the third knock I heard a car turn down the street and head toward me. I turned around, hoping it was Al in his Bronco. But what would I say if it were?

I could tell him I was worried about him after I heard that Winona had been killed. But what if he was responsible for her death? Or what if he was devastated by it and had been out driving aimlessly around town? What if he didn't even know? Maybe I could tell him that I'd been in the neighborhood and wanted to see how he'd done with his visit to potential clients that day. Yeah, right. That really sounded dumb.

The driver pulled to the curb a few spaces behind my car, turned off the engine, and killed the lights. I could make out the outline now, and it wasn't the Bronco.

It was a pickup truck like the one I'd chased through the streets of Denver the night before. The hairs on my head and arms felt electrified, and I was afraid the person in the truck could see the sparks radiating from my body. I jumped off the porch and slipped back into the shadows of some overgrown shrubs along the front of the house.

The driver got out of the truck, but the heavy network of evergreen branches made it impossible to see him. I heard his footsteps approaching the door, and I scooted back even farther into the bushes.

The person was on the porch now, and I could see the bulk of him through the tunnel I'd made as I burrowed into the miniforest of shrubs. He wasn't pulling out a key to open the door. Neither was he knocking or feeling for a doorbell. He was bent down looking into the deep shadows of my hiding place.

"Mandy, I know you're there," he said. "I thought you weren't going to go nosing around in this anymore."

Oh, damn, caught in the act. But while we were at it, Mack seemed to be no slacker himself in the nosing-around department.

"Come on out." He kept peering into the bushes, but I'm not sure he could see me.

I knew it was Mack, or I wouldn't have said anything, and although I couldn't really make out his face, which blended into the darkness of the porch, I'd recognize that deep, resonant voice anywhere.

"Speaking of interfering"—I brushed twigs from my face and made my way out of the shrubs—"what are you doing here?"

I could see his large shoulders as he shrugged. "Just stopped by to see if my buddy, Al, wanted to go have a beer."

I shook evergreen needles out of my hair and off my clothes. "You scared me to death. I told you it was a pickup truck that I followed from the plant last night, didn't I?"

He put up his hands as if I were a robber who'd ordered him to reach for the sky. "Hey, it wasn't my truck."

"I know," I said. I just wished there weren't so many pickups in Denver. And what was he really doing coming out here just after Manuel told us that Al had been dating Winona?

"So what's your reason for being here?" Mack asked.

"I wanted to see how many new customers he got today."

"Sure you did."

I was glad he couldn't see me scratching my nose, but if he did notice, I could always say the evergreen needles had scratched my face. Unfortunately it was true.

He started to leave. "Well, we might as well both go home. He isn't here."

"How do you know that? You just got here. You haven't even knocked."

"I came by earlier and no one was home, so I decided to check out the bar where he likes to hang out. He took me there a couple of times, but no one had seen him last night or tonight, so I thought I'd swing by here one more time and then give up."

I went over and tried the door.

"Mandy, what the hell do you think you're doing?"

I pulled my hands away and put them up as if he were the robber now, ordering me to stick 'em up. The door was locked anyway.

Mack started down the steps. I went over to the window and tried to look inside. It was pitch-black.

"Are you coming?" He waited for me on the steps.

I wasn't ready to leave. "Did you look around in back?"

"The place is locked up tighter than a bank vault. Trust me on this."

"You already tried the doors, didn't you?"

"No comment."

"What about the garage? Is his Bronco gone?"

"There are no windows in the damned garage. Now, will you just come on?"

I finally gave up, but I was glad to know that Mack was as meddling as I was. I'd use it against him later when he got off on me for butting in where I didn't belong.

"Let's go home," Mack said when we reached the street. "I think a good night's sleep will do us both some good."

"You know, we should have done a little coordinating tonight. You could have checked on Kim while I was over here."

Mack chuckled, a noise that seemed to rumble from deep in his chest. "Oh, you think I didn't try? Couldn't locate him either. It's terrible when all your friends are too busy for you." He stopped in front of my car. "How was the dinner with Mom and Herb, by the way?"

"I think Mom's back to her old self again now that she and Herb have reconciled." It was a reminder of that movie quote he'd thrown at me earlier from *Psycho* about Mom not being "quite herself today."

"Hey, I said I was sorry about that," he said, but he couldn't hide a smile. Now that we were out from under the cover of the trees I could see his teeth flash white in the night.

"They're going home tomorrow," I continued, "and I'm hopeful Mom will be too busy to try to get Larry and me back together."

I hoped that was true, and I wondered again if I should have put more emphasis on the fact that I didn't want any help, thank you very much, when my folks and I parted at Baby Doe's. God knows what kind of creative assistance they could think of from Phoenix.

"Good," Mack said, and climbed into his truck. He followed me home to my apartment as if he didn't really believe I'd go there. That was okay because if Mack hadn't followed me, I probably would have done the same to him.

"Now, don't forget," he yelled from his open window as he drove by my car. "Get a good night's sleep."

Unfortunately it didn't happen.

CHAPTER 25

I turned the corner to the flight of stairs leading to my apartment. That's when I saw the man hovering at the top of the stairs. My first thought was to leave, but then I noticed that he was sitting on the floor in front of my door like a skinny version of Buddha, his legs crossed in front of him in a double-jointed way I could never hope to achieve. He was also reading a newspaper, which was a dead giveaway.

"Hi, Nat." I started up the rest of the stairs. "I'm tired, and I'm going to bed, so you can't come in."

He dropped a copy of the *Trib* and looked at me through his granny glasses, which had slipped down on his nose as he read one of the articles in the paper, probably his own. "No 'Glad to see you? How you been? Nice of you to drop by'? Nothing?"

Nat was going to become my ex–best friend if he didn't quit dropping by at weird hours to see if he could wheedle information out of me to scoop the rest of the crime-hungry media in town.

"Nope, none of the above, Nat. I have to get some sleep tonight, or I'm going to collapse."

I was almost to the top step by this time, and he

launched himself from his cross-legged position like a missile being shot into outer space.

"Hey, you really look great. Been out on a hot date or something?"

I'd taken off my coat in the entryway downstairs and was standing on the step below him in my basic-black dress and a new pair of heels I'd purchased recently. It's strange how men always jump to conclusions when a woman wears a black sheath instead of a business suit or off-duty jeans or sweats.

"No, I haven't been on a hot date," I said, "and flattery won't cut it with me tonight. You still can't come in."

"Put your head down."

I didn't, but Nat reached over and tweaked something out of my hair anyway. "You can't kid me." He held up an evergreen twig like it was a clump of mistletoe. "You've been out in the woods with some guy."

The twig was obviously from my flight into the bushes at Al's place, but I wasn't about to tell him that. Instead I gave him a dirty look and took the final step up to the third-floor landing.

"Something's wrong with your chin. I noticed it last night." A shocked look came over his face. "Don't tell me it's a whisker burn and that you're back cavorting with Larry again?"

In my heels I was as tall as Nat, and I elbowed him aside so I could unlock my door. "That does it. I've had a hard day, and I want you to go home."

"Even if I have some information I think you need to know?"

I glared at this John Lennon imitation and realized this might be a hard-day's night as well. "What information?"

"Just something I thought we ought to talk about. Remember how we did that flow-chart thing on the other case, and it helped solve the murder?"

I sighed because I knew he'd never tell me what it was until I let him in. "Okay, one cup of coffee and that's it."

He grinned. "I promise, and seriously you really do look good tonight."

"One cup," I repeated, and opened the door.

Nat plopped down on the couch. I went to the kitchen, grabbed the kettle, and ran some water in it.

"Okay, what's in the paper?"

"Nothing you don't already know. The story's about Winona Morris's murder last night, and you already know that. But I did find out something strange today."

I turned the burner on high, but it was a toss-up which one would reach the boiling point first—me or the water. I went over to the couch. "Okay, shoot."

Nat sat up straight instead of slumping the way he usually did. "I talked to some people who worked for Farley Mills back in Missouri."

I was afraid of where this was going.

"They said Mills was a nut case who had an obsession about—and you aren't going to believe this, Mandy—Mack and your uncle Chet. They also said that all of a sudden last fall he sold his business and moved to Denver. Said he was about to even the score for his daddy's death and his mother's nervous breakdown." Nat was looking at me intently. "You already know about this, don't you?"

"Some of it." I stood up, not sure whether to yell or cry. "And now I suppose you're going to blab it all over town."

Nat sounded hurt. "As a matter of fact, even though it's against all my journalistic instincts, I decided not to use it."

I couldn't help it. I went over and hugged him. "Thanks. I think all those favors you owed me are paid in full."

Nat still had more on his mind. "Do you know about the fire at his daddy's plant in Alabama too?"

"Mack told me about it."

"I did some checking," Nat said, "and do you also know that the police down there finally arrested the kids who started the fire? Mack and your uncle had nothing to do with it."

I felt like giving him another hug, but I didn't know if our relationship could stand two hugs in one night. "Mack said they didn't do it, and I believed him, but I didn't know the police knew it too. Mack's going to be relieved to hear that."

"Yeah, Mandy, but it still looks bad, especially for Mack." Nat and Mack hadn't always gotten along, but I think they made an effort to be nice to each other because of me. "Farley's mother always blamed Mack and Uncle Chet for her husband's death, no matter what. It would help if we could figure out who killed Farley before some other reporter finds out about this."

"You're right." I dropped to the couch and put my head in my hands. "I keep thinking Farley was blackmailing one of my employees to work for him." I broke down and told Nat about the dirty tricks. "And finally that person couldn't take it anymore and killed him."

Nat nodded in agreement. "That sounds like a possibility, and I heard that one of your employees has dropped out of sight."

I noticed that he'd slouched back on the couch. "How did you find out about that?"

It was a silly question. After all, Nat never revealed his sources, and he ignored me now. "What I'm trying to tell you is that I had a P.I. friend of mine check her out. She had no identity until she showed up at your cleaners."

"She had a Social Security card," I said in my own defense.

"Yep, but before that there was no paper trail of credit cards, former jobs, nothing."

I can't say I was surprised, considering that I'd found out she lied about the job in California. "So how do you get yourself a whole new identity?"

"Oh, there are people who will sell you one for a price. How do you think illegal aliens get their green cards?"

I nodded because we had to be careful with that too.

"Or you can always go to the cemetery, find the name of a baby who would have been about your age if she'd lived, and apply for one in her name."

It made me squeamish to think about assuming the name of a dead child, and I couldn't imagine Sarah doing it, considering the way she seemed to love her kids, but I supposed she'd do anything she could to protect them.

"Do you think she could have killed Mills?" Nat asked.

"I don't know. I guess it's possible if he found out about her real identity and was blackmailing her." The kettle began its high-pitched scream, and I went to the stove to remove it. "But she was so small, I can't see her being able to put his body on the conveyor. She looked more like a victim than she did a killer."

Nat followed me to the kitchen and sat on one of the stools at the counter that separated what I called my "kitchen grouping" from the rest of the room. "So you don't think her disappearance and the murders are connected?"

I pushed a mug of instant coffee across the counter to him. "I don't know. Maybe she could have killed him if she thought her children were in jeopardy. She always seemed to get nervous when I talked to her about them."

"I need milk and sugar," Nat said.

I was already getting them for him, but it irritated me how he could drink his coffee laced with enough calories to make me gain ten pounds and yet never put on an ounce.

I put a milk carton and the sugar bowl on the counter and let him doctor the coffee himself. "You know how I always itch when I try to lie." I was sure Nat remembered all too well because I'd always gotten him in trouble when I tried to cover for him as a kid. "Anyway, when Sarah seemed to be lying, she'd start rubbing her neck. . . ." I stopped because that's when it hit, what had been floating around the edges of my mind at dinner with Mom and Herb.

"Go on. What are you trying to say?"

"It was the locket with the pictures of her children. It was missing from around her neck. That's why she kept fumbling with her collar and rubbing her neck when I asked her about the kids. I bet she missed the locket."

Nat looked confused. "So what does that have to do with anything?"

I shrugged. "I don't know. It's just interesting. That's all."

"One of the people I talked to said he was surprised at how fast Mills sold the business and moved," Nat said. "Why would he have come out here so suddenly after all these years?"

"Because someone must have told him about Dyer's Cleaners and that Mack worked here." I shook my head. "But I can't see Sarah doing that, especially if she's trying to hide out from something in her past."

Nat hunched over the counter. "I bet he'd have paid big bucks for the information. And you know what they always say about murders—follow the money."

"I thought it was 'Show me the money.'" I'd been around Mack too long not to think of the quotation from the movie *Jerry Maguire*, which would undoubtedly become another bit of trivia for the game we played.

"Whatever." Nat gave me a dirty look for my

digression. "And he'd probably have paid for the dirty tricks that you say were going on in the plant. That had to be an inside job. So did any of your employees seem to have more money than usual recently?"

I shook my head, but it wasn't a no, just a sign of bewilderment. "You never told me where Farley's business was in Missouri."

"It was in a Kansas City suburb, and he had a separate wholesale shirt laundry downtown." Nat was quiet for a minute. "Say, I bet Ingrid lived there at some point, the way she's such a Kansas City Chiefs fan. Maybe she knew him."

"She swears she didn't." But of course I had only her word for it that he'd been making a pass at her that day in the parking lot. For all I knew, they could have been talking over dirty tricks. "Ingrid did buy herself a convertible last fall. She said she hit a big jackpot in Black Hawk right after she came back from a vacation in Nebraska to see her sister."

"Bingo," Nat said, although he seemed disappointed. He'd always called her the sex goddess of the presses. "She'd have been strong enough to kill Mills, all right."

I was shaking my head. "But I don't know. Al Pulaski just bought a new Bronco, and, come to think of it, Larry has a fancy Jaguar that must have cost a bundle." Good Lord. What if Larry had something to do with this? That was a scary thought.

"Well, at least this has given us something to think about. I'll check with you tomorrow, and remember—follow the money." Nat took a last gulp of coffee and bounced to his feet.

That's what happens when you load it down with milk to cool it off. My coffee probably was still too hot to drink, but then I hadn't even tried it. I'd been too distracted.

"And a promise is a promise. I said I'd go, and I'm always good to my word."

With that he was out the door, and I was left with so many things to think about that I couldn't sleep for hours.

The next morning I put on a fresh white blouse, a blue skirt, and a red blazer. It made me look like a super-patriot, I realized when I looked in the mirror, but maybe that was a good thing. The bruise on my chin wasn't as swollen this morning, and seemed to disappear with a touch of makeup. Now the wounds were all on the inside.

I'd decided, somewhere around two in the morning, to have a talk with Ingrid and Al when I got to work and try to find out exactly how they got the money to buy such expensive cars.

I'd no sooner hit the back door than Mack waylaid me. "We need to talk."

"Not again." It seemed as if that's what we were always doing, but I motioned for him to follow me to my office. I tossed my coat on the couch at the side of the room and looked around for Mack. He was nowhere in sight.

He came in a moment later with a couple of cups of coffee and sat down. "Figured you'd need something to jump-start your engine."

"You know me too well." I grabbed the coffee as if it were a lifeline. "I did hear some good news last night. Nat found out about the fire in Alabama and he checked it out. The police told him that kids were eventually arrested for starting that fire."

Mack looked relieved, but only for a minute. "And I have some bad news. Juan called me last night when I got home, and he blew me away—said he'd worked for Farley for a short time back in Kansas City. The police had just talked to him about it."

"You're kidding." I sat down hard in my chair.

"He worked for Mills in a shirt laundry, but Juan said

he only knew him on sight. He never talked to him, and he didn't realize Farley owned the plant here in Denver until after Bobby got the job."

I steepled my fingers together in front of me as if I were praying, and in fact if I could have thought of a suitable prayer, I would have said it under my breath.

If this thing didn't get solved soon, people wouldn't want to come work for me at all, fearing they'd become suspects in a murder case just because they'd worked in the dry-cleaning business someplace else. It would give a whole new meaning to the term *Equal Opportunity Employer*. I had to find out who had means, motive, and opportunity—soon in order to protect the rest of my beleaguered crew.

"Juan swears he didn't have anything to do with the murder," Mack continued. "He says he was afraid to tell us about it after Mills was killed and that he'd never have sent his kid to try to get a job with Mills if he'd known the guy was loco."

"*Muy loco,*" I said to prove that I knew Spanish too. "Is he coming in today?"

"He said he'd be here, but speaking of which, Ingrid called a few minutes ago and said she wouldn't be in until noon."

"Damn." Maybe the police had called her in to talk to her about a Kansas City connection, too, and that's why she was going to be late. "We're never going to get all the orders done for Easter. People will be expecting to pick up their clothes, and they won't be ready unless I press again today."

The phone rang, and I reached for it.

"For what it's worth, Ingrid said she'd work late tonight," Mack said, and slipped out of the room.

"Is this Miss Dyer?" a woman asked in a shaky voice.

"Yes," I said.

"Thank goodness, I got you. This is Mrs. O'Neal.

You know, Sarah's baby-sitter. Well, not Sarah's—her children's."

The poor woman sounded as nervous as I felt, and all I could think of was that it was a shame to make Mrs. Santa Claus upset.

"You said if I ever heard from her to let you know."

"She called you?"

"No, but I do have something that might explain why she left. Do you have a minute?"

About a minute and a half, tops, but I didn't tell her that. "Go ahead," I said as if I had all the time in the world.

Her voice dropped to a whisper. "Not on the phone," she said as if it might be bugged, and the way things were going, she might be right. "I wonder if you could come over here. I need to show you something. I'm very upset about it."

I glanced at my watch. I had my priorities, and this seemed to take precedence over the unpressed clothes. Besides, I could work through the night if I had to. "Okay, I should be able to get there in about twenty minutes." Anything to ease Mrs. St. Nick's mind.

CHAPTER 26

As soon as Mrs. O'Neal buzzed me through the door to her apartment building, I could smell the aroma of cinnamon rolls in the hallway. It made my mouth water and my stomach cry out for food.

She was standing at her open door, wearing an apron with Easter bunnies on it. "I decided to make some sweet rolls," she said, wiping her hands on a corner of the apron. "I always bake when I get nervous. It helps to calm me down. I hope you'll have one with me."

What a pair we would make, since I always ate when I was nervous, but I tried hard to resist. "I really shouldn't take the time."

She looked so disappointed, I said, "Okay, just one." I'd been trying to lay off the sweets, but I didn't seem to have any willpower left. I followed her to her kitchen, which was not unlike mine, separated only by a counter from the living area. Except that mine never, ever smelled so sweet. A tray of rolls was cooling on a table. Icy white frosting dripped down the sides like an avalanche waiting to entrap me in its sugary depths.

She poured me a cup of tea and put it on the table, then motioned to the rolls and a small china plate that matched the cup and saucer. "Please, help yourself."

"First, what did you want to see me about?"

"Go ahead." She nodded at the rolls. "I'll never be able to eat them by myself."

My mind fought between grabbing her by her rounded shoulders and shaking the information out of her or diving into the tray of rolls and eating them all.

"Please, tell me what you wanted first," I said.

She put one of the rolls on my plate and brushed her hands on her apron again. "I don't know what to do. I've been so upset since I found it." She reached into the pocket of her apron. "I found this in my junk mail when I was going through it last night."

Talk about sleight of hand. She pulled out a coupon and thrust it at me. It was the same coupon Kim had shown me the day before. He'd stuffed it in his pocket, and now Mrs. O'Neal was pulling it out of hers as if by magic. A fifty-percent-off coupon for a pizza. I stared at it in disbelief. "I'm sorry, I don't understand."

"I almost missed it too." Her hand shook a little as she gave it to me. "Turn it over."

On the other side there were three pictures. One was a candid photo of a woman, obviously taken outdoors. The woman's face was half hidden by the shadow of a tree. The other two appeared to be studio portraits of children with "say cheese" smiles on their faces. *Have you seen us?* a caption asked above the pictures.

I made a calculated guess. "Sarah and her kids?" I could tell by the look on Mrs. O'Neal's face that I was right.

"I couldn't believe it when I saw the flyer," Mrs. O'Neal said. Her round apple-red cheeks had turned as white as the icing on the cinnamon rolls.

I took a bite of the roll to calm my nervous stomach. I guess I'd always had the feeling Sarah's disappearance had to be involved with something like this. Either she'd gone on the run with her kids from a husband or an ex-husband or she was running with kids who didn't belong to her. It was a damned good motive for blackmail if Farley had recognized her from some other place or from a wanted poster somewhere.

I read the flyer. It said the kids' names were Susan and James Jr., and the woman's name was Paula. The last names were the same—Woods, so Sarah was probably the mother. They'd been missing for nearly a year from Chicago. I took another bite of roll and absently licked the icing from my lips.

"Why would she do a thing like that?" Tears welled up in Mrs. O'Neal's eyes behind her thick half-glasses.

"You're sure it's Sarah and her kids?" I asked again. Frankly I couldn't tell from the picture of the woman, and I'd never seen the children except for that quick dash they'd made into Kim's house.

"I recognized the children right away." Mrs. O'Neal bent down to me and pointed with a stubby finger at the children's photos. "They're older now, so they don't look quite the same, but it's the same pictures that she had in that locket she always wore around her neck. And see that scar on the boy's forehead? It's the same as the one Sarah's son had. He said his daddy hit him, but Sarah said he fell out of a swing when he was too young to remember."

I studied the flyer as I finished off the roll. I guess I could see the resemblance to Sarah, although her hair was lighter, just as Mrs. O'Neal said her roots had been.

"Why would she do something like that?" Mrs. O'Neal sat down beside me, and I was vaguely aware of her serving up more rolls.

"She might have been running away from an abusive situation with her husband or maybe a judge had awarded custody of the kids to him in a divorce. You said so yourself—the boy told you his father hit him and that's how he got the scar on his forehead."

Mrs. O'Neal nodded, as if she needed to have someone else confirm what she wanted to believe. "Still, it's so sad. Sarah hiding away with those poor, sweet little ones where they never have a chance to make friends or have a real home."

I bit into another roll.

"I suppose she received the same flyer," Mrs. O'Neal continued. "They're delivered to 'Resident,' and the postman sticks them in all the mailboxes. It must have scared her to death."

I chewed thoughtfully. I was sure that the police swarming around the plant where she worked didn't help. No wonder she was frightened when they questioned her about Farley Mills, not to mention the fact that I'd followed up with my own interrogation. Some interrogator. When I tried to put her at ease by talking about her children, I'd honed in on the subject she most feared.

And what about that fight she'd had with Mills? Was it just that he'd come into the call office snooping around and trying to extract information about our operation, or was he talking to her about her children? Had he frightened her that night because he was threatening her in a way that reminded her of her husband, or was he threatening her with blackmail because he knew about her past? All I knew was that she'd refused to use the panic button that night, despite my order to employees to do so if a person was giving them trouble. No matter what the reason had been for his visit, I could understand now why she'd been reluctant to get the police involved.

"Would you like another one?" Mrs. O'Neal asked. "I like young people who have healthy appetites."

I looked at my empty plate in amazement. I'd eaten the whole roll. Or was it two?

"No," I said, holding up my hand to keep her from dishing up a third one. "You need some for yourself."

"Don't worry, I have more in the oven. I always make

a double batch when I'm upset. I'm making more to take over to my son's house for Easter. We all prefer them to hot cross buns."

I was glad she had a place to go on Easter. I wondered again if Sarah and her children would have time to dye Easter eggs, much less hunt for them on Sunday morning.

"Can I take this with me?" I held up the flyer.

She nodded. "I wish you would. I didn't know what to do with it. I was wondering if I should call the police about it."

"I'll take care of it." Much as I hated to blow the whistle on Sarah, the time had come. I drank the last of the tea and waved the flyer in the air. "Do you know when this came?"

She shook her head. "Sometime the past week. I let the junk mail accumulate and then I go through it all at once to see if there are any coupons in it before I throw it away."

"Did you happen to notice that Sarah hadn't been wearing her locket lately?" I asked, almost as an afterthought.

"As a matter of fact I did." Mrs. O'Neal pointed at her own throat. "It was only because she seemed to miss having it around her neck. I even asked her about it."

"What did she say?"

"She got all nervous about it, but then she said she broke the chain and was having it fixed." Mrs. O'Neal took off her glasses and stared into space. "I bet she took it off because she was afraid someone might look in the locket and realize that they were the same pictures that were on the flyer."

It was as good a theory as any. "Well, thanks for letting me know." I rose from the chair.

She nodded. "I want you to take the rest of the sweet rolls." She pushed the tray to me.

"I couldn't."

"Don't you have employees who would like them?"

Yes, I did, and if it would make her feel better, I decided to accept the gift. "Thank you." I slipped the flyer into my purse, where I could imagine it burning a hole in the lining the way Kim must have thought it was doing in his pants pocket the day before.

Mrs. O'Neal insisted on putting some Handi-wrap over the rolls, and while she did so, I asked if I could use her phone.

"Mack," I said when I reached him at the plant. "How's everything there? Did Juan come in this morning?"

"He called in sick, but Ramon should be able to handle the laundry."

"What about Al? Has he been in to pick up the clothes for his deliveries?"

"Now, don't panic about this, Mandy. . . ."

That was a good tip-off that there was something to panic about. "What's wrong?" My voice rose an octave.

"Everything's under control."

"What's not to be in control of? Tell me." I'd have gladly scarfed down another roll if it had been within reach.

"Al hasn't gotten here yet."

"Did you try to call him?"

"Of course I did. He's probably on the way to work right now, but if he doesn't get here soon, Harry's going to run the route."

"Harry's a presser. We need him to press clothes, and besides, we need Al's Bronco."

"This is just in case we need a backup plan. I'm sure Al will be here soon. If not, we can use my truck. It has a backseat."

"But Harry won't know where to go," I protested, but I had to admit that a backup plan was better than no plan at all.

"Look, Mandy, Harry used to be a milkman. He knows how to get around Denver. If worse comes to worse, I can help you press clothes tonight. We can work all night if necessary."

"Okay." I knew when I was licked.

I accepted Mrs. O'Neal's sweet rolls as soon as I hung up and promised to return the tray at a later date.

"Don't worry about it," she said, "although I always enjoy the company, and I would like to know if you ever hear any news of Sarah."

"I promise."

She followed me to the entrance and held the two sets of doors open for me so I could get out with my tray of goodies. I wondered if a bribe of high-calorie food would entice all my employees to work through the night with Mack and me.

The weather had turned cold and windy after the brief warm-up the previous day. They always say that if you don't like the weather in Colorado, wait a few minutes and it will change. That's the roller-coaster way my life had felt recently. No, my life was more like the other view of Colorado as Ski Country U.S.A. It had been all downhill for longer than I cared to remember.

I wondered about Al. Where was he? Had he fled the country after he killed Farley and Winona, or was he holed up in a bar someplace, grieving for his murdered girlfriend? I wanted to go by his house to check on him, but I couldn't afford the time. I needed to get back to the plant to confront Kim, and I didn't want to do that either. But, damn it, Kim should have told me about Sarah when he found the flyer. What else was he hiding? Whether Mack liked it or not, his shy assistant was going to have to explain a few things to me.

"Everything's under control," Mack said as I hit the door.

"Come into my office." I moved past him, and I guess he decided by the look on my face that I was having a panic attack.

He dropped the dress he was spotting and hurried after me. "I said everything's under control. Al didn't show up, but I sent Harry out to run the route, and Ingrid's here already. She promised she'd work overtime to help get out the work, and I'll see if the other pressers can work late too."

Obviously he didn't know I had other things on my mind. I handed Mack the flyer about Sarah and her children, which explained her disappearance but didn't explain whether or not she'd been pushed too far and had killed two people before she fled.

"Turn it over," I said. Mack nodded when he saw the offer for pizza on the other side, but I explained anyway. "That flyer's the same one Kim stuffed into his pocket yesterday. He recognized Sarah and her kids in the photograph. I'm sure of it. So why wouldn't he tell me about it right then instead of acting like he was a pizza junkie?"

"Like I said, I think he had a crush on Sarah."

"That's no excuse."

"He probably just thought he was protecting her."

"Okay, Mack, but I still need to talk to him about it. Will you send him in here?"

I was glad Mack didn't give me an argument about going easy on his assistant. A minute later Kim came into the room and took the chair Mack had just vacated. He was wearing jeans and a striped shirt, and he looked as if he were about to face the firing squad. Again I was struck by how small and thin he was. He was dwarfed by the chair, the way Sarah had been when she'd first applied for a job here. Physically at least they would have made a good pair, and I still couldn't see either one of them having the strength to hit one person over the head and strangle another.

"You knew about this, didn't you?" I pushed the flyer over to him, the pizza-discount coupon faceup.

All his emotions were on his face: pain, fear, anger. He turned the paper over as if he hoped the pictures of Sarah and her children wouldn't be on the other side. "Yes," he said finally. "It's Sarah and her kids. I found it in the trash, and I understand why she go. I think she left it for me to find."

"But why didn't you tell me about it?"

"I didn't want you to think it was a reason for her to kill Mr. Mills."

"Okay, I understand." And I really could accept Kim's reluctance to tell me. Hadn't I felt the same way about Mack when he told me about himself and Uncle Chet?

Kim handed the coupon back to me as if he couldn't bear to look at it anymore, and I tapped on Sarah's picture. "Did you know about this before you saw the flyer? Had she told you anything about it earlier?"

Kim brushed a lock of his straight black hair out of his eyes. "All I know is that she hate—" He seemed to be looking for a softer word. "She was upset when bad things happen. She said her husband beat her up, and she is afraid when bad things start happening here at the cleaners."

"Did she ever say anything to you about the bad things going on at the plant?"

Kim moved to the front of the chair. For a minute I thought he was going to bolt from the office. "She say—" He apparently was debating whether to tell me something or not. "She say someone lost something, and she's afraid to tell anyone where it is."

"Who? What was it?"

"I don't know. That's all she say."

"When was this?"

"Wednesday on the phone before I go over there and she's not home."

"Are you sure that's what she said—that someone *else* had lost something? It sounds as if she'd found it and was afraid to return it to them."

Kim shrugged, but he looked incredibly sad, as if he felt he were letting both Sarah and me down.

"You don't think she could have been talking about something she'd lost herself and was afraid to reclaim?" The locket came immediately to mind. Had she lost it but discovered where it was? Was she afraid to retrieve it for fear someone would see her do it and know it tied her to Farley's murder?

"No." Kim was emphatic, but I wasn't sure if it was out of loyalty to Sarah or because he really was sure he'd heard her correctly.

For that matter I wondered how much I could trust his understanding of English even when he was convinced he remembered what she'd said. Maybe she'd been talking about herself in the third person the way people do when they have something too painful or embarrassing to admit about themselves. That would surely confuse a person who wasn't fluent in English.

"Is there anything else she told you about it?"

"No, but I know she was scared."

When I told him he could go back to work, Kim ran from the office as if he'd gotten a last-minute stay of execution. Was it me or was Kim running from something else?

CHAPTER 27

I took off my jacket and placed it over the back of my chair, prepared to go to work. I was long overdue on the press line to fill in for Harry, who was still out running the route. I started down the aisle by the presses to Harry's work station, but Aretha, one of my other pressers, stopped me.

"I gotta go to the dentist in a few minutes to have a tooth pulled," she said, coming out from amid the clothes hanging on a slick rail waiting to be pressed. "I already told Mack."

What could I say? I could see that Aretha's jaw looked swollen. Either she had a dental problem or she had a wad of chewing gum in her mouth the way Ingrid usually did.

"Mack said you wanted us to work overtime tonight, but I probably won't be able to come back."

"I understand."

Bill, my other presser, must have overheard the conversation. He popped his head out from among the clothes on his line. "I can't stay either. It's my anniversary, and the wife will kill me if I don't show up for it."

I already knew that Harry wouldn't be able to stay that

night. He watched his kids while his wife worked nights as a nurse's aide.

Ingrid motioned me over to the silk press. Was she going to back out too?

"I'm sorry about not coming in yesterday and this morning," she said. "I just couldn't deal with it."

"I know what you mean."

"But I'll work late tonight. I already told Mack I'd make up for the time I missed this morning."

"Okay, thanks." It looked as it we were going to be a skeleton crew—Mack, Ingrid, and me—with a mountain of clothes to press if the orders were going to be ready as promised by the next day.

As I moved on to Harry's press, I noticed that the note I'd left for Ingrid was gone. "I see you got my message about putting your personal belongings in your locker."

She popped a bubble. "Sorry about leaving that stuff out here. I promise to do better in the future."

I thought about the gap in her work record. "By the way, Ingrid, I noticed that you filled out the new personnel form I asked for." I edged back to her press so that no one passing in the aisle would hear us. "It has a gap in it for a few months before Uncle Chet hired you."

"I didn't have a job," she said with a shrug. "I was living with a guy, but it didn't work out."

"Where was that?"

I thought she might get mad, but she didn't. "In Kansas City," she said. "That's where I got hooked on the Chiefs."

I wondered if my speculation had been right—that the police had discovered something about her time in Kansas City and maybe even called her in for an interview that morning, the way they'd done with Juan the previous night. She wasn't usually this forthcoming, and she was dressed up in a red skirt and form-fitting white sweater, which was unusual for her. A matching red jacket was hung at the end of the press. This from the person who had just promised to keep her work area clean. Already she was using the end of the press as a clothes hanger.

"By the way, did you know Farley Mills was from Kansas City?" I asked as I turned to leave.

"Huh?"

I repeated the question.

"No, that's news to me." She sounded as if she could have cared less as she finished a cream-colored blouse. Then she hung it on a hanger and put it over the screw conveyor that continued on to the inspection and bagging station up front.

I went to Harry's press, but Ingrid turned to me. "So how late do you think we'll be tonight, boss?"

"Till we get done."

She looked around at the clothes on hangers and in piles. "I may not be able to stay that long."

I had to smile. I wasn't sure any of us could since there might not be enough hours in the night to accomplish that task. "Okay, stay as long as you can, then. I'll appreciate it."

It was becoming apparent to me that it was probably going to be up to Mack and me to work through the night. What would I do without him?

Dozens of pants were hung over a cart at Harry's press. No matter how many I did, there were more to take their place. I was still at it in the late afternoon when Lucille dragged herself back to the presses to find me.

"That *detective* is out front again," she said in a loud, irritated voice.

Ingrid turned and winked at me. "God, he's a gorgeous hunk, isn't he?"

"Former hunk," I muttered. The thrill was gone now that we had such an adversarial relationship. To Lucille I added in a louder voice, "Just send him on back. I'm sure he knows the way by now."

"Can I go home now? Julia's here."

I nodded and kept on working. I'd just finished the first leg on a pair of tan pants when Foster found me.

"Could we talk in your office?" he asked. His face looked so serious I had a feeling it wasn't good news.

I sighed and lined up the other leg so it would have a proper crease. "Just a minute." Surely he'd let me finish what I was doing. I pushed the hand control to make the head of the press come down on the leg of the pants.

Foster looked around the plant. "Where's Mack today?"

I followed his gaze to the cleaning machines, but the only person I saw was Kim. "He must be taking a break right now." I finished the pants with a little touch-up with a steam iron, then put the pants over one of our hangers with a cardboard tube across the bottom. "Okay, I'm ready."

Now I knew how Kim had felt. As I led Foster to my office, I couldn't help but feel as if I were going to face the executioner.

He waited until he'd closed the door, and we were both seated across from each other at my desk. "I'm sorry to tell you this but Al Pulaski is dead."

I gripped the edge of the desk. "What happened?"

"His neighbor hadn't seen him for a couple of days, and he went over to investigate. He saw his body through an open bedroom window."

"But what happened? Was it a heart attack or something?"

"I'm afraid not. It appears that someone hit him over the head while he was sleeping."

I tried to release my knuckles from the table, but I couldn't seem to break their suction. Al must have been in the house when Mack and I had been there the night before.

"You—" I started to speak, but the words wouldn't come. I tried again. "You say the neighbor hadn't seen him for a couple of days, but he was here at work Wednesday. When do you think he died?"

"We won't know that for a while."

Goose bumps broke out on my arms. I'd been warm when I came into the room, but suddenly I felt cold and clammy. I managed to unclasp my fingers, and I reached around for my jacket and started to put it on. Tears welled up in my eyes, and I blinked them back.

"I'm sorry about this, Mandy, but the reason I'm here is that I have to take Mack downtown."

"Mack?" I was half in and half out of the jacket, and I froze. "Why?"

"Wallace Patterson, the neighbor, said he saw a black man outside Mr. Pulaski's place last night," Foster said. "It sounded like Mack, and we need to talk to him about it."

I felt a momentary relief as I pulled an arm out of the jacket, pulling the sleeve with me. "Mack and I were at Al's place looking for him. He didn't come in to work yesterday."

"What time was that?"

I fumbled with the sleeve. "About ten-thirty, I think."

"Mr. Patterson says this was earlier and that the man might have been coming out of Al's back door."

Any energy I had left seemed to evaporate. I didn't even have enough strength to put on the jacket. What should I say? Did I admit that Mack had been trying to find Al earlier, or did I let Mack speak for himself? I decided it would sound better coming from him.

Instead I tried another tack. "Look, since Al didn't come in yesterday, he must have been killed Wednesday night, the same night Winona died." I was making up a whole scenario in my mind as I went along. "Winona must have been blackmailing the killer, and he thought Al knew about it too. Manuel said Winona and Al were going together. Remember? Besides, it couldn't have been Mack because that's when he came down to see you—just before Winona's body was found."

"I just want to talk to him, Mandy."

I never got a chance to argue. The door burst open, and there were Mom and Herb. Mom was wearing a hot-pink pants suit that made her look like the first tulip of spring about to burst into bloom. Herb was still dressed like an escapee from the nineteenth hole in his blazer, plaid pants, and white shoes.

"Whoops," Mom said, looking between Foster and me, my jacket still half on and half off. "Are we interrupting something?" She smiled suggestively.

I jumped out of the chair and somehow pulled on the jacket. "What are you doing here? I thought you were on your way to Phoenix?"

Mom didn't answer. She fluffed her hair and sized up Foster as a suitable boyfriend for her daughter.

"We missed our flight and we couldn't get another one until seven," Herb said, hopefully more aware than Mom that this wasn't a romantic interlude. "We thought we'd come on down and see your plant, but if this isn't a good time. . . ." He had Mom by the arm and was trying to move her toward the door.

She wasn't having any of that. "Aren't you going to introduce us to your friend, dear?" She fluttered her eyelashes at Foster, which was an automatic reflex she had around men.

It didn't bother Herb, but it did me. "Mom, this is Detective Foster, and he's here on *business*." I looked from Foster to the two exiles from Arizona, to which I'd fervently hoped they had returned by now. "This is my mother, Cecilia, and my stepfather, Herb Smedley."

Foster made an effort to be pleasant. "It's nice to meet you."

"Aren't you the young man I talked to on the phone the other night?" Mom wrestled herself away from Herb's grip and came over to Foster. "You called to warn Amanda about the break-in here at the plant. Thank goodness it didn't amount to much."

Foster nodded helplessly.

"Well, I hope you've got some good news for Amanda this time. This whole thing has been very hard on her."

I stepped from behind the desk. "Why don't you and Herb wait in the break room until the detective and I are through talking?"

"Oh," Mom said. "Ohhhh." The final exclamation was said as if she still thought we were having some intimate tête-à-tête. "Of course, dear. . . ." She started backing slowly out of the room, but she had the audacity to wink at Foster as she did. "We'll leave you kids alone, but maybe we'll have a chance to get better acquainted later."

"Come on, Cecilia," Herb said, his face turning a deep shade of red. "Mom and I will just wait outside until you're through with your meeting." He had the door open. "Glad to have met you, young man."

Mom wasn't ready to leave without a parting shot. "I keep telling Amanda she works too hard. She needs to have more fun."

"Mother." My voice was strident. "Detective Foster and I are discussing a police matter." I shooed her away with my hand. "Now, will you two wait in the break room?"

They left, and Herb closed the door.

"I'm sorry," I said.

"That's okay." Foster seemed bewildered. "People always seem to be trying to get us together."

I assumed he was also referring to the incident with Manuel at Tico Taco's the other night. "In their dreams," I muttered and returned to my chair.

But there was one good thing about Mom and Herb's

unexpected appearance. It seemed to have given me a second wind. I was so mad I could feel my adrenaline pumping. "Mack didn't kill anyone, and while you're here, there's something else I think you should know."

I handed him the flyer about Sarah and her missing children and told him that, by my calculations, she had disappeared the same night that Winona and Al were killed. I emphasized Al because I was convinced he'd died the same night.

Foster sat back down in the chair that was too small for him and read the flyer. "So what are you saying—that you think she killed them?"

"I don't know. I just know it wasn't Mack."

"Where did you find this?" Foster tapped on the flyer.

I explained how the baby-sitter for Sarah's children had given it to me that morning. "Maybe Farley was blackmailing Sarah because he knew about her abducting her children. That would be a damned good reason for blackmail, don't you think?" I came out from behind my desk because I couldn't sit still any longer.

Foster got up too. "I still need to take Mack down to headquarters, Mandy."

"What are you going to do with him—handcuff him and force him to go with you?"

"I hope he'll come voluntarily."

He was at the door before I could stop him, but frankly I'd run out of any information to delay the inevitable. He opened the door, and there were Mom and Herb. Not in the break room where I'd asked them to go but blocking Foster's way as if they'd been eavesdropping or trying to keep him from getting away.

"I hope we'll get to see you again," Mom trilled as I followed Foster around to where Mack was loading one of the cleaning machines. Mom and Herb came too.

"I need you to come down to headquarters with me," Foster said to Mack. "I hope you'll cooperate."

Mack didn't ask questions, and much as I wanted to tell him what was going on, I didn't want to discuss it in front of Mom and Herb. "I'll get my jacket" is all he said.

He went to the break room as Mom approached Foster. "You're not arresting McKenzie, are you?" I thought for a minute she was going to hit him with her purse. "I'll have you know he has worked here for years—first for my brother-in-law and then for my daughter. He would never kill anyone." I could tell that this had lowered her estimation of Foster as a potential boyfriend for her daughter, no matter how good-looking he was.

"We'd better stay out of it, sweetie." Herb pulled her aside.

Mack was back by then, wearing his familiar old pea jacket, and we watched as he and Foster left by the back door. I could tell it was going to be a long night ahead for Ingrid and me.

"I can't believe it." Mom had her hands on her hips by then. "And he seemed like such a nice young man too."

"It'll be all right, Cecilia. We won't let this happen to Mack." Herb looked at me. "We'll see that he has the finest lawyer money can buy."

I thought of Mom's earlier effort to get me a lawyer. "No, please, I think it'll be okay. Mack went voluntarily, and I'm sure he can explain everything to the police."

"There must be something we can do," Herb said.

I looked at my watch. "Don't you need to get to the airport? You said you had a seven-o'clock flight."

Herb looked at his watch too. "She's right, Cilia. We'd better get going."

For a minute I thought Mom was going to refuse.

"We wouldn't leave you like this, but we do have that closing tomorrow . . . ," Herb said.

Thoughts of her dream house mixed with Mom's desire to stay and help Mack and me. For a minute she seemed torn. She fingered the heart-shaped locket at her neck.

I couldn't help thinking of Sarah's locket. I wished I knew where the damned thing was, and if that's what she'd been referring to when she said something was missing.

Mom twisted the chain on her locket. I could tell that her dream had won out. Thank you, God.

"I guess we'd really better go," she said.

"And if you need any help, Mandy Pie, you let us know. You hear?" Herb was urging her to the door as he spoke. "We can be back up here tomorrow night."

Mom came over and kissed me on the cheek. Herb gave me a bear hug, just as he'd done the night before.

I followed them out through the back door and watched as they climbed into their luxury rental car and drove away. I had never felt so sad and alone in my life.

CHAPTER 28

It wasn't even dark yet, but I felt as if I were in a deep, black hole and would never be able to find my way out.

I wanted to help Mack, but I was no closer to a solution than I'd ever been. I wrapped my suit jacket around me and stared across the parking lot to Tico Taco's as I thought about Manuel. He'd come over here and knocked on the back door when he saw the van Sunday night, and when he'd hurried Winona away from Foster and me a few nights later, he'd told her to go home to make up for working late Sunday. Maybe he'd left her to clean up, and she'd seen someone come out of the plant after Manuel left.

But who? Was it just a coincidence that she'd asked us about Ingrid before Manuel sent her on her way? What she'd said suddenly occurred to me—that she and Ingrid had to quit playing the slots last summer because they'd both maxed out their credit cards. But Ingrid hadn't quit. Not if she won a big jackpot while she was on vacation last fall.

That didn't mean much. I'm sure Mom's old neighbor, Evelyn Bell, vowed to quit gambling every day of her life. What it did mean was that Ingrid had been in debt last summer but rolling in money about the same time that Farley apparently heard about Mack and Dyer's Cleaners. Maybe instead of winning a jackpot she really had offered Farley information in exchange for money, and maybe he'd kept paying her to help him with his dirty tricks.

Suddenly the door popped open. I jumped a foot.

"I needed a smoke break." Ingrid pulled a pack of cigarettes from the pocket of a dark leather coat as short as her skirt underneath. She continued over to the shelter of the Dumpster to the right of the door. I'd been avoiding looking at the Dumpster since the police found Winona's body inside. I wondered if it bothered Ingrid.

She tapped on the bottom of her pack of Marlboros and pulled one out. Then she flicked on a lighter, and when it flared, she puffed until I could see a spark on the end of the cigarette. The glow seemed to hang suspended in the shadows of the Dumpster until she walked back over to me and shook another one out of the pack.

"Here, want one too?"

I shook my head, and I was proud of myself for having the strength to refuse. I needed any small victory I could get right then. "I'd better go back inside and get to work."

She towered above me. Nat had once described her as "stacked like a ten-foot hourglass." The description had irritated me at the time, but as he'd said the night before, she probably would have had the strength to kill Farley and Winona and even Al. Poor Al, who'd never met a man or woman he didn't like. All the time I'd been thinking he might be a killer, he'd been dead inside his house. I began to choke up again.

"What happened to Mack?" Ingrid put the lighter inside the cellophane on the pack of cigarettes.

"What?" I had a hard time coming back to the present.

"Did they arrest him?"

"No, they just wanted to talk to him." It was probably

both wishful thinking and a general unease that made me add, "He should be back in a little while."

"That's good."

I couldn't bring myself to tell her about Al. I mustn't even think about it right now—not until Mack came back and we could talk it through. I needed to concentrate on other things.

"I thought you gave up using a lighter," I said in that unfortunate way I have of bringing up something insignificant when there's really something else I want to ask. She'd told me that she quit using lighters because of the childproof safety features, hadn't she? Yet it occurred to me that there'd also been a lighter among the junk I'd tossed in her locker the day before.

She didn't answer, and I hoped she hadn't heard me.

I tried something more to the point. "I was wondering where you won that jackpot last fall. Was it in Black Hawk or Central City?"

"Why'd you want to know?"

I shrugged, which was easy because I was already shaking. "I was thinking of going up to Black Hawk Sunday, and I was looking for a casino with loose slots."

She took a long drag on the cigarette. "You're out of luck. It was in Black Hawk, but the casino's gone belly-up since then."

"Too bad." Surely the police could find out whether or not Ingrid won a jackpot at a Black Hawk casino before it closed.

"When did you hit the jackpot? Before or after you went back to Nebraska to see your sister?"

"After, but why the hell do you care about that?"

I coughed, and I wasn't even smoking. "No reason. Just making conversation."

She stomped away from the building, flipped the remains of her cigarette into the parking lot, and lit another one.

"I guess I'd better get inside." Not a moment too soon either. Ingrid was definitely hot under the collar, as Uncle Chet had been fond of saying.

"I'll be back in a few minutes," she said, not turning to look at me.

Unfortunately it might take her longer than that to cool down, and I couldn't say I blamed her. I had a lot of suspicions about her, but not a single shred of evidence.

I couldn't get into the rhythm of the pressing, although Ingrid seemed to be on a roll on the silk press in front of me. When she'd first come back inside, she'd hung her coat in the break room and begun attacking the clothes as if she were attacking me. But it was doing marvels for her production rate, and I let it go.

Theresa and Julia came by the presses.

"We're leaving now," Theresa said. "I locked the front door, and we'll let ourselves out the back. Do you want to turn on the burglar alarm now?"

"No, I'll do it later." I finished another pair of pants and sent it down the conveyor to the assembly station.

The only person with a connection to Farley that I hadn't talked to was Juan. Maybe I should try him. What had the police asked him about last night when they took him down to headquarters? Obviously they didn't find anything incriminating or they wouldn't have let him go. I wondered if he knew anyone else on my crew who'd ever worked for Farley.

"I have to make a call. I'll be right back." I brushed back my hair, which was beginning to droop around my face.

Ingrid glanced around at me, her blond hair all neatly held in place in a French braid that hung down her back. "Okay, boss." She blew a bubble with her gum, and I hoped she was over being mad.

I found Juan's telephone number in my purse and dialed it. A child, who sounded too young to be Bobby, answered and called his dad. "This is Mandy," I said, "and I wanted to talk to you about your time in Kansas City. Mack said you told him you worked for Farley Mills for a while."

It sounded as if he spat into the phone. "He was *loco—muy loco.*" And Mack kept saying I needed to learn Spanish. Hadn't I said the very same thing about Farley that morning?

"Why did you think he was *loco*?"

"He was—how you say?" Juan began to rattle something off in Spanish. He always did that when he got excited, and yes, I did need to take a crash course in Berlitz if I was ever going to understand anything more than *loco, gracias,* and *de nada.*

"Could you put Bobby on the phone, Juan? Maybe he can translate for us."

"Roberto," Juan yelled.

There was more background noise, and then Bobby came on the line. I explained that I'd been with his father and Mack the other day at the jail.

"I remember."

"Could you ask your dad some questions for me and then tell me what he says. That way there won't be any misunderstanding."

"Sure."

"Ask him what he said about Mr. Mills being *loco.*"

I heard Juan in the background.

"Dad says he was afraid to tell you that he'd ever worked for him when he found out how *loco* he was and that he might be doing bad stuff at your plant." I could still hear Juan talking in the background.

"What I really want to know, Bobby, is about your dad working for him in Kansas City. Does he know of any other employees of Dyer's Cleaners who worked for Mills?"

Bobby repeated my question to his father and waited for an answer. I glanced out in the plant and could see Ingrid staring at me. She dropped her eyes when she saw me looking at her.

Bobby came back on the phone, and I could tell Juan had his own agenda. "Dad says he didn't even recognize Mr. Mills without his—uh—little mustache—" Apparently Bobby paused to make sure that's what his father'd said. "Mr. Mills had a mustache back in Kansas City, and Dad says he didn't realize it was the same guy when he first saw him here in Denver. If he had, he says *no way* would he have let me work for him."

"But does he know of anyone else here at Dyer's Cleaners who might have worked for Farley Mills?" I repeated.

"He says no, he doesn't know of anybody."

I was disappointed, but I'd thought all along that Juan was a long shot. "Okay, thanks, Bobby. Thank your father too." I had another thought. "Bobby, did you ever see Mr. Mills with anyone that you might have recognized from here at your dad's job?"

"No."

"Did Mills ever say anything to you about Dyer's Cleaners?"

"Not that I remember."

We hung up, and as I glanced out into the plant, Ingrid's eyes seemed to dart away from me. I swiveled around to the window and stared at the dark hole outside. It seemed as empty as my mind. I needed to go in another direction. Maybe Sarah. . . . She'd told Kim that someone had lost something. She knew where it was but was afraid to call attention to herself by mentioning it to anyone. It must have been something in the plant. Yet the police had already searched the place..

Sarah wasn't one to go wandering around the plant. She would have had to see it in the break room or up front where she worked, and she'd only been here Wednesday afternoon. After Lucille left, I'd put her to work bagging clothes.

So where could the missing item be? A place where the police wouldn't be suspicious of it and bag it as evidence. Something that was bagged already. No, not bagged. Put inside an envelope. I jerked around in my seat and glanced at Ingrid. She was putting a dress on a hanger.

I'd even been talking about the envelopes with Mom and Herb last night—how we used them for the items we found in customers' clothes. Then we placed them in our lost-and-found drawer to be stapled to orders after the clothes were clean. Sometimes we even found items that had fallen out of the clothes when a customer came into the call office. We did the same thing with them, just in case a customer came in and inquired about them.

Could Sarah have assembled an order that required her to go to the lost-and-found drawer? Yes. Could she have seen something inside the drawer that belonged to someone she knew? Yes, yes, yes. I was sure of it. I even had an idea what it was.

Other things were beginning to come together, even Juan's remark about Farley's mustache. I took a few deep breaths in an attempt to calm down before I made my way past Ingrid to Lucille's mark-in table. I couldn't let it go until later. I had to find out. I grabbed a While You Were Out slip from my desk, and when I thought I was in control enough to pull it off, I got up and started to the front of the plant.

"What's wrong?" Ingrid watched me curiously as I walked past her. "Where you going?"

I waved the slip of paper in the air. "I have to check on a suit for a customer. He needs it for a business trip he's taking tomorrow morning."

When I reached the front of the plant, I punched in numbers so the conveyor would start. I took a quick glance at Ingrid, who was facing the other direction. I slipped over to the mark-in table and took another peek at her. Now she was almost hidden by a line of clothes waiting to be assembled.

I pulled out the lost-and-found drawer. There were only a couple of envelopes inside with customers' names on them. I couldn't believe it. I'd been so sure I was right. I slipped my hand deeper into the drawer and patted around to see if I'd missed anything.

My fingers touched another envelope in a corner. I could tell by the feel that it wasn't Sarah's locket inside, and even before I pulled it out, I knew what it was. It might not be a smoking gun, but it was close. Something that could start a fire if put to a trail of gasoline.

I opened the envelope and stared at the lighter inside. Not any lighter. A *red* lighter. Not incriminating in and of itself, but enough for me. It was the lighter Ingrid must have dropped when she killed Farley Mills and hung his body on the conveyor. That's why she hadn't had a lighter Monday afternoon—not because the childproof lighters were too hard to use. No wonder she hadn't answered when I started in on her about it again tonight.

The lighter was probably something Lucille had found just before I turned on the conveyor and saw the body. She must have thrown it in the drawer without even looking at it or giving it a second thought, but Sarah could have seen it and known immediately what it was. In her fear about being discovered herself, maybe the only thing she could think to do was leave the lighter where it was for someone else to find.

No wonder Lucille had complained about other employees hanging around her mark-in table in an attempt to get a look at the murder scene. She'd particularly complained about Ingrid, who'd been looking for the lighter she'd lost, not trying to view the place where Farley was killed.

And despite all her denials, Ingrid must have known Farley before he came to Denver. I thought he'd looked like an evil Howdy Doody. Howdy Doody didn't have a mustache. Ingrid had said Farley reminded her of Hitler. There was no similarity that I could see unless she'd known him when he had a "little" mustache.

I was still staring at the lighter when I realized the conveyor had stopped. How long ago? I closed the envelope and started to put it in my skirt pocket.

"I've been looking all over for that." It was Ingrid, and she was standing only a couple of feet away. I hadn't even heard her come up behind me. "Give it to me."

CHAPTER
29

I shoved the envelope and its lighter in my pocket and grabbed another envelope from the drawer. "What? You want this?" I shook it, and some coins jingled around inside.

"Not that." If looks could kill, I'd be dead already. "The lighter. I realized that's where it had to be when I saw you go over to the drawer. I knew you'd figured it out."

"Figured what out?"

"Oh, cut the crap." I saw that she had a belt, and she snapped it taut between her hands. The fact that Winona had been strangled with a belt wasn't lost on me.

I dropped the envelope of coins on the floor, hoping she'd think the lighter was inside and try to grab it. "I don't know what you're talking about." The coins clattered across the floor.

"Sure you do. I never should have bought myself some new lighters after I told you I didn't use them anymore. That's why you asked about them tonight, wasn't it?"

Guilty people sometimes give the rest of us too much credit. Maybe I should have thought about it even earlier, when I saw the new lighters at her work station, but I didn't know anything was missing then.

She still hadn't moved. "I didn't think the police had

found it, so I figured it had to be around here someplace. Now, give it to me."

I kept a viselike grip on the lighter as I edged away from her. "You're not making any sense, Ingrid."

"Just give me the damned lighter." She lunged at me, but I was ready for her. I sidestepped out of her way, just as a toreador would do in the face of a charging bull. I might not be any good at Spanish, but I was dynamite when a big woman in a red skirt was coming at me.

I had a plan, and I took off on a dead run. I'd get to the light switch and douse all the lights. Then I'd hide among the equipment until I could make a run for the back door and Tico Taco's.

Admittedly it wasn't a very good plan, and I wasn't even halfway to the back of the plant when she overtook me. She tackled me with a hit around the knees. I kept skidding down the aisle for another three or four feet. Then I did the only thing I could think to do. I rolled over and heaved the lighter as far as I could throw it. It was a Hail Mary pass, and Ingrid went out for the interception.

She let go of my legs and tried to make a midair catch. I didn't wait around to see if she caught it, but I knew she didn't. I heard the lighter, still inside the envelope, thud to the floor somewhere out of her reach. I got to my feet and started running again.

I could hear her behind me, and I ducked into Harry's press station. She scooted in after me, and we circled like we were bulls in a ring. I knew she couldn't afford to let me get away once she'd said as much as she had about the lighter.

I tried to stare her down from the end of the press. "Why did you do it, Ingrid?"

Her face contorted in anger. "I needed the money, but it got out of hand. The jackass said he was going to tell Warren unless I started putting out for him."

We kept circling, and finally when I was on the side

closest to the back door, I took off running again. I was almost to the light switch, but by that time I'd decided just to keep on going to the back door. My mistake. Ingrid shoved me into Mack's spotting board. I saw the belt come down over my head as she rammed her body into mine. I grabbed one of Mack's spray bottles of spotting solution, twisted around, and squirted her in the face.

"Damn you," she screamed.

She doubled over, dropping the belt, and tore at her eyes.

I headed for the back door just as someone pounded on it. I yanked open the door and came face-to-face with a huge man I'd never seen before. I didn't care. As far as I was concerned, he was my salvation.

"Help me," I gasped as he reached out for me.

"Stop her, Warren," Ingrid yelled, tears streaming down her face. "She just tried to kill me."

Damn, I'd never seen her husband before without his blue-and-orange makeup.

The next thing I knew Warren had one arm around my neck and the other one was pulling my hand behind my back.

"What was she doing to you, baby?" he asked.

"She hurt me." Ingrid cowered in what was an Academy Award performance. "She killed those other people I was telling you about, and she was trying to kill me too."

Warren tightened his hold on me. "Go call the cops, honey. Nobody's going to hurt you now."

In some air-deprived recess of my brain, I realized that Warren must not be Ingrid's partner in crime. If I could just break his stranglehold on me, maybe I could make him understand I wasn't the bad guy here.

"Call Nine-one-one," he said. "I've got her, and she won't get away."

"Ingrid's the murderer," I tried to say, but my voice came out sounding like a parrot that had never learned how to speak.

"No." Ingrid slumped over the spotting board. "She's going to frame me for the murders, and we can't let her get away with that. We've got to get rid of her."

Warren loosened his grip on my neck.

"She killed 'em, Warren," I squawked.

I still didn't think he could understand me, but he must have heard something. He dropped his hand down to my collarbone, and I gasped for air.

"Ingrid killed them," I said.

Damn. Why hadn't I turned on the burglar alarm when Theresa and Julia left? If I had, it would have started screeching the moment I opened the door for Warren.

"She's a liar," Ingrid screamed.

"Don't believe her, Warren. She's the one who's lying."

Ingrid had come over and was standing with her face bent down to mine and the belt circled into a noose in her hands.

"Why would Ingrid kill anyone?" Warren must have been addressing me, but I couldn't see him, only Ingrid's bloodshot eyes.

"For money, Warren." He'd loosened his grip on me enough that I probably could have gotten away, but I didn't want to let Ingrid know.

"She's insane," Ingrid said, spitting the words at me. "That guy that was killed was threatening her business. She killed the other two because they were blackmailing her about it."

I said the only thing I could think of that might convince Warren that Ingrid was the guilty party. "She came into a lot of money last fall, didn't she? It was from the guy who was killed. He was paying her to sabotage my plant."

Warren dropped his hands away from me. I'd been

planning to point out that Ingrid couldn't have known there was a third body, Al's, unless she was the killer. I didn't have a chance. Ingrid grabbed me from the front and swung the leather belt around my neck.

She pulled it tight as she dragged me away from him. "You have to help me," she sobbed. "She's going to frame me for the murders if we don't stop her."

I didn't think she needed any help. She was doing a good job all by herself. She'd pulled me in front of her once she had the belt around my neck, and we were both up against Mack's spotting board facing Warren.

He was coming toward us, holding out his hands and saying something to her, but his face and voice were fading in and out as I tried to kick back at Ingrid's shins. I didn't think I'd hit her very hard, but the blows seemed to pound in my ears.

It wasn't until I saw the blurred figures of two men that I realized the pounding had been coming from the door. God, please let it be Foster bringing Mack back to work.

I fell to the floor, dragging Ingrid with me. She let go of the belt, and I clawed to loosen it and get it off my head. I gulped for air, but I was gagging and coughing so much, it was awhile before I became aware of anything around me.

The two newcomers came slowly into focus. They looked like George Hamilton and a chubby Woody Allen. I had to be hallucinating because it sure wasn't Foster and Mack. It was Larry and his cohort, Brad "The Cad" Samuels.

"What's going on here?" Larry asked, taking a tentative step toward us.

"Stay back." Warren was now as wild-eyed as Ingrid. He grabbed her and pulled her to him.

Larry and Brad both stopped in their tracks.

"She's crazy, Warren," Ingrid cried into his chest.

Larry and Brad were staring at us as if we were all nuts.

"It's going to be okay, baby." Warren patted Ingrid on the back. "We'll get help now."

"Ingrid's the killer," I squawked again. A parrot with a very limited vocabulary.

"We've got to get out of here, Warren." Ingrid tugged at his jacket and tried to pull him to the door.

He looked as confused as Larry and Brad, but at least Brad moved over to the door in an attempt to stop them.

"Get out of the way, I'm warning you," Ingrid yelled, still tugging at Warren.

Brad held his ground, but Larry the Intrepid backed up at least six feet.

I scrambled from the floor and reached over to Mack's spotting board for his steam gun. "Don't move," I said, aiming the gun at them. "This will scald you alive."

Warren pulled Ingrid toward him in an effort to protect her, but fortunately he didn't move.

"Larry, call the police," I yelled.

He started to my office just as the door opened again. This time it was Mack, and a uniformed officer was right behind him.

I motioned to Ingrid with the steam gun. "Officer, this is Ingrid Larsen, and she killed Farley Mills."

Brad never missed a beat. He stepped forward and handed Ingrid one of his business cards. "I'm a lawyer, and I think you should be advised that you have the right to remain silent and have an attorney present."

CHAPTER
30

Mack and I both wanted to believe that Al had had nothing to do with Winona's blackmail threat. But Ingrid had been sure he knew about his girlfriend's get-rich-quick scheme, so, after she killed Winona, she went over to his house and lured him into bed with her, then killed him while he slept.

That's what Nat told us when Mack and I had dinner with him at a restaurant called The Front Page, which Nat liked for obvious reasons. It was a few days after Al's funeral, and by then Ingrid had confessed to the killings and Brad the Cad was thinking of entering a temporary insanity plea in her defense. I didn't see how it would work in the murder of three people, but what did I know about the law?

"Apparently Ingrid worked for Mills for a little while in Kansas City, but he must have paid her under the table because there's no record of it," Nat said.

"Except in her resume," I said. "I bet she'd listed his cleaners as one the places where she'd worked and that's why she broke in and stole the personnel files."

"Anyway," Nat continued, "she knew about his obsession with Mack and Uncle Chet, but even when she went to work for Dyer's Cleaners and discovered that they both

worked here, she didn't do anything about it until she became desperate for money. She says she didn't mean to
kill Mills, but they got into a fight when she realized he
was going to burn down the plant, not just play a few
harmless pranks."

I had a feeling that her killing Farley had more to do
with his threat to tell Warren what was going on, but I
guess it really didn't matter.

Nat couldn't resist playing reporter. "By the way, have
you ever heard anything about Sarah McIntyre?"

I shook my head. I'd decided not to tell him about the
flyer with her picture on it. I guess we'd never know
where she went, just as we'd never know about Al. Or
even the reason why Farley had asked Kim to spy on Ingrid. Maybe to keep track of her husband and when he
was going to be out of town so Farley could make his
move on her.

Nat seemed disappointed that I didn't have any information, but he bounced right back. "I want to point out,
Mandy, that I was right. Didn't I tell you to follow the
money?"

"I thought it was 'show me the money,' " Mack said.

Nat gave us two movie buffs a dirty look, but he continued in what was a surprisingly sympathetic tone. "It's
just too bad the whole thing caused Mack so much grief."

Mack shrugged it off, but I knew the last few weeks
had taken their toll on him. "At least," he said, "it's good
to finally put that fire in Alabama behind me." He looked
over at me and couldn't resist giving me a piece of fa-
therly advice. "Now that it's over, I just hope you'll quit
detecting and take up some other kind of hobby."

"Maybe I could start a dating service like a dry
cleaner I heard about on TV who takes Polaroids of his
single customers and posts them on a bulletin board."

They both nearly laughed themselves under the table.
That was even after I pointed out that Mom and Herb

were now happy as peacocks in their new home in Arizona, thanks to me getting them back together.

I decided maybe I'd better stick to cleaning clothes. After all, most of my customers seemed to be standing by me despite the fact that some of their clothes hadn't been ready for several days after Ingrid's arrest. I'm sure Nat's lengthy article in the newspaper helped them understand, not to mention the twenty-dollars-off coupons I handed out for their next visit to the cleaners.

Mack and Nat were still laughing about my dating-service idea. And I had to admit that it probably wasn't a good sideline for a woman who'd decided to swear off men completely.

Later that night I made these feelings known when Larry the Lustful Law Student called me. I told him I wasn't interested in reestablishing a relationship with him, legal or otherwise.

"But I think you ought to appreciate the fact that I went to a lot of trouble to get Brad to represent Mack when your mother called me from the airport that night," he said on the phone.

"I do," I said, "but it's over now."

"I still think we need to talk so we can have some kind of closure in our personal relationship."

I hated the way he always threw around words like *dysfunctional* and *closure*. "To me, closure means having a zipper that stays closed on a pair of pants." I like to think it was the dry cleaner in me talking, but if the womanizing Larry chose to think it had a double meaning, so be it. "But if you want some other kind of closure, this is it. Right now. This minute. Good-bye." I hung up, and when the phone rang again, I pounced on it like Spot trying to slam-dunk a mouse.

The poor cat had been curled up on a chair, being halfway sociable for once, but I scared him with my unexpected outburst. He jumped down and darted into the closet as if he'd been attacked by a crazed pit bull. I'd have to get him a kitty treat after I tied up this loose end.

"Larry," I yelled into the phone. "I don't want to talk about it anymore. Understand? It's *fini*, kaput, over. *Arrivederci*." Good grief, I was beginning to sound more like Nat every day, which is what I get for hanging out with people who always use trite expressions as a form of communication.

"Don't hang up. This isn't Larry."

I could tell it wasn't Nat either. After all, I'd just seen him. He'd ended dinner by asking me if I'd ever gotten around to telling Stan Foster that there was nothing going on between him and me. I'd said no and to butt out of my personal life.

So if the caller wasn't Nat and it wasn't Larry, who was it? I thought I knew, but I wasn't about to guess.

"This is Stan Foster," the caller said nervously, as if he feared I was going to yell at him, too, and I might have if he'd given me a chance. "I need some advice on how to get blood out of a shirt."

Oh, sure, now that he needed my professional help, he was calling, but back during the investigation, the handsome detective couldn't have a kind word for me. My anger was tempered only slightly by concern that he might have been wounded in a shoot-out or stabbed in the apprehension of a suspect.

"What happened? Whose blood is it?"

That stopped him for a second. "You mean it's different for different blood types?" Then realization dawned. "Oh, you thought I got it on the job. No, I poked myself with a needle trying to sew a button on my shirt."

Good grief, this guy really was a walking disaster when it came to caring for his clothes, and I couldn't help grinning. I hauled out one of my oldest books on spot removal and quoted from it. "Well, you might try soaking the shirt in cold water for fifteen to thirty minutes."

"Okay, thanks."

"Wait. I'm not finished yet. Then you apply ammonia. Rinse. Soak in warm water and an enzyme presoak for another fifteen to thirty minutes. After that you apply detergent to the stain and rinse. If the stain remains, soak it for another fifteen minutes in an oxygen bleach or a hydrogen peroxide solution and launder."

"Slow down. I'm still back on 'soak in cold water.' "

I started to repeat the part about ammonia.

"Just a minute." There was a pause on the other end of the line. "Do you suppose we could go out for dinner sometime and you could explain it to me? It sounds complicated."

We made a date for him to pick me up at the cleaners the next night, but I chose to think of it as a professional consultation over food. In keeping with the business theme, I dressed in a tailored gray "power" suit as opposed to my basic-black dating dress. Foster showed up straight from work in wrinkled pants and sports jacket. I think it was his rumpled look that appealed to me after I spent every day trying to make customers look well turned out. That and the fact that he had a Clint Eastwood face I would love to try sketching sometime.

Before he arrived, I collected the clothes he'd brought to the cleaners in December and had them ready for him. If he forgot them again, I was giving them to a homeless shelter.

He carried the clothes to his car, and we went to the Black Angus, where they have secluded booths without any nosy restaurant owners like Manuel to interrupt. We ordered drinks, a beer for him and wine for me, and I asked for the latest news on Ingrid.

He'd told me right after she was arrested that I shouldn't visit her in jail. After all, I would be the chief witness against her when she came to trial. I'm not sure I would have wanted to see her anyway, but I probably would have felt guilty about it.

When he said there was nothing new on the case, I said I had one question.

"Figures," he said.

"I know you found the keys to the plant and van in her possession, but how did she get them?"

"She said she lifted them from Al and had copies made."

I'd been relieved when the police finally released the van. I found out they'd kept it so long because they'd found some stains on the floor where she'd apparently hauled away rags she'd used to clean up after she killed Farley. There were no fingerprints, though, and I assume she used latex gloves, the way we do when we remove blood from clothes.

"Another thing I can't figure out is why she drove the van back to my place after she killed Farley," I said.

Foster gave me his lopsided grin. "Is that another question?"

"I guess." I squinted at him and decided he didn't really have a crooked smile. The cleft in his chin was definitely a little off-center.

"Apparently she met Farley at a bar on Colfax that night, and she didn't have any other way to get back to her car."

I nodded. "Okay, that's all. Now it's your turn to ask me questions about how to get blood out of a shirt."

"I have a confession to make. I brought the shirt with me tonight. It sounded too complicated to get out the blood myself. Just don't let me forget to give it to you when we leave."

A busboy came right then with water and a basket of bread.

"And speaking of questions," Foster said after the man left, "I've wanted to ask you out for a long time, but I thought you and Nat Wilcox lived together. Nat called me last night and told me he made the whole thing up." So much for Nat staying out of my personal life. Bless him.

Foster seemed ill at ease, and I must say, I kind of enjoyed his discomfort. "Nat said you were just good friends—that you'd known each other since junior high."

I nodded.

The waiter brought our drinks and left again.

"He told me that the two of you wrote your own comic books when you were kids and that you even made up epitaphs about people you knew."

Oh, please, not the epitaphs. I had just taken a sip of wine, and it was all I could do to keep from spitting it out. Instead I choked in my effort to swallow it.

"Are you all right?"

I nodded and coughed at the same time.

"That's kind of weird—the epitaphs, I mean."

Not as weird as the fact that I might kill Nat when I got my hands on his skinny neck. Why did he have to tell Foster about the epitaphs?

"They weren't weird—just funny," I said, taking another sip of wine in an effort to soothe my throat.

"Like what, for instance?"

"Oh, you know." I paused, remembering humorist Erma Bombeck's caution once to make fun only of yourself or or the guy with the little mustache—Hitler. "Okay, how about 'Here lies the body of Mandy Dyer. Out of the frying pan into the fire'?"

Foster laughed. "That's good," he said. "Now make one up for me."

I thought about it for a minute, but before I came up with something to rhyme with Foster, he slapped his hand on the table. "I have it," he said. " 'Here lies the body of good old Stan. Into the fire from the frying pan'?"

I must say I was pleased. I hadn't realized how well

our names went together. Maybe there was hope for us after all.

A slight doubt arose during our after-dinner coffee when he mentioned his dog, Sidearm, whom he declared "the most friendly mutt in the world."

Could a man with a dog, friendly or otherwise, and a woman with Spot, the grouchiest cat in the world, ever have a future together? That was the biggest question of all.

Mandy's Favorite Cleaning Tip

To remove blood from colorfast fabrics that can be laundered, flush the fabric in cold water as soon as possible and use hydrogen peroxide on stain. Let set for a few minutes and wash out in cold water. (For a longer method, see pages 244–245.)